Bν
6.4

THE WITCH'S BOY

The Witch's Boy

MICHAEL GRUBER

HarperTempest
An Imprint of HarperCollins*Publishers*

The Witch's Boy

Copyright © 2005 by Michael Gruber

www.harpertempest.com

Library of Congress Cataloging-in-Publication Data
Gruber, Michael.
    The witch's boy / by Michael Gruber.—1st ed.
        p.   cm.
    Summary: A grotesque foundling turns against the witch who sacrificed almost everything to raise him when he becomes consumed by the desire for money and revenge against those who have hurt him, but he eventually finds his true heart's desire.
    ISBN 0-06-076164-4 — ISBN 0-06-076165-2 (lib. bdg.)
    [1. Mothers and sons—Fiction. 2. Witches—Fiction. 3. Foundlings—Fiction. 4. Nature—Fiction. 5. Characters in literature—Fiction. 6. Fairy tales.] I. Title.
PZ7.G93187Wi   2005   2004020845
[Fic]—dc22

Typography by R. Hult
2 3 4 5 6 7 8 9 10
❖
First Edition

To witch mothers everywhere

Witch

Once upon a time, in a faraway country, there was a woman who lived by herself in the middle of a great forest. She had a little cottage and kept a garden and a large gray cat. In appearance, she was neither fair nor ugly, neither young nor old, and she dressed herself modestly in the colors of stones. None of the folk who lived nearby (not the oldest of them) could tell how long she had dwelt in that place.

One spring morning, the woman set off to collect some plants she needed. As she glided silently along, she studied a list she had made, for she tended to be absentminded about small things. She passed the old oak tree, lightning killed and half hollow, where the local people were accustomed to leave things for her, and there she heard an odd little cry. She stopped and looked, and saw that in the hollow was a wicker basket. Have they left me a piglet? she wondered. But when she came closer, the basket shook and she heard the unmistakable cry of a new baby. There was a note in a crude hand tied to the handle of the basket, which read:

THE DEVIL'S CHILD
FOR THE DEVIL'S WIFE

"Well, well," said she to herself, "let us see what some rude person has left." She opened the basket and looked in. "Oh, my!" she said aloud, as she beheld the ugliest baby boy that she, and perhaps anybody, had ever seen. He had a piggish snout and close-set eyes of a peculiar yellowish color. His mouth, wide and floppy, was already full of square little grinders. He was covered in coarse dark hair resembling the bristles of a hog; and his ears were huge and pointed like a bat's. His body was also oddly shaped, like a sack of stones, and his feet were far too large. Of all his features, his hands alone might be called good, their long delicate fingers flexing as the stubby arms waved.

He seemed healthy enough, and when the woman reached down and touched his cheek with the backs of her fingers, he gave a lusty cry and rooted with his mouth for her thumb.

"Hungry, are you?" she asked. "Don't you know that witches are supposed to eat babies, not feed them?" The ugly baby gurgled and pushed harder against her hand. His yellow eyes looked hungrily into her gray ones. She felt a magic older than even her own flicker between them, and it startled her.

"What am I thinking of?" she said. "How could I keep a baby? I have never been sentimental before." She addressed the baby. "You will make a meal for the lynx or the gray wolf. This is your fate." She moved her hand away and turned to go, but the little thing, feeling the withdrawal of the woman's warm presence, began to whimper again. In an instant, almost without thought, she had drawn the baby into her arms and pressed him to her bosom. The baby gurgled and stared with mindless intensity into her eyes.

"Ah, well." She sighed. "It seems we are stuck together, little lump. I have no idea how we shall get on or what will become of you. I have never heard of a woman of my sisterhood rearing a child before, but lately the world is full of new and disturbing things— and perhaps this is one of them, dropped into my very lap. Perhaps we shall both learn something from it."

She placed the child carefully back in his basket, and carried it back the way she had come. The few people she passed all nodded cautiously at her and made room on the path, but none attempted to start a conversation, as they might have with almost anyone else. The people of that neighborhood were woodcutters, trappers, charcoal burners, and a few farmers who worked the small clearings. They thought her strange; she had the disconcerting habit of appearing without warning around the turn of a path; or you might be working and suddenly be aware of her presence in a corner of your sight, like smoke from a distant fire. You could not hear her coming, not even in autumn, when the very rabbits made a crunching as they traveled their underbrush roads. Although she greeted people politely on these occasions, she was short of speech and soon glided onward, out of sight. Her voice was deep and clear and not accented with the local twang. She kept no company, nor did she trade, as far as anyone could see.

Tongues wagged about her, of course, as they will in a small place. One fellow said he saw her pop out of a cleft in a rock in broad day, and when he looked for a passage or cave had found nothing but the smooth black stone. Another said she had seen her walking with the shy roe deer often and once with an enormous brown bear, chatting away and pausing as if to listen, as if she were conversing about the weather or the year's chestnuts. The local boys dared each other to go down the path to her cottage and peer in the windows at night. None ever did, although they lied a good deal about it. Some of the older women brought little baskets of fruit or crocks of cream or preserves and left them in the hollow tree by the head of her path, where today someone had left a more strange and less welcome gift. The rough men of the forest left her clever fur bags they made of whole marten skins or stone jars of the spirit they distilled from elderberries in the fall while they waited for the ricks to burn down. These were plain people who still felt the weirdness of life's twists, and, God-fearing though they might be, they were also in the habit of making small sacrifices to keep on the good side of powers more strictly local.

They made up stories about the woman to pass the evenings and frighten the children into bed: how she could change her shape, becoming a raven or a red fox, how she could sour milk with a glance or spoil traps, what she did in her cottage to little boys and girls who did not mind their elders. These tales grew richer with the years; in the end, they called her a witch.

Such things used to happen often to women living alone and mostly no harm done, although when some old goose is treated as a witch and given little presents, she may get it into her head that she really has the power to make rain drop from the sky or two people fall in love, and then she might find herself in trouble.

But this particular woman was a real witch.

She was not wicked; but neither did she often go out of her way to do good. She was like some venerable mountain that in winter holds a cap of snow, which at any moment might send forth an avalanche. Around such a crag, therefore, one ought to walk tiptoe, although ordinarily the snow will relax into the full streams of spring without troubling the country.

This woman had a name, but no one in the forest knew it; a good thing, too, for if any there had uttered it, their tongues would have been scorched from their heads along with a good portion of the surrounding country. The people called her the Quiet Woman or Mrs. Forest or, more commonly, with a peculiar roll of the eyes or a shake of the head, "That One" or "Her."

Everyone knew which Her was meant.

What the woman actually did with her time was quite different from what the people imagined. She did not ride on a broom nor visit the devil nor dine on children. Mostly she studied the world, both the parts that we all see—made up of rocks and flowers and rain and beetles—and the parts we don't see but which we may sometimes feel by a prickle of the scalp and a shiver down the back when we stand in a rustling wood and the clouds race across the full moon.

She knew how to listen. Even the stones had no secrets from her. Not only could she hear the words of animals, which many people can do, but also the voices of the flowers in the fields and the trees of the woods. And she could speak their various languages as well, and so was able to learn the secret wisdom locked in the great river of life that runs unbroken back to the making of the world.

With what she learned, she made magic and not just what we think of as magic nowadays—making the small large and the large small, making the soft hard and the hard soft, making up and down change places—although she could do that and more with less effort than you make to scratch your nose. No, what she spent most of her time doing was so strange that even the memory of the words that describe it has utterly vanished. You might say, if you had to say something, that she adjusted the pattern of things so that life flowed smoothly through time, the sun becoming the sunflower seed and the sunflower seed becoming the mouse, the mouse becoming the weasel and the weasel becoming the horned owl, the horned owl becoming the carrion fly, and round and round, ever changing, the patterns crisp and balanced as they danced to the unknowable tune.

To hear the sound of that tune was what the woman lived for. It was her life's work and her only pleasure. Lately, its sound had become fainter. The woman worried about it; she felt changes coming, but distantly, like the clang of an axe on the other side of the mountain. There were more people coming into the forest, for one thing. A village had grown into a real town at the forest's edge; it was sending out roads like the cables of a spider, and where the roads went farmsteads grew mushroomlike into actual villages, filled with strangers who scoffed at the old ways. It made her irritable, and she worked ever harder.

The local people had no idea of any of this, of

course, although part of what she did touched their lives. They called it luck, and indeed the forest was a lucky place. The trapper's traps were full enough to earn them a living selling furs, yet many animals escaped them. The woodsman's axe bit true, so the tree always fell in just the right place and in falling threw its seed into the most fecund cranny of earth. The horses never slipped at their chains, so the logs skidded neatly into the river, and hardly a jam slowed them in their passage to the mill. The cows in the little farms gave without stint; the hens were prodigious layers; and the local butter, cheese, and eggs were famous in the towns that bordered the forest. All this came from what the woman did, although indirectly, as the fire from a great forge will help to hatch the eggs of the swallows nesting in the rafters high above.

Now carrying the basket with the baby in it, she returned to her cottage. It was a small high house, made of weathered wood. It had a steep thatched roof, and it rested on a foundation of dark stone, cleverly locked together without mortar. One corner was supported by a living oak tree; and the door and doorframe bore carved figures—serpentine forms of women, men, and animals. These figures were not always in the same place each time you looked at them. Besides that, the woman's home appeared to be an ordinary cottage of the district.

A large, ragged gray cat with grape-green eyes was sunning himself on the warmed stone of the front step, and as she approached he looked up. His whiskers twitched when he saw the basket she carried.

"I hope that's something to eat," said the cat.

"It most certainly is not," said the woman. "It's a baby. See?" She placed the basket on the ground and opened the cover. The cat peered in at the baby, now asleep.

"What fun!" said the cat, grinning. "Are you going to chase it and tear it to pieces?"

"What an idea!" the woman exclaimed. "I'll do no such thing." She paused and regarded the cat closely. "And neither will you. I mean it, Falance. If I find one scratch on this child—" she leaned over and put her face close to the cat's—"I'll turn you into a *dog*."

The cat shuddered and began washing himself in the offhand manner of cats who have been embarrassed and don't wish to acknowledge the fact.

Between licks he said, "Well, then, what do you

propose to do with the thing?"

"I shall bring it up, of course. It will live here with us."

The cat stared at her, aghast. "What!" he cried. "Impossible! Whatever has possessed you?" At this, he stopped, frozen. Then he placed his forepaws against the woman's knees and stared deeply into her eyes.

"You're not, are you?" asked the cat hesitantly. "Possessed?"

"Oh, of course not, you nincompoop," she snapped. "I'm perfectly fine." She brushed the cat aside, picked up the basket, and stalked into the cottage. The ground floor was mainly one large room, with a hearth and latticed windows on the three other sides. Chairs and a round table stood in the center of the room, with cupboards for dishes and things against the walls and a bookcase that went up to the low ceiling. The tabletop was littered with twisted bits of paper holding herbs and seeds; dried bunches of plants; colored glass vials, some containing liquids, others with shriveled brownish objects in them; a tilting stack of leather-bound books; and a quill pen stuck in an ink bottle. The woman cleared a space with a sweep of her arm and set the basket down on the table.

She turned to the cat, who had followed her in, and said, "This baby was flung at me like a curse. By taking it in, I avert this curse and carve a different channel in fate. Who knows where it may reach? Besides, I have always wanted to raise a child. Was that a snigger, Falance?"

"Not at all. Perhaps a hair ball." The cat jumped up on the table and peered into the basket again. "Charming creature," he observed. "Something like a pig, something like a bat. Aren't babies supposed to be pretty?"

"He will grow out of it," said the woman confidently. "It is a stage they all go through."

The cat gave her a sharp, incredulous look, which the woman did not catch. Instead, she took the baby from his basket and sat down in a comfortable chair, cuddling him in what she imagined was a maternal way. She had no experience with babies at all, having come into her vocation at a very early age and never having been interested in any aspect of what she had regarded as a messy business. How messy she now found out; the baby had not been tended for some time and stank. Nevertheless, she maintained the pose, largely for the benefit of the cat, who was watching the demonstration with a baleful eye.

"You're actually serious about this?" said the cat.

"Yes, I am," she replied. "There is no reason I can't be a mother. After all—"

"*Be* a mother? My lady, you *are* the Mother—"

"Don't be blasphemous, cat!" she shot back. "At my best, I am merely Her shadow on earth."

"I beg your pardon," said the cat with more sincerity than was his wont. "But think, my lady! What about our work? Who will watch the baby when we are away? Who will feed it when it's hungry? Shall we halt our journeying among the worlds because you must change its sopping clothes? And, again, this house is not a safe place, not a domestic place, as you well know. You know how hard it is to guard ourselves. How, then, will we protect a helpless kitten?"

"Baby," said the woman. On her smooth, wide forehead, two deep vertical lines had appeared.

The cat saw this and pressed his case again. "Lady, I have served you all my life, which through your good grace has been longer by far than cats are used to living, and I say: what you will, I will; but, I beg you, think on this!"

The lines on her forehead faded, and her face took

on a more determined look with a tight knotting around her jaw. "I *have* thought, Falance, and my mind is settled. But all that you say is true; it will be hard on us and on our art."

At that moment, as if by way of demonstration, the infant's gurgling became the full cry of a hungry baby.

"It starts," remarked the cat in a low voice.

The woman rose and jiggled the baby absently. She said, "You are right about one thing, cat. It will definitely require a nurse. Now, who shall it be?"

Baby on hip, she strolled out into the garden and lifted her free hand above her head, palm uppermost. A brown sparrow flew down from its perch on the eaves of the house and lighted on her finger. She brought the little bird close to her lips, whispered briefly, and then tossed it into the air.

In less than three minutes, the sound of creaking boughs and snapping twigs broke from the wood, followed soon by the appearance of an immense brown bear. With heavy tread, the animal approached the woman and stared into her face, which was only a little higher than its own.

"You called, my lady?" asked the bear in a voice stranded between a cough and a thundery rumble.

"Yes, Ysul. Thank you for coming so quickly. I have a favor to ask."

"At your command, madam."

The woman held the squalling baby before the bear's nose. "This is my own dear child," she said, "and he needs a nurse. I would like you to care for him as if he were one of your own cubs."

The bear squinted at the baby through nearsighted eyes and sniffed it all over. "Of course. I would be honored," replied the bear. "A very healthy and strong-smelling infant, if I may say so, madam. What is its name?"

"Name? Well, of course, I haven't had time to find out his proper Name. In the meantime, I think . . . *Lump* will serve."

"Lump it shall be. Now, as to arrangements, will I be staying here or at the den?"

"Oh, here, by all means. Please, how discourteous of me! Do come in. Door, there! Open!"

At the woman's command the doorframe writhed and stretched to admit her and the bear. She darted forward and moved a chair. "You'll have to stay here by the stove for the while until I can get an addition built. A nursery, in fact. Imagine that! But, oh my! Listen to him wail! Could you give him his milk?"

"Of course," said Ysul. The bear waddled over to the indicated corner and settled herself comfortably. The woman placed the baby, Lump, on the immense living rug with his mouth convenient to a nipple. Immediately he began to imbibe the rich milk, nor was he quiet about it.

The woman watched with satisfaction. "I trust it will agree with him," she said. "They do say bear's milk is the best."

"I have never doubted it, madam," said the bear. "One question, though, if you please. Is he to be raised as a bear or as a man?"

"Oh, at this point it hardly matters," replied the woman, gazing fondly at the nursing baby, who, if truth be told, resembled a baldish bear cub more than he did a human infant. "Use your own judgment in such matters."

The bear nodded. The cat, who had observed all from a pantry shelf, sniffed and began to wash himself in disgust. At this moment, the sun lifted over the tops of the tall trees that ringed the cottage clearing and sent a shaft of buttery light into the room.

"Oh, my!" said the woman.

"You forgot about the star grass, didn't you," said

the cat snidely. "While you were being a mother. And it
has to be picked before noon, or it's no good—"

The woman shot him a look that made the fur
stand up along his spine. "Cat, I'm warning you . . ."
she began, and then, throwing up her hands, she turned
and dashed toward the door, which barely had time to
get out of her way. A moment later she stuck her head
through the window and addressed the she-bear. "Ysul,
take good care of baby, and I'll be back in no time. I
must fly!" She vanished from the window; shortly
thereafter, a large raven flew over the tops of the trees
toward the west.

The cat dropped from the shelf and padded over to
the bear and her charge. Wrinkling his nose, he
remarked, "Ysul, I hear that bear cubs are born
unformed, so that their mothers must lick them into the
proper shape. If so, you will wear your tongue out on
this one."

"I will not dignify that with a reply," answered the
bear.

"But seriously, Ysul, you're a sensible creature. Tell
me what can have gotten into her to have brought such
a misshapen manikin into our house? I fail to understand it."

"For me, I do not even try to understand her. Nor should you, cat."

"Still, you agree it makes no sense," the cat persisted.

"Not to you it doesn't," the bear responded shortly, "but that is why she is the Woman of the Forest and you are only a cat. Now, be quiet and let me get this child to sleep!"

The woman returned, not after a few moments, as she had said, but near dusk. She was breathless and redolent of leaf mold and cut vegetation. She threw off her gray cloak and knelt beside the bear. Little Lump was asleep in a crook of a furry forelimb. The woman touched his cheek lightly and said, "I see all seems to be well. It only remains to construct the nursery."

Then she rose and lifted to her lips a silver whistle that hung from a chain around her neck and blew upon it three uncanny notes. Immediately there sounded a great groan from behind the house, followed by a curious sliding noise, as if a gang of workmen were dragging a heavy crate up a ramp. Then the door opened, and there entered such a creature as, if glanced at but once, would make for a lifetime of nightmares. It was not merely that it had tusks and horns and an indeterminate number of glowing, sparking, spinning eyes. No, what made it so awful was that it kept changing the number, shape, and position of its various features, so that its face was like the roiling surface of a cannibal's stewpot. Just as one had gotten used to one face and concluded that nothing could be more hideous, it slithered into another, and it always was. The only constant in this phantasmagoria was a bright-blue bushy beard. Its body was in general the size and shape of a very large man's, although the number and position of the limbs was subject to some variation. Its skin was iridescent, the color of the scum on an abandoned canal.

He was an afreet, a kind of demon that inhabits desert places, and his name was Bagordax. He had been sent to the woman many years ago by an evil wizard far to the south, who desired a certain charm that she possessed. But the woman had tricked the afreet (which is another story) and pinned his tail in a cleft boulder, where it now remained. The woman used the afreet occasionally as a servant, to do heavy work. He was not a good servant, but since he was impossible to release without causing great harm, the woman put up with his ways.

Bagordax entered the room, dragging his boulder,

and made an elaborate bow.

"Sister of the moon, all-knowing, queen of sorcery: Bagordax, prince of djinns, greets thee and waits upon thy whim!"

"Oh, stop doing that!" the woman snapped. "I can't think when you're writhing in that disgusting manner."

The afreet settled his form into mere monstrosity.

"That's better," said the woman. "My whim, as you put it, is to have an addition built onto the cottage. I have a child to raise now, and he must have his own little nursery."

The monster's gaze darted around the room until it fell upon Ysul and the baby. An expression of hideous delight crossed his face. Ysul pulled the baby closer to her, growled softly, and showed a fang. Bagordax turned to the woman.

"Oh, majesty, before the night has passed, a jewel-encrusted palace shall stand here with gardens and fountains, suitable for this handsomest of all princes and a wonder to the world. Yet it cannot be a tenth of what it should be for such a thrice-blessed infant while the full scope of my art is stunted by this slight embarrassment of stone that clings to thy servant's tail.

Release me now, and I swear by all the Powers that—"

"Oh, do shut up, Bagordax!" said the woman impatiently. "Now, take heed! No palace, no jewels. Just a room. Large and airy, with windows on three walls. A door leading to this room and one leading outside to the garden. Painted walls. Carpeted floors. Furniture suitable to a child and a bear. And, Bagordax—"

"Yes, serene one?"

"No tricks. If anything nasty turns up in that room, you'll find your head in that stone along with your tail. Do I make myself clear?"

"Crystalline, highness, like unto the River Styris when it falls cascading into the Pools of Ixmir, like—"

"Enough! Begone!"

The demon abased himself again and backed out of the room, its boulder rumbling.

The woman fell into a chair and sighed. "I don't see why domestic arrangements always become so complicated. Including a child in a household cannot be any more difficult than—than—"

Her thought was interrupted by a cattish cough from the pantry shelf. She turned to find Falance gazing at her with an expression even more smug than usual.

"Yes, Falance. Did you have a comment?"

"My lady," purred the cat, "it may have slipped your notice, but in less than an hour it will be moonrise and the moon is full tonight."

The woman shot to her feet and clapped hands to her cheeks in alarm. "Oh, blast! And I had it written down, too."

It was, in fact, astounding that the woman had forgotten this; the moon is as essential to magic as seed is to a farmer. It was the most powerful indication of how the arrival of the baby had upset the woman's schedule.

"I have no doubt that it is written down somewhere," said the cat. "Perhaps the note is under the bear. In any case, do you intend to work, or will you be rocking the cradle?"

"Falance, one more word . . ." said the woman menacingly.

"I beg your pardon," said the cat smoothly. "Merely a figure of speech. Nevertheless . . ." He indicated with a movement of his head the waning light at the window.

"Yes, I know, I know! Give me a moment." She went over to the bear, moved a fold of fur away from the sleeping Lump, and kissed his cheek. The kisses of witches are supposed to be icy cold. This is a lie, or was in the case of this particular witch. It was as warm as any baby could wish. Lump stirred comfortably in his furry nest and blew a tiny bubble.

"Ysul," said the woman, "take care now. I'll be back before the dawn. Mind that Bagordax does his work and doesn't make a wreckage."

The bear grunted sleepily in assent. The woman gathered up some necessary items in a woven bag and went out into her garden. A breeze had sprung up with the setting of the sun, and it brought the scent of new grass, pear blossoms, and violets. The frogs were starting to peep by the river. The woman dropped her head and started to focus her powers. She found it more difficult than usual. Thoughts of the day's odd events disturbed her concentration, and she could not help thinking about the child and how strange it was that she, for so long the unchanging center of all change, should be herself transformed. She found herself longing to be with the baby.

"Well," she said to herself, "I'll be able to spend more time with him when he's older."

Lump

Bagordax delivered the nursery as promised, constructed in a single night, after the reputation of its kind; and so Ysul and Lump were able to move in the next day. Your afreet is a reasonably good architect, as is often told in the *Arabian Nights,* although the showy habit of nearly instantaneous construction requires that they fudge some of the details: the floors may be of marble and the walls may be draped with perfumed silks, but the windows are apt to stick, while the plumbing often leaves much to be desired. Besides that, you can imagine that a nursery designed and built by a demon would be an unusual sort of place to pass a childhood.

The room was large, as ordered; in fact, it was somewhat larger on the inside than on the outside and never seemed to have the same dimensions from one day to the next. It was also airy, with small lunettes on two sides and two broad windows giving on the small meadow behind the house.

Ysul was not entirely happy with the room. The decor was lushly Oriental, which might have been expected. The cradle was carved sandalwood, and needless to relate it rocked by itself and crooned in Parsi. The nurse's divan, in pink brocade, was large enough for an enormous pasha, and had in fact lately belonged to an enormous pasha until it was magicked out of his palace on the green Nile. The walls were decorated with paintings of lords and ladies, heroes and monsters. Out of the corner of one's eye, they seemed to move, which Ysul found irritating. Where she drew the line was at the windows. Here she felt obliged to call the woman, who arrived bleary-eyed and testy, having been up working most of the night. Ysul pointed at one of the windows with her snout and sniffed loudly at the soft breeze flowing in from outside.

"Madam," she asked, "what do you smell?"

The woman closed her eyes and breathed in deeply. "Myrrh," she said after a few moments. "And lotus. And jasmine."

"Exactly. May I point out that these are not the characteristic scents of the region? And also note, madam, that while there is a breeze blowing in through these windows, it is nearly still outside, with not the smallest leaves trembling on the trees. The other window is worse. Observe!" The bear pulled aside a yellow silk curtain. Through the window could be seen rolling dunes and a small oasis with three tall palms in front of a low caravanserai, or inn. As they watched, a line of camels approached, their bells gaily tinkling.

"Yes," said the woman, "I see. And, Ysul, I'm sure you noted that painting on the far wall. When I came in, the maiden was feeding an apple to that centaur, and now she is up on his back, with an expression on her face that I am not at all sure I like." She blew the strange notes on her silver whistle.

The djinn appeared at the window, grinning horribly, and in his usual cringing posture. "Empress of the Twelve Kingdoms, suzeraine of the ineffable—"

"Oh, do stop that! I said no tricks, Bagordax. And what do I find? Magic pictures, perfumed breezes from nowhere, the wrong view out the window . . ."

The afreet looked alarmed. His features spun like a wagon wheel. "Excellency! Keeper of the whole world! This is no trick, and there is no harm in it. It is merely an amusement for the little lord, may he live a thousand years! When the window is opened, as might be in summer, we have the homely meadow. When closed, as now, we see Caravanserai of the Three Palms. Or, on the left there, the Lagoon. Thus it was in the grand hall I built for the prince of Trebizond, except, of course, in that case I devised—"

"Yes, yes, Bagordax," the woman broke in impatiently. The djinn had a habit of running on about his accomplishments. "But get rid of the magic windows. The rest, I suppose, will have to do. I don't want him quite so *immersed* in magic. I would like him to have as normal a childhood as possible."

A half-stifled guffaw sounded from the doorway. Falance had entered and now remarked, "I fail to see, really, how a household consisting of a witch, a cat, a bear, and a demon could be considered normal by any thinking person . . ." At this, the woman shot him a glance so ferocious that his teeth ached. He continued, blandly, "But I'm sure it will be, actually, as normal as one could wish. Truly."

It was not quite that, but no one could say that Lump had anything but a happy childhood, at least to begin with. A large bear makes a very good nurse, being at once food, bed, blanket, and bath. A human child raised by a bear is, of course, quite safe from nearly all danger and is apt to be taught good manners as well. Bears are serious creatures; they brook no nonsense from their young and do not spare the paw.

The baby grew like a weed, becoming strong and agile, if no less hairy. Ysul carried him down the forest paths for his daily outing in all weathers, at first in her hot damp jaws, and later, when he was able, astride her broad neck. There are few who have ridden through a forest on such a mount, but these few declare it a pleasure beyond compare; horseback is nothing to it. A bear makes its own trail through the woods, and all creatures flee before it, especially if it is a she-bear with young. The ramblings of Ysul and Lump were accompanied by thrashing and crashing and the squawks and cries of animals and birds. Naturally the little boy thought, in the manner of all small children, that this scattering and crashing was his own doing. There arose in his mind an unshakable self-confidence, verging on vainglory, which had he been a real bear cub would have been proper, for someday the cub *will* be a full-grown bear and a monarch of the forest in his own right. But since to be a bear was not Lump's destiny, it led him astray.

This, it must be admitted, was the fault of the witch,

who not only knew nothing about child rearing but also was disinclined to find anything out. It was clear to her that the local women, who were the only convenient sources of such information, had nothing to teach, since their talents appeared to stop at churning butter, feeding animals, sewing crude garments, and making baskets; whereas she was free with the deepest mysteries of the earth and the heavens. Surely, she thought, being a mother could not be that difficult or these simple women could not do it, not to speak of bears and the other animals. So she was content to see the child at bedtime and tell him stories, feed him his breakfast porridge on occasions when she was not too busy, and make sure he was clothed and washed. Ysul was a trustworthy nurse, and, besides, a young child is not, to the studious sort of person, a very interesting thing. And she continued to think, when his prattling bored her, that it would be very much more amusing when he was older, when she would be sure to spend more time with him.

So disaster struck. One summer's day, Ysul set off with Lump, then three and a half years old, for the great convocation of she-bears that was held four times a year to mark the seasons. It was the first time she had

judged him old enough to attend. These fêtes were con-
ducted on the rocky slopes of the black mountains that
rose above the forest where Lump and his foster mother
and his bear nurse lived. The place was as wild and des-
olate as can be imagined, a vast field of huge broken
stones and boulders, tossed about like blocks on a nursery floor. This rock field had deep crevasses on either
side. Above, there rose only sheer rock; below, to the
south, a narrow patch of scrub firs and pines and some
blackberry brambles bordered a rushing stream. Thus
the area was a perfect, sheltered park; and the cubs
could be allowed to run nearly wild within its precincts.
The great stones were also most convenient for a meeting of bears, for if the day was fine there were many flat
surfaces on which to bask or seek shade in the heat of
the day, while if it rained, there were plentiful dens and
sheltering overhangs.

This particular morning was hot and fair, the air
thick with the smell of pine and wild rose, and mint
growing by the bordering brook, and, in the boulder
park itself, the must of the bears. The lady bears sat at
their ease in small groups in the cool of the rocks and
conversed, while their cubs played around them. As a
rule, bears can take society or leave it alone, but they

do enjoy an occasion. Every creature in the forest possessing a tooth or a claw—from the fox to the male bears (especially the male bears!)—knew that this was a good day to stay far away, no nearer than the other side of the brook.

The conversation of the lady bears was of a homely sort, concerned largely with food and cub rearing, and many would have found it dull; the bear is not noted for wit as a rule. The presence of Ysul and her small nursling, however, provided an irresistible subject of conversation. It had never happened that a bear of the district had raised a human child, if that was what it was—there seemed to be some doubt, and this was itself a novel topic—nor had any of their tribe ever become so close to a figure that all of them regarded with something near to worship. They gathered about Ysul, shyly asking questions about the woman, and her den, and what she ate and drank, and wasn't Ysul frightened of the magic, and also paying compliments to Lump, although, since the bear has no guile, the only qualities of his that they thought worth mentioning were his agility and the coarse brown hair that ran from his crown down his little back. Ysul, though a level-headed bear, was quite overcome by this attention and the audience for her theories on cub rearing; as a result she did not keep as close a watch on Lump as she had planned or as she ought to have done.

At social events, young cubs sensibly keep entirely with their age mates, and Lump, asked by the first cub he met how many summers he had seen, answered proudly "three" and accordingly was directed to the Club of Three, disporting themselves on a lower slope, at the farthest remove from the mothers. Lump was forward for his age—large, sturdy, and intelligent, speaking fluently the languages of both bears and men—but he should have been playing with the small cubs of the year and not with three-year-old bears, who were near twenty times his size and weight.

They regarded him with many an odd look and suspicious sniff when he reported to the captain of the Club of Three, a cinnamon-colored boy bear named Os.

"You are three?" asked Os. "It is hard to believe, as you are so tiny and have hardly any hair. Didn't your mother feed you?" All the bears snuffled in the way that bears do when they find something amusing. Lump looked around in confusion and wished that Ysul were not so far away.

"It is Ysul's nursling," said a girl bear, Nol by

name. "It is the child of the Woman."

Os sniffed at this, not knowing quite what to do about this novelty, and, to cover his own doubt, he turned and crashed through a low stand of wind-shriveled pines. The other Threes followed him, and Lump followed them. While far better at running through country than any ordinary three-year-old child, Lump was not a bear. Soon he was trudging unhappily along the broken path made by the others, far behind.

When he caught up with them, they were playing knock-me-off-the-log around a great deadfall of broken trees that had accumulated on a sandbar in the brook. Fearless as he was, Lump charged into this game; and, as you may well imagine—a little boy in a herd of bears—he was roughly handled.

Nol found him leaning against a stump, covered in tears, scratches, and mud. She was a tenderhearted creature and used her tongue to lick him clean, giving particular attention to his face, for bears do not weep, and she was fascinated by the tears, their delicate taste.

"You are not much of a bear, for a Three," she remarked. "I am to choose a mate when the leaves fall next year, and unless you grow a great deal, I would not choose you."

"I am not a bear at all," Lump snapped. He seethed with unfamiliar and unpleasant feelings, most common, unfortunately, in children who have not had playmates to teach them that they are not the center of the universe; although, in fairness to Lump, having it taught by bears is somewhat harsh. He stared knives at Os, who was balanced on a log, easily knocking back all the challengers. Nol sought to touch up his ear, but Lump knocked her snout roughly away.

As he did so, a honeybee flew by, and then another and another, all sailing from the dog rose bushes nearby. Lump watched them glitter away. Nol did, too. The paths of bees are noticed by bears—and boys raised by bears—at a deep and barely conscious level. In a few moments, Lump and Nol realized that they were on a bee road, and immediately, without thinking or speaking, they both got up to see if they could determine where it led.

It led to the brook. Nol raised her nose and sniffed. Lump did, too. Her nose was better; his eyes were far keener.

"It's across the stream," she said sadly. "Too bad. It smells a rich one."

"Yes!" shouted Lump. "I can see it." It appeared as

a faint, shimmering cloud, like smoke, drifting about the dark shadow of a stump embedded in the high sandy bank of the opposite shore.

The other bears were sniffing, too, and at Lump's shout they directed their snouts to the opposite shore; and whether they could see the hive or not, they now fixed the position of the source of that exquisite perfume.

"Too bad," said Os, licking his chops.

"Why is it too bad?" demanded Lump. "The stream is shallow and slow. Why don't we walk across and get it?"

They looked at him, shocked. Nol said, "Why, because it is out of bounds. We never cross the brook. The mothers have said it."

An idea flashed instantly into Lump's mind, and it was as sweet as the promised honey. "*My* mother has not," he crowed. "I will cross and get the honeycombs. And," he added, with a sharp look at Os, "I will think about who will share the honey."

"Lump!" cried Nol, "Don't be a fool! The protection does not carry to the far shore."

But he was already in the stream, wading strongly across, his waist lapped by the summer-slack current, his hard, hairy feet sure among the rocks. The Club of Three watched him in horror and amazement. None of them would have thought for a moment of defying their mothers. Leaving came at the proper time, and the time was not yet. So they stayed on the far shore and shouted for him to come back, not to be a stupid frog, and so on. He forged across, unheeding.

The hive lay deep in a hollow of the sandy bank behind a huge oak stump that had washed down in some long-ago spring flood. Lump crawled into the damp, bee-smelling passage. He was not stung; the bees, too, knew the woman. He broke off a small piece of comb and let the honey flow into his mouth. Bees gathered at his lips, gently murmuring. The cries of his age mates grew louder through the buzz. Whatever were they shouting about? he wondered, and he filled his hands with dripping comb.

Thus encumbered, he found it hard to turn around in the tunnel; when he did, he saw that it had grown strangely dark as if something blocked the light. He heard a low rumbling that turned into a snarl; and with a shock that chilled his heart, Lump understood that what blocked his passage was the head and shoulders of an old male bear. Instantly, there sprang into his head all the stories he had heard from Ysul and her friends of what became of little cubs who ran afoul of the great he-bears when their mothers were not close by.

"Lord, let me by," said Lump to the bear in a little voice. "I have taken only a little of your honey, and that I will put down now."

As if in answer the massive head jerked forward, teeth bared and gleaming in the scant light. Lump scuttled away at the same time so that his back was against the warm wax of the combs. The bear's jaws closed with a horrible wet clack only a hand span from Lump's drawn-up foot. The bear seemed to smile at him.

"Why, you are a very small cub," the bear rumbled. "You have not learned your lessons very well, I find. Here, let me withdraw, and you can run back to your momma. And, please, take some honey along with you—there's plenty." The bear took his head away and pale light, flickering with watery reflections, returned to the little cave.

Lump felt his heart relax. He broke another honeycomb from the hive, stuck it in his mouth, and with a comb in each fist he began to crawl. An odd sound from the outside made him pause, a scraping sound, as if something was digging away the earth. The air around him was thick now with angry bees. Suddenly, the passage went dark again. Without an instant's thought, Lump reversed direction and crawled backward as fast as he could, until his back was once again pressed into the hive.

A breeze fanned his face, a finger's breadth from his nose, and he heard the sound of something heavy smashing against the wall of the tunnel. Bits of earth sprinkled down upon him and he made himself as small as he could. Without seeing, he knew very well that what had barely missed him was the great spiked paw of the old bear, reaching for his flesh. There was light again, and again Lump's ears brought him the sound of digging, a continual angry snarl, and over all the war song of the bees. The bear was clearly being badly stung, and it was slowing his work, but Lump well knew that no amount of stinging could keep a bear from a fat hive. The bear, he now realized, would dig until the passage was wide enough to admit his shoulder and then he would claw out the hive and eat it, along with the smashed pieces of a foolish little boy.

And then he heard splashing water, a scream of outrage from the old bear; the spine-chilling cry of a she-bear protecting a cub; the sound of heavy bodies pounding the earth, making the walls of the passage shake and crumble in little avalanches; and then at last the sound of a bear crashing away through the underbrush.

"Lump? Oh, child, are you there?" It was Ysul's voice. Nol had run and brought her to the river.

In a moment, he was clinging to Ysul's fur while her familiar, gentle tongue washed away the crust of mud and honey.

That evening, as soon as Lump had fallen into a deep and exhausted sleep, Ysul and her employer discussed the day's events.

"It is outrageous!" cried the woman, when the story had been told. "For a great idiot of a bear to attack my child! Where were *you*, might I ask?"

The bear bowed her head. "Clearly, I was remiss, and, of course, I take full responsibility for the unhappy occurrence. I will understand perfectly if you wish me to leave the position."

"Oh, don't be a ninny! I'm upset, of course, but you know very well I could not possibly get along without you. Now, turning to this particular bear—shall he be called and suitably chastised?"

"Madam, you will forgive me, but I have already

made enquiries. The errant bear, Gloor by name, is a very old bear and not quite assembled in his intellect. He had been watching this hive for some time, was looking forward to the honey, and quite lost his head when he saw Lump a-raiding. And, besides, in fairness, Lump had strayed outside the precincts—outside the protection, that is."

"Ah, that is a different thing entirely. Well, as long as Lump was not harmed . . ."

"No, madam, fortunately not," said Ysul, "yet I believe that such incidents will become far too common in the future. For," she added at the woman's questioning look, "I believe it is inadvisable to continue raising him as a bear."

"Oh? And why not, pray?"

"Because he is . . . how shall I put this, madam? Of insufficient size. He is not as large as a three month cub, yet he is rising four years. As a bear, he would naturally be with his age mates, but to allow this would be a cruelty, as we now see. In fact, I believe that he was ill-used by some of the Threes today, and this made him wish to perform some bold exploit, so as to rise in their regard."

"Then I shall make him larger," said the woman

immediately, as casually as if she were considering adding a pinch more salt to a stew. And here was the problem on a plate, thought the bear: If everything is to be touched up by magic, how will the poor child learn anything about the world or about right behavior? This she did not say, but rather, "I fear that will not serve, madam. Besides being the wrong size, the child will not be controlled, at least not like a cub of the same age. Making him the size of a three-year cub would not help him make his way—far from it, unless you will also give him a bear's claws and teeth and a bear's heart and mind, in which case . . ."

"Oh, yes, I quite see. In which case, why bother having a child at all? Well! I really had no idea," said the woman, pacing to and fro in the narrow room. The cat Falance was pretending to ignore the conversation and he kept his face turned away, so that his mistress would not see the unpleasant I-told-you-so expression on it.

The woman stopped pacing. "Of course! He must be raised as a man from now on. He is just the right size for *that*. Naturally, Ysul, you will stay on as nurse, but we must also have a tutor to teach him"—here she paused, halting against her profound ignorance of ordinary human society—"all the things that tutors are able to teach. That is the solution." She held her silver whistle to her lips.

"Surely not!" exclaimed the cat. "Surely not Bagordax!"

"I don't see what is wrong with Bagordax," replied the woman coldly.

"You don't? Well, in the first place, he is not a tutor. He has no references at all, and we have no idea whether or not he can teach the things a boy ought to learn. In the second place, how can you trust him? He lives in the hope of escape."

The woman dismissed these objections with a wave of her hand. "You are mistaken," she said. "Bagordax does what he is told; he is a bound spirit, that is his *function*. As for his talents—we have never found him wanting in any respect, not counting a certain unwarranted exuberance of creation, a tendency to misunderstand. Compared to his usual line—conjuring palaces out of thin air, magic carpets, and such—teaching Lump will hardly be taxing." She blew on her whistle, and the afreet appeared and made his usual flowery obeisances. She told him what she wanted, and he readily agreed.

"He shall be a sage among sages, O ineffable one. The deepest wisdom of all ages shall be as a preface to him."

"You've done this before?" she asked.

"O majesty, Bagordax has done everything that has been done and will be done. His power knows no limit, save for the temporary embarrassment of this bit of gravel clinging to his person. Should it be removed, his gratitude—"

"Yes, yes," said the witch impatiently. "We know all that. But specifically, what is your experience as a tutor?"

"Hear and be enlightened, serenissima," said the afreet, his voice dropping a register. "Once upon a time, I was summoned by the cham of Tartary, to instruct his four daughters in the mantic arts. Now, these daughters were more beautiful than any other women the memory of man records, but the most beautiful of all was the youngest, Madille by name. Now, it happened one morning, that Madille went to the—"

"Enough!" the woman interrupted. "We will be here all day, and I have much to do. So—that seems to be an adequate reference"—here she cast a satisfied look at the cat—"and therefore it remains only to construct a schoolroom, with appropriate supplies, and . . ." She looked at the afreet critically. "Could you not modify your appearance? You do not look like someone responsible for the development of a child. You do not appear tutorial."

The djinn bowed and spun into a blur, reappearing as an elderly gentleman of a vaguely Eastern cast, with a white robe and turban. His beard was white, but with cerulean depths.

"Good," said the woman. "Ears not quite so bat-like. Yes. And not so much orange in the complexion. Obscure your tail and stone. Yes, just so. And, Bagordax—we are not so interested in the wisdom of the ages just now. Reading and writing, and figuring and comportment, of course, and"—this rather vaguely— "the arts. And sports. With balls. Sports are so important to happy school days."

The cat Falance cast a startled look at his mistress when this last remark fell from her lips. He had no idea from where this odd bit of information had entered her mind, but he was fairly sure that she had never seen a sport in her life, much less played one. She was being foolish, and this was so unusual, so *dangerous,* that for a moment he could not speak. At last he remarked mildly, "But he cannot sport, madam; he has no play-mates. Kittens have other kittens, and cubs have cubs, but he is alone."

She was not listening; that is, she was not listening to him, but he could tell from the cant of her head and her rapt expression that some message from the unseen world was coming through. He felt it himself—a prick-ling of the fur on his back and a desire to sneeze. She drifted out of the nursery, and soon the others smelled herbs burning and heard a low, musical chant begin. The air thickened, and objects took on a soft glow. The afreet vanished in a puff of silvery smoke, presumably to begin construction of the schoolroom.

"Ysul, mark me: this will end poorly," said the cat.

"We must all help the best we can," answered the bear, cuddling the sleeping child to her broad chest.

Falance sniffed rudely and left to join his mistress at her task.

Being a bright child, forward and curious, Lump proved a willing pupil. In reality, he had been Bagordax's student since the first day he had arrived at the witch's cottage, since the nursery itself was designed to amuse and entertain an infant, and to an infant this is the same as education. As early as he could remember, he would wake in the deep of the night with moonlight shining through the window and the bed singing to him in a language not his own and rocking slowly in time with the music; nor was the moon the same as the one that floated in the sky above the little cottage. Bagordax had obeyed the woman, after his fashion, and the windows were now nearly always ordinary glass. But either some magic clung to the panes, or else the djinn was acting the trickster, for by holding his head just so and squinting in a certain way, Lump could gaze into another world.

When he was old enough, he would climb from his crib and look out the windows at the caravanserai with the three palm trees and at the Lagoon of Pearls. He was young indeed when the bed whispered to him one night, in the midst of the music, that neither Ysul nor his mother was able to see these scenes, and that if he told anyone about them, the windows would lose their virtue and show only the dull garden and the line of dark woods beyond. He did not tell. It was his first secret, and by it the lesson of secrecy was laid down at the foundation of his character, and shaped the whole, as the first course of bricks determines how the wall will lean.

In time, the stories began, whispered for his ears alone, and illustrated, not by still pictures in a book, but by the moving decorations on the bedroom walls. A centaur fell in love with a princess, so her father the king hid her away in a castle on a crag, and the centaur sought her out and came to her through many adventures and slew the king and married the princess. A beautiful girl was kept in a tower by an evil witch, but a noble prince rescued her, when she let down her long hair. A lovely girl was stolen away by a troll and brought to its burrow under the roots of a great oak, but a clever shepherd boy heard her singing a sad song and outwitted the troll and saved the girl.

In the pictures, all the heroes had hairy faces, pig's noses, snaggle teeth and bat's ears, and were called handsome by the voice from the walls, but all the ladies were smooth and lovely, with very small features and waists like wands. Lump accepted this as the way things were, just as he thought it nothing strange that all the tales the bed told and the walls showed were about the hardships of captivity and how the highest good was the release of a prisoner.

It was no surprise to Lump that the voice of his new tutor was the same as the one that had long whispered from his bed. In fact, few things ever surprised the boy, for when you are raised in a household where magic is thick in the air, like the smell of cabbage, you grow used to nearly anything happening. Thus, when the infant Lump flung his porridge bowl to the floor, it leaped back onto his tray unspilled. When he climbed up on a chair to steal a cake and fell into the hearth, he was not burned, for the burning coals hurried out of his way. Until his rough treatment by the young bears and his narrow escape from the old bear Gloor, he had led, literally, a charmed life.

Why the witch allowed this would be hard to say, for it was the worst possible preparation for life, depriving the child of the possibility of learning from his own errors, that greatest of tutors. Perhaps she felt sorry for him. Perhaps she felt ashamed that she had not spent the time with him that she had meant to spend; for as it turned out, her resolve to do so "when he was older" remained merely a resolve, forever pushed into the future.

Meanwhile, the boy grew froward, and as the years passed his studies did not advance well. Bagordax managed to teach him his letters and numbers, using a variety of enchanting tricks—colored figures marching down the slate, announcing their sums in squeaky voices, and so on—but Lump was easily bored and distracted by the usual curriculum. He would start off well, at drawing or playing upon the flute, say, but he would toss the thing aside when his achievement did not come out as he thought it should: that is, perfect. Many a flute and mandolin were broken or flung at Bagordax's head, or both. At one of these times, with Lump building up to a tantrum, Bagordax picked an ant up off the windowsill and cried, "Watch!" Instantly, the ant changed into a little black horse, which danced and pranced along the djinn's palm. As the boy watched, his tears forgotten, it sprouted tiny wings and flew around the room, neighing. The boy raced after it, and when at last he caught it, it changed into a jelly tart in the shape of a horse. Lump laughed and gobbled it down, with the tart crying all the while, "Don't eat me, don't eat me!"

"Did you like that, Lump?" asked Bagordax.

"Yes! Do it again!"

"As often as you like, little prince. But let this be between us two. Your mother desires that we work, work, work, with no time for nice fun. She would make me stop."

Lump solemnly promised not to tell, nor did he; and afterward there were many more amusing displays of Bagordax's little tricks. Gradually, Lump became aware, from various hints that his tutor dropped, that magic was a thing that could be learned. He was furious when Bagordax refused to teach him any, and he secretly resolved to bring this up with his mother.

He chose a certain Friday evening in his tenth year. Lump and his mother were at the worn round table, and she was rolling out pastry dough. (Friday was her baking day; although meals in the cottage tended to be irregular, the woman was a competent plain cook and especially enjoyed baking.) Friday evening was also the time appointed for Lump to exhibit his progress. As usual, there was little to show.

The woman was not pleased and said so.

Lump put on the sulky look she knew so well and said, "Mother, it's because I don't wish to learn what twelve nines make or the direction of Thule."

"Oh? And what would you desire to learn, child?"

"Magic!" said the boy, and his eyes sparkled. "If one knows magic, all things are possible and with the greatest ease. One can . . . one can *fly* right to Thule, or anywhere, without having to learn the direction and the capital city. And you could teach me it, couldn't you?"

The woman put down her rolling pin. She said, "I am sorry to tell you that I cannot do that. There are two reasons. First, the sort of magic I do can be done only by a woman, and you are not a girl."

"But boys, men, are also magicians," he objected. "Bagordax says so. Bagordax himself can do all kinds of magic."

"That is interesting," said the woman after a significant pause. "What sort of things have you seen him do?"

"Oh, just little tricks," said Lump, realizing he had said too much. "But, please, couldn't I learn from him?"

"No, for Bagordax is not a man either, and his magic has nothing to do with skill but flows from him like our breath does from us. You might just as well ask Ysul to teach you how to be large."

"Then get me another tutor," he demanded pettishly and stamped his foot. He was angry, and also a little confused, for he did not know quite what the woman had meant about Bagordax not being a man.

"I said there was another reason," she went on patiently, "and here it is. You think magic is easy, like wishing or dreaming, but it's not. It is the hardest thing in the world, and dangerous as well. If you miss what is twelve nines, it is nothing—a frown from the tutor, no more—but if you make a mistake in magic, it can be dire. There are forces in the unseen world that could pluck your soul from your body like a raisin from a cake." And she demonstrated, snatching a cake she had just made from a rack, plucking a raisin from it, and holding it up before his startled gaze.

"You can be *eaten*," she continued, her voice low and urgent. "Do you understand? Not just your hand or your whole body but *you*! Like this." She popped the raisin into her mouth and chewed it up.

He shuddered and said weakly, "Then I will study hard and not make any mistakes."

She regarded him bleakly. "Will you so? Will you, Lump?" Then she sighed and said in a kinder voice, "Look, my dear, do you know what magic is, what it *really* is?"

Lump thought of a number of answers, but the look on his mother's face dissuaded him from using any of them. He shook his head.

She rolled a little ball of dough and held it in front of his face. She cast her other hand over the fingers holding the ball and it became two balls, then four, then six. Lump grinned with delight. Given his features, this was not a fetching sight, but, she told herself, he has sweet eyes.

"That was a trick, not magic at all, strictly speaking. While you watched me roll the first ball, I had made the five others behind my back, and then, while you were distracted by my other hand, I affixed them to the back of the hand that held the first ball, producing them by swift movements of my fingers. Now, watch again!"

Quickly, she mashed the dough balls into a single mass and from this made a little doll, which she stuck upright on the table. Then she began to sing a rhythmic song in some husky language he did not know. The air thickened and the dust motes in the air seemed to take on odd colored lights. Lump's eyelids felt heavy. It was not an unfamiliar experience.

The doll shivered and began to move, to dance in a circle, and it began to sing in a piping voice:

> *"Round I go,*
> *Made of dough,*
> *Ho, ho, ho!"*

"This is real magic," said the woman. "Now, what have I done?"

Lump watched the dough baby, fascinated. "You have made it alive!" he cried.

"Have I? Surely, it seems alive. You can see it move; hear it, too; and feel it if it were to dance on your hand. But how do you know that what you are seeing and hearing is really happening? Perhaps it is only your senses that have been confused, as with the dough-ball trick."

He looked doubtful. "But I can see it dance. It is real!"

"And, pray, what do you mean by 'real'?"

Lump had never thought about things in this way before; the question brought confusion but also a kind of thrill. He answered with a sweep of his hand around the room. "All this: what we can see and feel. And . . ." he added after some thought, "what all the other people in the world can see and feel."

"Very good," said the woman. "And you will allow also the animals, for as you know, they can see and feel things that we cannot."

"Oh, yes, the animals, too," agreed Lump.

"So what is real comes from the body, you say, ours

and the animals', although these are not exactly the same. Now, what about your mind? Is that real as well?"

"Of course it is," Lump answered. "It's what tells my body what to do and what my body is seeing and feeling."

"And therefore what is real and what is not is determined by our minds. Good. Now, what about dreams? They must come from our minds, yet you would not say that they are real."

Lump laughed. "But dreams are when we are sleeping. Our minds are shut off when we are sleeping."

"Still, dreams affect us as if they *were* real, do they not? If we have an ill dream, do we not wake all a-sweat and trembling in our limbs?" Lump nodded, not sure what to say. He had had many such dreams and did not like to think about them. She resumed, saying, "Listen, then, when I tell you that you are still asleep, even now, and this that you call real is a kind of dream. For even as the dreams you have when you sleep are but shadows of the sunlight world of true day, so the world you see by day is a mere shadow of an unseen world that lies beyond it. This unseen world is the source of true magic. For, as one might whisper in your ear while you dream, so that your dreams should take on some desired form, so by my enchantment I changed your waking dream so that this little lump of dough seems to leap about and sing."

Lump was now confused and growing angry, too. He pointed to the dancing mannikin. "So this is not real either?"

"I ask you again, what is real? If I were to conjure an ogre, let us say, instead of a dough baby, and he were to savage you, you would be just as dead as if a wolf from the forest had done it."

The little dough baby was still capering across the table and piping. With a casual swat of her hand she crushed it; it made a sharp final squeak.

"There *is* an unseen world. In places it penetrates this dream we call life, what you call real, and some have learned to cross over the borderlands between. These the vulgar call witches, mages, wizards, but they are merely travelers, bringing back a few treasures. Also, beings from that world have learned to cross into this one, and we call these elves, fairies, bogies, trolls, djinns, and so on. Bagordax is such a one. Tell me, have you never sensed anything odd about Bagordax? No, you have not. I can see it in your face. And this, perhaps, is yet another and final reason you may not learn magic. Some people have the gift; others have not. Were you gifted in this way, you would not have had to come to me asking to learn magic; you would have been making dough babies yourself from the time you could crawl. In this house the barrier between the worlds is as thin as gold leaf; it does not take great skill or concentration to pierce it. Yet you have not done so, even once. Besides, you were lulled by Bagordax's capers, the storytelling bed, and the moving figures on the walls. You did not venture to examine their magical roots, which you would have done had you any natural inclination for the magical arts."

The woman spoke matter-of-factly, and without any hint of reproach, yet to Lump her words were worse than blows. He had thought himself clever, keeping a secret in league with his tutor, yet she knew all and counted it as nothing. And for her to so lightly dismiss his dearest ambition was intolerable. Tears filled his eyes and he cried, "I will do magic! I will! Better than you! Better than anyone!" And he ran from the room, slamming the door.

"That child is spoiled," said the cat from his comfortable perch in a stone niche near the hearth.

The woman looked at him crossly and was about to make an objection, but a tiredness came over her suddenly, of the sort well-known to those whose children have not turned out as well as they had expected, and she simply sighed.

"I think you are right, Falance," she admitted. "I cannot see why, however. The boy has had everything that is proper for a child—food, warmth, shelter, well-fitting shoes—"

"What *we* say," the cat said, interrupting this litany, "is, cuff and cuddle cats the kitten. This child has had little of either cuffs or cuddles."

"That is untrue," said the woman. "I have spent many hours with him, baby and boy."

"Yes, and when he grew fretful, or you bored, you called for Ysul."

"What! Am I to be taught mothering by an old tomcat?"

For once, the cat did not flinch; cats have a keen sense of who has the moral advantage, and, having once seized it, he was not about to give it up. He ignored her angry gaze. "In fact," he continued, "you are not fond of him, or rather you are as fond of him as you are of everything. His little achievements bring a smile to your lips, but it is the same smile you bestow on the first iris or a passing badger. You are correct that I am no expert, yet I don't think this is the usual case among mothers of men. Instead, they dote. With us, it sometimes happens that a mother will ignore one of her kits, and it will grow into a runt, snarling and ill-mannered, yet still it has its brothers and sisters to heap among, be warmed by, to play with and learn from. You will observe that Lump has never had this chance. He has no sibs, nor even friends of his own kind."

"*I* had no friends!" the woman blurted out in a strange, harsh tone that surprised both her companion and her.

Then they were both silent for a period, while she tended to her pastry. She made a tray of strawberry tarts—Lump's favorite—stoked the fire, and popped them into the oven. Wiping her hands, she settled herself in a chair facing the hearth. When she spoke, her voice was weary. "I suppose you will say I should have known better. You will say you warned me of this."

"No cat would be so rude," said Falance. "You followed your heart, which, despite all, cannot be entirely ill. Nevertheless, it is a fair puzzle. Something must be done. The child is what? Ten years old?"

"Something like that," said the woman, suddenly conscious that parents elsewhere were not so vague and made much of their children's birthdays and held parties to celebrate them. The woman had never thought to do this and regretted it, now. Witches do not attend many parties, and those they do go to are hardly ever suitable for children.

"Then it is time you thought about what he will do to make his way in the world," the cat went on. "He cannot stay here forever."

"No, of course not," the woman murmured. "I had always thought that when the time came I could send him to Parmelka or Arminius or one of the western wizards, as an apprentice. I thought that he would develop some talent, and it was hard to admit that he has none at all. I kept hoping . . ."

"Surely you must have realized that if he did not show *here* and early, he would not show at all; this house is a compost heap for magic—the very *mice* can do wonders."

"Yes, yes—I beg you, do not lecture me, Falance. I feel sad enough about it. I have been neglectful and a fool, and now I must make it right. Let me see. . . ." She mused for some moments. "He might do as an apprentice to some trade. Surely, he has no great talent for learning, beyond reading and simple figures."

"You would have to cast a glamour on him for any master to take him," observed the cat. "I am no great judge of human loveliness, but he has, I think, less of it than anyone I ever saw."

"Yes, I thought he might improve with age, but he has not, and there it is. Although, now that you mention it, those who have little talent at doing magic are nearly always highly receptive to a cast spell. I could cast him clever in some trade, I suppose."

"You could," agreed the cat, "but you will agree that bearing a glamour that makes him pretty and a clever-spell on top of that is a mort of magic for a little fellow to carry, with no talent of his own, and especially for his whole life through the wide world. He would glow like a lamp to those who can see such things; and some of them, I do not have to tell you, bear us, and by extension him, no goodwill. Trolls would follow him down the street at noonday."

"Yes, of course, you are right. I don't know what I can be thinking of. It must be pretty or clever, but not both at once, to be sure. But which?" She rose and opened the oven door and brought out the tarts, which filled the whole cottage with their rich odor. The woman looked toward the door to the nursery in some hope that Lump might be lured back into good humor by the treat, but he was in the deepest sulk. She could feel it, like a heavy cloud through the planks of the door.

"If I may suggest it, my lady," said the cat carefully, "magical gifts are all well in their place, but the charms you have already cast to protect him have not done him much good with respect to his character. The main thing now is for him to be able to get along with his own kind. And none of us here are his kind. He needs companions, real ones, of the race of men."

At this the woman stiffened and answered coldly, "I will do what is necessary." And they spoke no more about it that evening.

Magic

A year passed. Lump was nearly eleven, the age when to ordinary children the company of friends is the dearest thing in the world. But Lump had no friends. Now, such children will often invent companions; in Lump's case this natural tendency was supported by his two magic windows. In the early mornings in cool weather when the windows were shut, Lump would glide lightly from bed so as not to disturb the sleeping Ysul and press his cheek against the panes.

In the near window, on such a morning at the Caravanserai of the Three Palms dawn still stained pink edges on a sky of the palest imaginable blue, utterly cloudless. Lump could hear the chuffing and pawing of the camels in the stockade and an occasional raucous bleat. A tall narrow door opened at the side of the inn, and a small figure emerged—a boy of about Lump's own age, dressed in a white robe and a white skullcap. Lump watched as the boy fed and watered the camels.

Lump seemed to be right behind him as he worked and murmured to the beasts. "I don't speak your language," Lump said in a low urgent voice, "but I know so much about you. I know your name in Djer and you have two sisters, Mahli and Zera, and your mother is Leila. Your father is dead, killed by bandits, you believe, and you help your mother run the caravanserai. It is a lonely place; and while many people pass through, no one stays for long, and the friendships you make are only passing ones. You are lonely, I know; sometimes at night you come out by yourself and sing to the camels, playing music on a harp with two strings. How I wish you would look up just once and see me! Please look up! I am so lonely, too!"

And then it seemed that Djer *did* look up, and that their eyes met and that Djer smiled at him, but it was only that a hawk had flown across the dunes, as it were, behind Lump, where he could never look. Then the bird flew over the caravanserai and away, and Djer lifted his empty bucket and went back inside.

Lump could have wept for vexation. He ran over to the far window and set his cheek against the glass. Looking through, he saw that it was late evening at the Lagoon of Pearls. The fires were lit in the little village above the shining beach. People were sitting and eating fish off huge green leaves, and the girls and boys were weaving garlands of pale flowers for their hair and to drape around their necks.

One girl sat apart from the others and threaded blossoms onto a thin vine. She looked out to the sea, and the rising moon lit her round face and shone on her long, black hair. Her name, as Lump well knew, was Pa'aili, and she was a pearl diver, as were all the girls and women in the village. Many times he had watched her row her little log canoe out into the pale green waters of the lagoon and fall over the side, clutching a rock, with no more splash than a leaf would make; and then his heart would nearly burst in his chest as he waited for her to break the surface, smiling, with a net full of shells.

Lump could now make out the sound of a drum, shouts, and the start of a song. Pa'aili placed her flower garland around her neck and joined the line of dancers. As he watched her, Lump's mind carried him across the seas; and he felt himself there next to her, her small brown hand clutched in his own; and also, through the same heartfelt wish, there was his other friend Djer and his family, with their camels, watching him dance in the moonlight and the firelight with Pa'aili to the beat of the great drum.

Into this delicious reverie there intruded the sound of another sort of thumping, and for some moments Lump incorporated this into his daydream; but at last he could not, and recognized that it was Ysul's heavy tread.

"Farewell, my friends," he whispered through the glass; his breath clouded over the dancing scene like fog from the sea. Here was the real reason that he had wanted to learn magic, to command dragons and flying carpets, as he had seen and heard in the stories Bagordax had caused to play on his walls. Yes, he was a prisoner, too, a handsome prince cast away from all he loved.

But now a disturbing thought entered his mind, not for the first time. Ysul had entered the room, and he turned to her, saying, "Tell me, Ysul, am I handsome?"

"Why, yes, I would say so, for a man-child," answered the bear. "You have a good dark pelt and your teeth are fine and long and yellow. Your claws are not what they should be, to be honest, but I have every hope that they will grow in time."

"But—" he began, and checked himself. It was

clear that if he was handsome, then Djer and Pa'aili's father and brothers and all the boys and men of her village were sadly deformed. He wondered if being handsome were quite so rare as that, and asked, "Do you think that there are many who are as handsome as me?"

"I could not say, my child," answered Ysul, "since I have never seen any of your kind, except your mother and once, when I was a cub, some men who were trying to kill me and my mother with arrows, but they were far away. Now, I have not come to pay you compliments, you know, but to fetch you for your lesson. Your mother awaits you outside."

Lump groaned. The woman had decided that neither glamour nor clever-spell would be necessary if Lump were to become a herb leech—one of the folk who wandered the countryside, curing diseases of man, woman, beast, and crop. No one expected a herb leech to be comely; the opposite was more usual, and a truly odd appearance might well add to the efficacy of the medicine dispensed. The woman felt quite pleased with this solution, as it both promised a livelihood for her son and gave her an opportunity to make up in part for what she now saw as a certain neglect.

Unfortunately, like many naturally skilled people, she was not a good teacher; and there was a great deal more grit than joy in learning when they came together for lessons.

She was at a garden table in the bright sun when she heard Lump's dragging step.

"You are late again," she said, regarding him sternly. "You must not lose track of time if you expect to excel in herb lore. Many herbs must be picked at a certain time, when a certain star is ascendant, or in a certain phase or elevation of the moon, for them to exhibit their full virtue." She then embarked on a lecture, paging through a large leather-bound herbal she had, in which there glowed many paintings of plants in their true colors, together with dried specimens. He listened glumly, knowing what was to come. At last she put up the volume and said, "Now, let us review. I have laid these out, both fresh and dried. Say what they are."

"Enchanter's nightshade," Lump began, "rosebay willow herb, salad burnet, lady's mantle—"

"That is wood avens."

"Wood avens, dead nettle, cowbind, corn gromwell, convulsion root, corpse plant . . ."

"Yes, go on."

He sighed. "Greater celandine—"

"Lesser celandine. A serious error. The plants are not at all similar in their principles or uses."

Lump flung himself onto a bench, his elbows on his knees and his face in his hands. "Oh, greater or lesser! I cannot do it; it will not all fit into my brain!"

"Yes, it will. You are just starting out, and, you know, you don't really apply yourself. You should study the book and make drawings of your own." She continued in this way for a time, but it was as if every well-meaning suggestion was a bag of stones placed on his back. His shoulders sagged and his head drooped, until she stopped, controlled her temper, and said, putting on a smile, "Well, perhaps it is too fine a day for such heavy work. I tell you what: let us go a-gathering. It will be a good study for you and I have need of some things."

He brightened. Since his babyhood with Ysul, Lump had found pleasure in field and forest, and, more than that, a walk would be a relief from the endless memorizing. The woman took up a basket and they set out through the garden and into the woods.

The forest was cool after the heat of the garden, and smelled pleasantly of pine and leaf mold. The marsh lilies were out, adding their heavy perfume to the air. It was late in spring, a warm day and fair.

"What are we looking for, Mother?" Lump asked.

"We are nearly out of cuckooflower. And there should be a patch of crow poison near that great, blasted beech. See if you can find it." She was about to say, "Mind the nettles," but then recalled that she had placed a ward against nettles on him, which still must have some power.

He darted ahead. Somehow, finding plants in the woods was a different thing from trying to recall their names when they were spread upon a table. He quickly found the spiky white-flowered plants and carefully dug out several with their bulbs, while she watched. As they continued down the path, she described the uses of the plant and its relatives—the false asphodel, the poison sago, and the death camas.

Suddenly, the woman halted, sniffing the air, her head tilted as if listening to some secret sound. "This is well met," she said. "It is time you learned something about this. Follow me closely, and be silent!"

The woman ducked under a low-hanging hawthorn and crawled down what appeared to be a well-beaten tunnel in the underbrush. The boy followed her, puzzled but with a growing anticipation. Neither of them made more sound than a squirrel.

The tunnel opened into a substantial hollow, damp and roofed with thorn, backed by black boulders. There was room to spare for both Lump and the woman to sit. Greenish light filtered down and cast coin-sized patches of brightness on their bodies.

"Listen well, my child. There are plants that are not in any herbal. They grow in the meadows and forests of the unseen world. This is one of the places where the ordinary world and the unseen world come close together."

"Like our house?" asked Lump, breathless.

"In a way, although our house is as it is because *I* am there and not through any virtue of place. This place is an actual . . . the word is *permalion*, a kind of gateway. It has uncovered since the last time I was this way."

"I don't understand. Uncovered?"

"I will explain. Do you see my apron? In one corner, here, there is a lily embroidered and in the opposite corner a violet. Now, suppose I twist and crumple the apron, like this. That is how the ordinary world and the unseen world behave, flowing past each other, touching at places, then separating. See, now the lily and the violet meet, and the two worlds are joined."

Lump looked around him doubtfully, trying to see marvels in the dappled gloom. "This . . . *this* is the unseen world?" he asked.

"Yes, but of course *you* cannot see it; no more could you see a banquet in a chamber barred by a thick oaken door. You would say, 'There is no feasting here!' Nay, the door must be opened for you. Now, look into my eyes and do not move!"

Frightened, yet terribly excited, Lump did as he was told. His yellow eyes locked with his mother's gray ones; the hair stood stiff on his scalp and along his spine. She began to sing in a low hoarse voice—not at all like her everyday voice—a rhythmic song, beating the measure on her thigh. The words of the enchantment seemed to emerge slowly from her mouth and burst over him like bubbles. The air grew warm and curiously thick, like goose down rushing through his nostrils, and along with it came a heavy smell, sweet and rancid at the same time; and the motes of dust floating in the air took on colors—red, green, violet, and some he could not identify. This is like falling asleep, he thought, and then, no, it is like *falling awake*.

She blinked her eyes, and he was able to look around. The sunlight pouring in through gaps in the foliage overhead seemed a stronger, more buttery yellow. There were blue-purple seedpods hanging from the thornbush overhead. He reached for one, but his mother cried, "No!"

She seemed a figure in a dream when he looked at her. He noticed, without really taking it in, that she had changed: she glowed, and her plain, country garments were now covered with an angular script, picked in silver.

"Don't touch that plant!" she warned. "It is called come-devil vine. Its juice attracts the trolls as nothing else does in either world. You do not want to get any on you. This is a troll den, in fact, in this world and in ours. Mind the droppings. Now, here is what I was after." She pointed, and he saw that the floor of the den was covered with a dense carpet of ordinary looking yellow-green plants, some of which had tiny yellow flowers on them.

"What is it? It does not look like much."

"No. But looks can deceive. This is wizard's tansy, extremely rare and extremely hard to obtain even when located. It only grows near come-devil, and since there are always trolls around come-devil . . ." She left the remark unfinished, and, as she knelt to gather the little plants, she added, "Fortunately, it is day in both worlds, which is not always the case. As I am sure you have learned, trolls are inactive during the day. Help me gather these."

Lump knelt and pulled. After some minutes working, he asked, "Mother, if the troll came back, could you . . . could you make it go away?"

"In my own place, with Falance to help, I could. You need earth power to fight trolls. Here, it would be touch and go. I might save you, though."

The significance of this last remark gradually penetrated his mind. "Wha—what would happen to you, Mother?"

"Oh, killed and eaten, killed and eaten without a doubt. Raw. Look, there is a good well-grown one behind you, Do not tread on it, please."

He turned and plucked the plant carefully and placed it in her basket, his head abuzz with uncomfortable thoughts. He had not really considered whether his mother loved him or not, but he was aware that quite often he did not like her very much. Now, almost casually, she had said that she would sacrifice herself to a dreadful death to save him. It was an unsettling thought; quickly, therefore, his mind put it aside.

Then a sudden notion struck him, and he sat up and tugged on the woman's sleeve. "Mother! If it is day, and trolls sleep in the day, and if this is really a troll's den, then where is the troll?"

"The troll? Why, it's just over there." She pointed toward the shadowy rear of the hollow. "Can't you smell it?"

He sniffed. There was certainly a stench. He looked. The dark wall was twice as high as he stood and four times as broad. In a small voice he asked, "Do you mean it is behind that great stone?"

"That is not a stone," she said. As she spoke, the wall rippled horribly and shifted as the monster stirred in its sleep.

Later, as they were striding across a meadow in the sunlight and he had stopped trembling, he said, "You haven't told me what this wizard's tansy is for."

"Have I not? Well, then, it is made into a tea, like common tansy, which, when drunk confers the power to—this is hard to explain—*draw* Names. It is used in the naming ceremony." Observing his blank expression, she continued. "Every person, beast, and thing has a real Name, different from and higher than the word we use to call it in the speech of every day. Magic depends on these Names, for we say, 'When name you sing, you sway the thing.' And learning your true Name is the first step in the higher magical arts."

"But I know my name," he exclaimed. "It is Lump."

"No, child. That is what you are called. But your real Name is that which was hammered into your soul when it was forged in the First Days. It can be learned; and once learned, it is the foundation of all the high magic that can be done by you. Or to you."

"Then if I knew my real Name, could I do magic, like you?" the boy asked.

"No, child," said the woman gently. "You have no gift for it; and a Name, while conveying many good things, will not give you that of itself."

The boy said nothing but walked on stolidly. After a while he said, "We are going to the river."

"Yes, we will find the cuckooflower there. What is the matter?"

The boy had stopped, gazing in fascinated delight across the meadow at a low mound of grass. He pointed.

"What are those, Mother? What are those?"

"They are the fay. That mound is a fairy hill, or fort," she answered. And after a pause, she asked, "And can you truly see them?"

"Oh, yes, I can! Aren't they lovely beyond anything? Can we go to them, Mother? Can we?"

"Not today. And, my dear, you should understand that while the fay are the most beautiful of all creatures, they are petulant, cruel, and violent beings. If it ever happens that you see them another time, keep your eyes on the ground and go about your business; do not heed their songs and cajolings, for once inside that hill, there you will stay and not see the true sun for a hundred years."

They walked on, but not without Lump casting many a secret backward look at the flashing wings and glittering costumes of the fairies. Soon these were obscured by a rise of ground, and Lump held tight to his mother's hand and rejoiced in her presence and that she was paying him attention. The woman seemed to be in high spirits as well, for she sang as she walked, one of her favorite songs. And Lump joined in the chorus:

"I am the girl called Sleeping Beauty.
I never answer to that name,
For I am slave to love and duty.
It was the kiss that brought the chain."

As they entered the birch woods that bordered the river, they heard a growing racket that soon resolved into the clang of axes and the crashing fall of trees. The woman stopped her song and said, "This is odd; I had not realized that men had come so far upstream. Lump, walk carefully now and do not show yourself through the trees."

Coming to the edge of the wood they peered through the white bars of the trees. There was the river, muddier now than they were used to, and on the other side a large clearing had been made and a log house had been constructed. A crew of men was chopping down trees; others were working in a sawpit, cutting the trees into logs; and still others were loading the logs onto a cart drawn by eight white oxen.

"Why are they cutting down the trees?" asked Lump.

"They will carry them in that cart and on the river to a market, where they will trade them for things they desire—food, clothing, tools, and so on. And gold."

"What is that?"

"A metal they love. Stay you here and be still. I will get the herb."

The woman vanished among the trees. Lump was content to stay there forever. He had never seen other people before, and everything they did was new and strange. The rough noises of the logging excited him as much as the visit to the troll den and the sight of the fairies.

Then, to his amazement, the door of the cabin opened and out came two children, a girl of about six and a boy of about ten years, slim and golden headed, both carrying buckets. Shouting, they dashed down to the river, filled their buckets, and went back into the house. They returned a moment later, and Lump saw that they now had dippers with their pails and were going from one crewman to another, giving them water.

Lump's heart was in his throat, and he wondered for a moment whether this were an enchantment. These were real children, not on the far side of the world, to be seen through magic windows, but here, an hour's walk from his own home.

The little girl came out again and went to the streamside, where she squatted and dabbled in the sand with a stick and drew pictures. The boy came out again, and after watching the girl for a few moments, he smeared her picture with his foot. The girl's face grew red and wrinkled; she made hooting noises and threw her stick at the boy, who laughed at her. She ran squalling back to the cabin.

The boy threw stones into the stream, making them skip across the water. A fat woman called to him from the cabin; he continued to throw stones, ignoring her. Shortly thereafter, a much larger boy came from the sawpit. He was heavy featured and broad shouldered, red faced and dark haired, with an angry look on his face. His hair and rough clothing were covered with a pale layer of sawdust. He strode to the blond boy, who, seeing him come, attempted to run away, but was quickly caught, thrown to the ground, cuffed, and dragged by an arm, crying, back to the cabin.

"We must go," said the woman, appearing just behind Lump.

"No, Mother. I want to watch the children. They are so strange in their ways and so ugly, the poor things. Their noses hardly show at all, their ears are but little bumps, their teeth are all worn away, and they have pelt only on their heads. Of course, they may be ladies."

"No, not ladies," said the woman carefully, "but in the wide world people may have appearances different from those you are used to. You have not seen many people."

"I have not seen *any* people! Oh, please, may I stay? Perhaps I could"—he reached for an unaccustomed word—"*play* with them."

What am I feeling? the woman asked herself. I have always known what to do; I see the Pattern clear as my own hand, and I follow it and am content. But there is no guide here, and every path I can see leads to some pain. Perhaps this is part of having a child; the Pattern is of no use, and there is this aching in my heart.

She looked across the stream to where the fat housewife was scolding her little boy; as they watched he got a clout across the ear that made him wail. The woman wondered if that woman ever felt so, ever had this aching, and for the first time she regretted never having had any human creature to whom she might unburden her heart.

"May I, Mother?" Lump asked, bringing her back to the issue.

"No, child, you may not. Not now, for we must

return. I have things to do before nightfall. But," she added, when she saw his face, "perhaps another time."

Despite this disappointment, Lump thought that this was the best day he could remember. He felt showered with attention; even the cat was kind to him. Of all the little household, only Bagordax seemed grumpy; the afreet crouched in a corner of the schoolroom and gave short answers when Lump tried to tell him about the wonderful excursion. Lump could not see the granite mass that bound the djinn now reached to his knees.

His mother even came to tuck him in, a rare treat, and Lump felt encouraged to try for one even rarer.

"Will you tell me a story, Mother?"

"Yes, I suppose so. Which would you like to hear?"

"The one about when you were a little girl and your grandmother and the wolf."

The woman smiled and began. "Once upon a time, in the middle of a great forest, there lived a poor family with a little girl, and that was me. I loved the forest and all its creatures, and they loved me. I was out in all weathers, and to keep me warm and dry, my mother made me a riding cloak, with a hood to it, of red wool woven close, for which reason I became known in those parts as Little Red Riding Hood. Now, one day my mother said to me, 'Take this basket of goodies to your grandmother's house, but be careful not to stray off the path. There are wicked huntsmen in the forest, and not only might they mistake you for a hart or roe deer, and shoot you down, but they might wish to carry you off and sell you, since not everyone has a lovely little girl like you, and many want one.' So I said I would take care and went out with my basket of goodies. Halfway to my grandmother's house, I met a great gray wolf. I did my curtsey and said, 'How d' you do, wolf?'

"'Well, am I,' said the wolf, 'but not so my pack, for we are sore hurt by these huntsmen. Many are shot down, nor are they eaten but left for the crows. It is a sadness. But where are you bound, child of men?'

"'To my granny's,' said I, 'to bring her these goodies in my basket. Would you care for a slice of sausage?'

"'Yes, I would,' said the wolf, and I gave it to him and he snapped it up, one-two.

"'Now I will give you something for being a friend to the wolves,' said the wolf. And he pulled three hairs from his tail and wove them with his clever mouth into a love knot that he fixed to the tie of my hood.

"Then he said, 'If you are ever in danger, place the

knot in your mouth and chew it, and I will be pulled by the tail. Then I and mine will come to you with all the help we have.'

"I thanked the wolf and went on my way. But the day was hot and the path long, and soon I saw a place where I could cut through the forest and shorten my trip, and, forgetting what my mother had told me, I left the path and walked through the shady woods.

"There a huntsman spied me, who marked my direction and hurried to my grandmother's house, as fast as his legs would carry him. There he climbed in through the window and seized the poor old lady, tied her up, and stuck her in the cellar. He dressed himself in her bed cap and gown and got in among the bed-clothes, arranging his fat leather game bag across his belly, where it would be handy.

"Soon I came in and did my curtsey, saying, 'Grandmother, here is a basket of goodies for you, except a bit of sausage I gave to a wolf. But, Grandmother,' I said, looking hard, 'what big eyes you have!'

"'The better to see you with, my dear,' said the huntsman.

"'And, Grandmother, what big ears you have!'

"'The better to hear you with, my dear,' said the huntsman.

"'And, Grandmother, what a big belly you have!' said I.

"'The better to bag you up, my dear,' cried the huntsman, and he leaped out of bed. He seized me by my little red riding hood and stuffed me headfirst into the bag.

"'Oh, huntsman, huntsman!' I called out. 'Why do you stuff me in your bag?'

"'Why to take you to market,' said the huntsman.

"'And will you sell me there?' I asked, for I recalled my mother's words.

"'Oh, yes. I will sell you to a man, to be his wife.'

"'And what will become of me then?' I asked from inside the bag.

"'He will nail you with four nails,' said the huntsman. 'He will nail a pot to one hand and a broom to the other, a stove to one foot and a washtub to the other.'

"'But then I shall not be able to run the wild woods in my riding hood,' I said, 'and sport with the birds and the beasts.'

"'No, nay, never,' said the huntsman, 'never no more, but you shall have many babies to sport with and a fine dress to wear. And I shall have the gold for you, so it is all right.'

"But I did not think it was all right at all, and so I chewed down on the knot of hair that the gray wolf had given me, and the wolf was pulled by the tail and he howled and summoned all his kin. Running like the wind they came to my grandmother's house and came in through the doors and windows and ate up the huntsman, one-two, until not a scrap was left. Then the wolves let me out of the bag, and I untied my grandmother and we all had a nice supper with the goodies from the basket, and never again did I disobey my mother and go off the path."

Lump sighed and wriggled deeper into his bedclothes. There was something about hearing a story from his mother that was so much nicer than hearing a story from a magical bed or from Bagordax. But Lump was not satisfied with this oft-told tale.

"And what happened after that?" he asked. "Did you live happily with your family ever after?"

At this the witch's face grew dark, and she was about to tell an easy fib; but lies always fell uneasily from her tongue, and, besides, she thought, with these people we saw today crowding in, it's as well he learned something of the world.

"No," she said, "sadly, I did not. The next winter my mother was carried off by a fever, and my father grew morose and drank; and when drunk he railed at me, saying I recalled too well his lost wife and blaming me for living, while she was dead. Also, about that time, I was coming into my power and weaving little spells of my own, and this made him frightened of me. One day at supper there was a stranger, a woman, who admired me and spoke charmingly, and gave me to drink yellow cordial, which was the nicest thing I had ever had in my mouth. But it put me into a deep, deep sleep, and when I awoke I was in a strange bed. He had sold me to a witch."

"Were you frightened?"

"A little, but there was such a pulse of magic in that house that in a little while I dried my tears and was entranced. Then the witch, whose name was Meregild, told me that I would be her servant for seven years, and in return she would teach me to control my art. This I later found was a lie; she wished instead to make me her slave, my power subject to her own, and steal my youth and live longer, for she was then a very old woman. She beat me often and would not let me out of her sight, and never another soul did I see those seven years."

"How did you escape her?"

"She had a weakness. She loved honey but was deathly afraid of bees—I don't know why, but she was. She said her spells did not work on them, and they stung her. So she sent me to the bees to draw her honey from their stores, and thus I made friends with them and had many pleasant conversations with the queen in the buzzing glades. And I said if she helped me, I would see to it that her hive was never raided again by bear, badger, or witch, for Meregild was greedy and demanded too much honey. So one day they came in a mighty swarm and drove her out of the house, and I slipped in and stole her great book of spells, the same that sits on my shelf to this day, and with it I cast a magic that won me my freedom."

"What happened to the witch?" Lump asked.

"She is small and dried in my blue jar, the one on the chimneypiece."

"Oh," said Lump, and this got him thinking again about the power to bind. It occurred to him that he had not had lessons from his tutor for some time, and so he asked, "Mother, is Bagordax still my tutor?"

"No, dear," said the woman. "I believe Bagordax has taught you all he can. In fact, I suspect that some of what he has taught you might best be unlearned. It was perhaps an error to employ him, as I see now."

"*You're* my teacher, now," he said confidently, and then, as his mind flitted idly, he asked, "Mother, little girls and boys in stories are always beautiful, aren't they?"

"Yes; it is the way of stories."

"And I am beautiful, too. But those little children we saw today, if their mother tells them stories, are they not sad when they think how ugly they are, and not like the children in the stories?"

"Perhaps. But perhaps if their mother loves them very much, as I love you, it does not matter a great deal."

Lump smiled and closed his eyes. The woman kissed his eyelids, said a little charm for pleasant dreams, and left the room silently. Ysul the bear snored gently on her pink sofa.

The woman set the kettle on to boil and reached down for a tea caddy to make herself a cup of tea, for she was much disturbed in her heart. The caddy's lid stuck, however. In trying to force it, she ripped a nail, which caused her to utter a malediction and fling it to the floor, where it vanished in a ball of blue flame and a stench, appearing a moment later among a group of shepherds in a far country, who treated it with the utmost reverence thereafter.

"You are upset," said Falance. "Pray sit down in your chair, and I will make you a soothing cup."

The woman was so surprised by this offer that she immediately went and sat down in her favorite place, a high-backed armchair draped with rugs. The cat was perfectly capable of making a cup of tea, by standing on his hind legs and using his paws, but he had never offered to do it before. It was a service one does not expect from cats, especially not tomcats.

"This is good. Thank you, Falance." The woman sipped gratefully at her cup. The cat had used camomile, raspberry, and widow's vervain, for there is nothing more suitable for calming the nerves.

"My pleasure," said the cat, jumping up to his shelf by the hearth, where he could look her in her eye. "What is the matter? I thought you passed a pleasant day. The boy at least was singing like a sparrow. I nearly warmed to him myself."

"It was a lovely day, and he is a lovely boy. But his heart is about to be broken. There is nothing I can do to prevent it, and it is like an icicle through my own heart. I know you don't like him and that you don't approve of my being mother to him, but there it is. I am at a loss. I see now that you were right, my dear cat, that it was a grave error to raise him away from his own kind, and now the timbermen have come over the near ridge, and there is a homestead on the narrow river, a homestead with children, and of course he wants to go to them. He thinks they are ugly and he is handsome, and he feels sorry for them."

"You are not to blame in this, if I may say so, madam," said the cat. "You yourself know so little of human ways: sold as a child to a witch, raised with a stick and a curse, alone in the forest . . ."

"Oh, stop! Yes, all that, but still, there remains the child and what to do with him. I have an urge that before all, he must have protection."

"Protection! By my whiskers, madam, the child is covered with wards enough to shield a province from the whole cavalry of hell."

"Oh, those are country magics, *piseogs*, to block fly

bites and falls," said the woman. "I mean a Great Magic, a true ward. And for that, of course, he must be Named."

The cat sighed; they had been through this before. He said, "You are thinking of clever spells and glamours again, are you, my lady? I presume the herbal lessons do not go well."

"Well enough, although he has no great love for the study of it. He has an affection for the woodland, though, and all natural things. He loves the beasts and they love him. Ysul is his slave. It is a great compliment, and in the matter of his character I must have some hope at least, if only from that. But it seems he does have one talent, of a sort. We were down in the troll den—"

"What! There is a *troll*?"

"Yes, I forgot to mention it. There is a *permalion* in the beech wood. It is fat with wizard's tansy and there is a troll in it. Yes, yes, don't stare at me as if I were a kitten that had messed its coat! We will tear out the come-devil and set trollbane around and about. But what I was going to say: while we were there I Opened him, so he could see the unseen herbs, and then when we were out in broad sunlight, I expected it to fade, as it does with ordinary people; but when we passed

Tiptree Hill, he saw the fay."

"But—but Tiptree Hill is a shut hill, by your order, my lady. The fay are not to show themselves to mortals without your leave."

"And shut it is, Falance. They were not showing; he *saw* them. It was the Opening I did on him. I have never seen the like: he holds a cast spell like white iron quenched in oil holds the hammered shape. When is the full of the moon? I will name him then and cast him a ward so strong that the scoffs and harms of the world will roll off it like rain. Now, what shall it be . . . ?"

"The next full is Wednesday, but it is Midsummer Moon, madam," observed the cat, after a pause. "And you are off tomorrow to Merrymount, to light one of the Seven Fires."

The woman slapped her thigh in irritation and her tea spilled. "Devil!" she cried and then made an averting sign. "I had forgotten. Yes, well, then the one after Beltane, the very first one."

The next morning, Lump learned that the delights of the previous day were not to be immediately repeated and that his mother would be gone for a week or more.

"Can't I come with you?" he pleaded.

"I'm afraid not. Midsummer Moon is not for little

boys. You will be fine with Ysul. There is plenty of food in the larder and garden."

"But Falance may go," said the boy with his former sulkiness.

"Yes, but Falance is a colleague; he is my familiar. You know that, Lump."

"You love him better because he can do magic and I cannot."

She sighed and took his hand and tried to maintain her patience. She did not need a cranky scene on this of all mornings, when she had a thousand tasks of last minute preparation for the great week of the witches' liturgical year. "It has nothing to do with love, dear. And I will promise you this: when I return in a week's time, I will take you to the heart of the forest and there I will draw down your Name. You will be named! How would you like that?"

The boy brightened. "Then I will be able to do *some* magic, won't I?"

"Ah . . . well, in a manner of speaking," she temporized. "You will certainly be able to do magical feats."

With this he had to rest content. The remainder of the day was consumed by the gathering and packaging of herbs and simples, the copying down of spells, and performance of a series of rituals behind the locked door of the woman's workroom.

The aura of the magic was annoying, so Lump left the house and wandered off, through the garden to the wood line and into the forest itself. It was a warm morning and, except for the invisible warbling birds, the forest would have seemed deserted to the ordinary walker. It was not so to Lump. He had keen ears and a keener sense of smell, so he heard the high-pitched conversation of the tiny creatures below the leaf litter, the scrumblings of the wood burrowers in the trees, the tread of the rabbit, and the more stealthy tread of the weasel that stalked it. He was perfectly at home.

His feet seemed to know their own way and gradually he became aware that he was moving toward the little valley and its river, where he had seen the wood-cutters and the children. He entered the birch wood and peered through its edge. He saw, to his surprise, that what had been a wooded hill was now bare and raw as a wound, all red earth and the ragged stumps and branches of the fallen trees. Some men were trying, with many a vile curse, to rip up a stump with a team of white oxen. Huge bonfires had been lit to consume the stumps and scrap and to make ash to fertilize the soil of what was clearly meant to be a farm. The two youngest children were dashing around the fire, screaming and waving brands, while the older boy was bringing armloads of branches and flinging them in. They were calling to one another, and this is how Lump learned their names. The little girl was Tippy, the little boy was Lons, and the big lad was Mank.

In a while, two men approached with a barrow loaded with stumps. They shouted the two smaller children away and enlisted Mank to help them unload the stumps onto the blaze. Lons ran off to the river, followed by his sister. There they amused themselves by throwing stones into the water and at whatever birds flew by, although there were not many birds about. They found a mole in a stump hole and battered it to death, and then Lons threw the body into the water. Lump watched all this in growing puzzlement. The children were clearly amused by what they were doing, but Lump could not understand why. He knew that animals killed other animals to eat them, but the children did not eat the mole. Perhaps there was something in the activity that he could not see. But he very much wanted to, for until he understood these new people he would not venture to make himself known to them, and that was what he now wanted more than anything else in the world.

The men stopped their work for their dinner. They sat at a trestle table outside the cottage's front door, while the stout woman of yesterday and a younger woman he had not seen before brought them bowls of food, with Tippy's help. The men shouted orders at the women, although Lump thought the women were moving as quickly as they could. Neither Lons nor Mank helped to serve, but sat at the table with the men. Lump now grew hungry himself and left the birches, waving a good-bye that the children could not see. Crossing a glade, he saw some crows in a tree, and decided to try the new game he had learned. He picked up a pebble and threw it as hard as he could at the crows. They arose, squawking and flapping heavily. He threw another and another, and actually struck one on the wing. Lump smiled; yes, that was fun, to see them jump like that. It reminded him of his days with Ysul, when all the forest creatures fled from their path.

"Why do you stone us, child of men?"

Lump turned and there was a crow king, a big, raggedy bird the color of midnight in a coal mine, sitting on a low bough of an ash tree, regarding him with his bright black eye.

Lump felt a hot blush rise to his cheeks and he shrugged.

"We have not harmed you, have we? We have not eaten your grain or garden, not more than a little, and we have never stolen the chicks from your nests. Are you injured in your mind, to thus attack us with no reason? Son of such a mother, for shame!"

Lump turned and ran home, while the crows shouted his crime to all the world. Far worse was the look on his mother's face, when he came into the kitchen, breathless and famished.

"Is this true what I hear? You have been stoning the crows?"

Lump returned the same shrug he had given the crow king.

"Why?" the woman persisted. "What has gotten into you? Look at me, please! How could you bring such shame on our house? *Cruelty to birds*? You have always loved the birds. Lump! Speak to me!"

He sat down at the table and looked away from her. "I'm hungry," he said.

She stared at him for a moment, silent. "If you are

hungry, Ysul will make you something," she said coldly after a time.

"Ysul can't make anything but porridge, and I don't want porridge."

"Then take yourself something; there is plenty in the larder."

"No! I don't want to! I'm tired," he said petulantly. "I want *you* to make me something. You're the *mother*. You're supposed to. That's what *real* mothers do. That's what *real* people do. They don't care about silly birds."

He glared at her with his face flushed and such a look of arrogant condescension in his eyes that for an instant, a fraction of an eye blink, the heavy barricades that she had emplaced to shield ordinary beings from the true fires that flared within her slipped, and she *looked* at him, right into his eyes.

The children of the public executioner do not see in their father the terrifying masked figure that strides, blood reeking, through the shambles; to them he is just Dad, a good old fellow dozing with his ale before the fire. Likewise, it had never occurred to Lump that he was being raised by the dreadful Queen of Air and Darkness.

In that terrible second the magical wards that had sheltered his childhood from the ordinary harms thereof were stripped away like so much tinsel. He felt as if he had been struck by a hot black wind; his mind reeled and he tumbled backward from his chair, bruising his elbow and his cheek painfully on the rough flagstones of the floor.

And just as swiftly, she was overcome with remorse. She knelt down beside him, reaching out to him. But he shrank away, sliding across the floor, blubbering with terror and unaccustomed pain. Staggering to his feet, he ran from the room.

For the rest of the day he sulked on his bed. He suffered Ysul to lick his wounds and bring him some bread, cheese, and milk, but spoke not a word. Nor did he look through his magic windows; the faraway children no longer satisfied, not when real children were close by. He fell into an exhausted sleep soon after sundown, and in the morning his mother and her cat were gone.

"I tell you what it is," said the cat as the two of them flew over mountain, plain, and sea. They were not on a broomstick, but if any person had looked up and caught a glimpse of them against the waxing moon, fat with creamy light, that is what they would have seen: a cat and a woman flying on a broom.

In any case there was a wind, and the cat had to

raise his voice to make himself heard. "I tell you what it is: it's those new people in the valley, the woodcutters. He has seen how they behave and he wants to be like them. It is like a young bird who imitates the songs it hears until it learns the proper music of its kind. It will take some time and explanation to correct this, but, after all, my lady, it is not your fault."

"It *is* my fault, Falance. I will never forgive myself. The poor thing! We had passed such a pleasant day, and he was so excited that I was taking an interest in him at last, and I was glad, too. And then the very next day I must ignore him again, because of this duty."

Yes, thought the cat, but you did not send to the Wise and say you could not come to the fires because you had to go lollygagging after plants with your little boy. He did not say this, and she went on. "You know, I might have killed him then. He was so hurt. I cannot understand how I allowed myself to get into such a fury. And stripping away his wards like that!"

"Well if a cat may be allowed to offer advice, it would probably have been no bad thing for him to skin his knee from time to time or bump his head. After all, he must get on in the world, and pain is the great teacher."

Friends

At one level of his mind, Lump knew he had behaved like a fool and had deserved his mother's ire. But he had been given so little close rearing that he was unable to deal with this thought head-on. Instead, he made up a story in which he, the handsome prince, had been stolen by the wicked witch—his mother—who did not understand him. His real home was in the valley, with Lons and Tippy and Mank and the big bearded men with axes and the stout woman who ran in and out of the doorway bringing steaming plates of food. That Lump's mother actually *was* a witch (although far from wicked) gave his version of this common story unusual power.

In the morning, he gulped down a bun and a bowl of milk in the kitchen and set out for what he had half convinced himself was his true home. It was another pleasant spring day. As he walked he was fixed on this dream and was not paying attention. He did not notice that the birds, instead of dancing around his head and sharing the gossip of the forest with him, as they had before, stayed in their trees and sang warnings to one another.

He walked until he came to the birches and threaded his way through the close-set trunks. The bonfire was still burning but lower now. A man was spreading ashes on a field with a wooden rake, but Lump barely looked at him because there was something far more fascinating going on by the river. A crew was heaving at ropes and tackle, lowering a log onto a cradle made by other logs, which had been stuck upright in the bed of the river. They were building a bridge, but Lump did not know that, as he had never seen a bridge. From the foot of this bridge, they had laid short-sawn logs crossways to make a road, which now extended back over the far hill. Lump wondered why they had left the logs lying on the ground that way; he had never seen a road before either.

He watched the men work, at the same time looking out for the children. He saw Mank with the bridge crew; he was carrying a bag of pegs and running from one crewman to another when called, handing out the pegs, which the men hammered into holes to secure the logs to their supports and tie the whole together. Tippy and Lons he did not see.

The sun moved across the heavens and the day grew hot. Lump became hungry and thirsty and thought he would gather blackberries for his noon meal. He walked through the birches for some distance and found a loaded bush among the birches. He began to pick handfuls of the ripe berries, jamming the sweet cool fruit into his mouth. As he picked and ate, he was still lost in his dream world—in his imaginings he had reached the place where he came running up to the cabin, and all the people stopped what they were doing and embraced him, and were astounded at what a lovely child he was, and made him welcome—and so he did not notice that someone else was picking on the other side of the bush and making a good deal of noise doing it.

He pulled a branch down to get at some higher berries, and there, her face as smeared with juice as his own, was little Tippy. He smiled delightedly. "Good day," he said politely. The color drained from her pink cheeks, her blue eyes widened, and her tiny purple mouth formed into a perfect O. Then she let out a shrill cry and vanished.

Lump heard her crashing through the bushes and

ran to follow her. As he ran, he looked wildly around to see what had frightened her so badly. But there was no scent of bear or wolf in the air. Perhaps she was simply startled by seeing a strange boy. He burst through the bushes to a narrow beach of small stones. Here, he saw, the river ran foaming through a line of flat, tumbled boulders. Over these the little girl dashed lightly, making a continuous din with her piping cries. He watched her disappear into the birch wood that lined the opposite shore.

Lump ate some more berries and then walked back to his vantage point. Tippy had arrived at the cabin. She was crying and pointing to the opposite shore, while the bearded man from the field and the two women—the younger and the elder—and Mank and Lons, listened and looked in the direction she was pointing. The bearded man went into the cabin and came out with an axe. With Mank at his heels he strode off in the direction of the ford. The elder woman slapped Tippy to make her stop crying. Lump sighed and slipped silently out of the birch wood toward his home. He did not want to speak to the man with the axe. Tomorrow he would come back to the berry patch early and pick a great pile of berries. Tippy would return and then he would give her the berries and they would become friends and then he would walk hand in hand with her to the little farm and all would be as he imagined.

"Where are you off to?" asked Ysul the next morning, as Lump raced for the door after gobbling his porridge.

"Out. The woods," Lump replied, slipping a bun into his shirt for later.

"Then be sure to stay on this side of the birch woods. There are strange doings there, I hear—odd folks and tearing up the woods."

But that was just where Lump was headed. He arrived breathless at the birches and looked down. The bridge was nearly complete. Men were pounding spikes to secure the split logs of the roadway. Mank was not among them, nor could Lump see either of the two younger children.

He watched the work for a while, hoping to see them, but, growing bored, he left the birches and walked upstream to where the blackberries grew. He made a cup of a large coltsfoot leaf pinned closed by a thorn, and filled it with choice berries. As he picked, he became conscious of an odd sound, a snuffling, faint whimper. He pushed through the tangle of blackberries, heedless of the prickles, and there, in the little clearing where he had first encountered Tippy, he found her once more.

When she saw him, she started to scream and jerk about in a peculiar way, and Lump saw that she was tied to a birch trunk by a thick rope about her waist. He approached her, smiling and holding out the cup of berries. Her cries and movements became all the wilder.

"Who has tied you this way, Tippy?" he asked kindly. "Here, let me help you get untied." He took a step toward her. There was a crashing behind him. He turned to see what it was. It was Mank, his face a grimace, holding a cudgel over his head.

"What is it?" cried Lump and looked wildly about, to see what beast might be poised to attack. Then he felt the blow, and fell into the dark.

"He's killed," Lump heard a voice say. "You hit him too hard, Mank."

"Shut your stupid face!" said a deeper voice. "He's not dead. Look, he stirs."

Lump opened his eyes. His vision was blurred and the light was dim. It came from a horn lantern, held by Mank.

Lump moved his head, and was shaken by a stab-bing pain. What has happened? he wanted to say, but discovered that his mouth was blocked by a thick leather strap that went around his head. Nor could he stir his limbs. He was bound, sitting, to a post support-ing a low ceiling in some sort of cellar.

"You're right, Mank. He's alive," said Lons.

The smaller boy was standing next to his brother. He held a hayfork. "Can I poke him, Mank? Can I?"

Mank grunted assent, and Lons jabbed Lump painfully in the flank.

Tippy, who was standing on the other side of Mank, cried, "I want to poke, too!"

"No, you're too small to hold the fork," said Lons.

"Am not! And I found the goblin myself. It's *my* goblin."

"Shut up, Tippy!" snapped Mank. "It's all of us's goblin. And we're going to be rich off it. Tomorrow, we'll go to the village and tell all that we have a real goblin in our cellar, and when the folk come we'll charge them a copper piece for a look and two to poke him."

"I want to poke him now," said Tippy. "I was tied up to catch him." She snatched up a stick from the cel-lar floor and flailed at Lump's head.

"Look, he's crying," said Lons.

"Don't be stupid!" said Mank. "Goblins can't cry. She must have poked his eye. Stop that, now, Tippy! You don't want to ruin him."

"Where do goblins come from, Mank?" asked Lons.

"Ma says the witches make them. They steal babies and cut 'em up, and then they throw 'em into a big pot with pieces of dog and pig and whatever they can catch and boil it all up and make spells, and then what walks out, see, is a goblin. Look, you can see he's part pig in his snout and he's got doggy ears. My foot! Did you ever see ugly like that!"

"He can talk," said Tippy.

Mank laughed. "Nah, he can't. Goblins ain't people, see, and only people can talk."

There were shouts outside. Mank said, "They're wanting us now. Hurry!"

The children left, leaving Lump alone in the darkness.

Hatred breeds best in the soil of ruined dreams. Lump now felt for the first time in his life the hot pangs of that emotion. It was directed at his tormentors, not so much for what they were doing to him but because they were not what he had hoped them to be, a loving and admiring family. And at his mother, too, for not foreseeing this, for allowing him to believe that he was something other than a hideous monster. And, worst of all, at himself: self-contempt gripped at his vitals and also shame, and his free boy's heart was strangled in his bosom.

That was the first horrible night. It rained, and the cellar flooded, soaking Lump and chilling him to the bone. The next day was worse. A train of yokels came and stared and dropped their coppers in Mank's cup, and stabbed at Lump with pointed sticks and forks and laughed when he writhed. The children's father, the bearded man, soon found out what was going on in his cellar; and he beat the children soundly and took all the money and made himself the impresario of the show. Lump was dragged from the cellar and tied in the yard so that a larger crowd could see him, jeer, and throw stones and clods of filth. And Dad had his two savage dogs worry Lump, tearing off his clothing and wounding his feet. The crows circled overhead and they seemed to be enjoying the sport, too, screaming and laughing as he was tortured. Then he was tied in the cellar again.

No one thought to feed him or give him anything to drink, because it was well known that goblins ate only human flesh and drank only blood. So, tied to his post in the dark, his mind dulled by abuse, his body a mass of bruises, Lump began to die.

In the meantime, Ysul was frantically searching in ever-widening circles around the witch's cottage. The rain had quite washed away all scent, and so she blundered along every little trail she could think of, bellowing for her lost lad, and stopping from time to time to weep and moan. "Oh, dear, oh, dear, whatever will she say when she returns! Oh, dear, oh, my . . . !" It never occurred to her to visit the farm by the river, for she had told Lump to stay away from there and she believed, without any good reason, that he was an obedient cub. A kindly bear, and brave, but somewhat slow-witted, was Ysul.

At dusk on the second day of her search, she was slumped in a clearing, quite baffled as to what to do next, when a large crow fluttered down to the ground before her.

"Why do you weep, bear?" asked the crow.

"Oh, for I have lost the man cub that the woman charged me to keep, and I don't know what to do or how to find him again," Ysul replied.

"My folk," said the crow—and it was the same king crow that had complained when Lump threw stones—"my folk say there is a new nest of men by the deep river, and they cut down all the trees and destroyed many villages of ours."

"I'm sure that was a trial to you," said Ysul politely, but in her misery she had no real interest in the affairs of crows.

The crow king went on, saying, "Yes, and there we saw today a sight we never had seen before, and we did not know what to do. We held parliament to decide."

Ysul grunted. The crows were perpetually holding parliaments to decide issues of interest only to other crows.

"One said," the crow king continued, " 'What concern is it of ours if the boy is tormented? Did he not torment us with stones?' But another said, 'Yet the ills brought on us by these men are far worse than what he did, and, therefore, we should favor him; and, besides, many times his mother has been good to the crows and their kin.' But then a third said, 'What of the precedents? Is it not true that in the time of—' "

"Crow! What are you saying?" Ysul interrupted

with a growl. "Have you found our Lump? Who is tormenting him? Enough of your debates—tell me!"

And the crow king told her what the crows had seen at the farm, and flew off.

Now the red fire blazed up in the eyes of Ysul, and she roared and started to run in the shambling, slow-seeming but deceptively swift and irresistible charge of the bears. She came to the bridge and crossed it, causing the workmen to leap into the water in their terror. In the farmyard, before the cabin, a ghost of a dear scent wafted past her nose, and she roared again and headed straight for the cabin. Dad stuck his head out the door to see what was happening, then let slip his two fierce hounds. But they might as well have been rabbits for all the good they did. One was smashed like a rotten apple and flung lifeless to the ground. The other leaped at Ysul's throat; she bit its head off with one snap of her jaws.

Then she was crashing through the door to the cellar, beating it to kindling with mighty swipes of her long claws. Now she found Lump. A flick of a claw disposed of his gag.

"Oh, child, how did you come to be here! How dirty and pale you are!" Her teeth sliced through his bonds, and she licked his face.

"Ysul," he croaked weakly, "take me home. They hurt my feet, Ysul. I cannot walk."

"There, there, my child. Grasp my fur, and you shall ride bear back, as you did when you were a little thing."

So they left, while all the people of the farm and the work crews peeked from hiding and trembled.

Ysul took him home and laid him in bed and washed the blood and dirt from his body, tutting and fretting over his wounds. She dripped water into his mouth, and he drank some, but he would neither eat nor speak, but turned his face to the wall and lay still.

The next morning, he was no better. Ysul smelled death on him and was afraid. She ran into the open air and called out in her loudest voice, "Oh, folk of field and forest, Ysul the bear begs your help. The boy of my mistress, the lady of this house and of this our forest, is dying. Who of you, fleet of foot and swift of wing, will go and bring her from Merrymount home to save him by her art?"

She waited. Soon, there was a muttering and a fluttering, and the crunch of leaves and grasses, as all the creatures within sound of her voice came flying and running and creeping and crawling to stand in ranks deep around her. And there they conversed and chose from among them a gray goose, who was swift of wing and tireless and also had the power of never becoming lost. So she flew off, calling into the western sky, and disappeared behind a little cloud, while they all watched.

The woman arrived home in the middle of the darkest hour of the night, riding a whirlwind, with Falance clinging to her back with all eighteen claws and his teeth. She went instantly to Lump's bedside, at the same time demanding of Ysul how this had happened. But the bear could tell her little, and so she held her temper.

A gasp escaped her lips when she saw what had been done to him. She gathered herbs and rare ointments, boiled water in two kettles, applied soothing poultices, and poured healing drafts through the boy's bruised lips. He slept for three days, murmuring and sometimes shouting in his sleep. When he awoke, the first thing he saw was his mother's face; she had watched him and nursed him all that time, barely sleeping.

The first thing he said was, "Why didn't you tell me that I was a monster?"

"You are not a monster," she replied. "You are a boy."

"I am ugly!" he cried. "I am a goblin!"

"You are not a goblin."

"But I *am* ugly?"

"You are . . . unusual looking," she said. "But you are strong and healthy, and you have beautiful eyes."

"Pah! Why can't you say what is the truth? I am hideous. Everyone hates me because of it. I wish you had never found me or had let me die."

"I love you, as does Ysul . . ." she began, but he was not listening.

He demanded, "What will you do now?"

"Do? I will nurse you, of course, until you are well again and then . . ."

"No! No, I meant what will you do to *them*!"

She paused a moment before answering. "I suppose they will have ill luck. It will not be a prosperous farm, and after a few hungry seasons I have no doubt they will all leave. And I would not be surprised if the bridge were washed away next spring in a flood. And they will all have unpleasant—*very* unpleasant—dreams."

"Is that all? Ill luck? Dreams? Is that the only punishment they will have for what they did to me, your son? See! I knew you didn't love me."

"Lump, what would you have me do?" she asked calmly.

"Destroy them!" he shouted hoarsely. "Rain fire on them! Turn them into worms! Send trolls to crush their bones and tear them into pieces! You have the magic for it, don't you?"

She sighed unhappily and tried to stroke him, but he pulled away. "Of course you are angry," she said, "but if you think that what you want is possible, then you have entirely misunderstood the nature of my magic and my powers. My power exists within the Pattern, and the Pattern has its cruelties. Would you have me punish the wolf because he tears the deer? Or the raven because he steals the nestling from the sparrow? No, for that is their nature, as it is the nature of these people to hate and torment anything that is strange. The Pattern itself will repay them with misery, disease, and death."

But the boy would not listen, and turned his back on her, hoisting the quilt over his head and curling into a ball. She watched him in silence for a while. His shoulder under the quilt heaved with stifled sobbing.

"How is he?" asked Falance, when she returned to the hearth.

She sat in her chair and rubbed her face with both hands. "In his body? Well and mending. I can cure that, but his heart and his mind are hurt beyond my power or anyone's to soothe."

"He must lick himself and lie in a quiet place then," said the cat. "Time and nature are hard but sure cures for all such hurts."

"Yes, but will he allow them to work? Do you know, he wanted me to utterly destroy those wretched people who injured him?"

Falance was shocked, and immediately began to smooth a patch of belly with his tongue. "You can't do that," he said through his fur.

"Of course not. But he wouldn't understand."

"Their farm cannot succeed. You told him that?"

"Yes, but you know that road worries me more than the farm. Lately I have felt an oppressive presence in the Pattern. It was much discussed at Beltane; the other Wise have felt it, too. A shift is taking place—and not for the good, either."

"It's all the iron," said the cat. "And men are boiling into the forests in greater numbers, which the road will speed."

"Yes, well, the forest has always held men, but

formerly they were *of* the forest. These people seem to not want the forest to *be*. They cut without replanting; they waste half what they cut; they clog the streams with their filth."

"Perhaps we must move deeper inward," the cat suggested.

She laughed, suddenly and sharply, surprising her companion. "Yes! That is always good advice, my dear cat. Move deeper inward, indeed! If only it were as easy as that!"

In the next weeks the boy grew stronger. He left his bed and hobbled weakly about the garden, sitting for long hours silently in the summer sunlight. He spoke little, and it was as if a cloud hung about his head. He refused all invitations from the woman to study or to walk the woods and collect. His life before his captivity seemed but a distant dream, forever lost.

His magic windows no longer gave him much pleasure. He watched the lives of Djer and Pa'aili unfold, for something to do, but dully and without the delight of imaginary friendship to enliven the experience. Of course they would not wish to be his friend; of course they would run screaming from him should he appear.

Late one afternoon, bored, he wandered into the old schoolroom. He scuffed his feet, watching the dust rise. A voice said, "Young prince, I am happy to see you up and in the full bloom of health."

He turned, startled, and there was the djinn, making a deep bow.

"What! Are you still here?" exclaimed the boy.

"Where else would I be, my precious master? Her excellency, may her name be thrice enobled, your mother, has cast me into this stone." Here he tugged aside his robe, to show that he was engulfed to the knees in a boulder. "How I long to be gone," the djinn continued, "now that my work—not that it was work, say, rather, my joy in forming your mind is at an end. But no doubt your esteemed mother is correct in this, as she is in all things." He sighed theatrically and examined the boy closely for a moment. Then he said, "Nor do you seem in the best of spirits, my delight. Will you not tell your old tutor what is the matter? My powers, although cruelly curtailed by this clinging megalith, are entirely at your disposal."

"What do you mean, your powers?" asked Lump.

"Oh, delight of my heart, my *powers*! You have not seen a tenth part, a hundredth part of my powers.

To get riches! To travel far in the blink of an eye! Or," he added slyly, "should you have an enemy you wished to punish, to utterly destroy and vanquish, to torment with the most exquisite and unendurable agonies; well, you would have only to say a word to your Bagordax and it is done." A pause. "Surely, O worship of the world, your dear self can have no enemies? Surely no one would dare to brush the hem of your garment?"

"Those people hurt me," Lump blurted. "Those children at the river—Mank, Lons, and . . . and Tippy. And I did nothing to them." Now he burst into tears and the whole sad story came out, concluding with, "And she says we mustn't hurt them back, because it's the Pattern and they don't know any better and they'll leave soon anyway but . . ."

"But what, my master?" asked the djinn in a velvety voice.

"But I want them to know that I am not a goblin but a boy," said Lump softly, "and that they hurt me very much, and that they might see what it is like to be hurt. That is fair."

"Fair! It is *generous*, oh, most merciful of princes! I would teach them such a lesson that they would not harm even a ladybug without looking over their shoulder in trepidation. Yes, I would," he added with a wistful tone, "if I but could."

"Why can't you?"

"O my princeling, by reason of my stone. My magical stone, which the good lady has seen fit to ensorcel me with, for a trifling misdemeanor I accomplished, oh so long ago. Could I be free of it for just the half part of an hour, then would I teach a lesson to those naughty children!"

"But you would have to come back then, wouldn't you?"

"Oh, most assuredly, my master, most certainly. I would promise to on my mother's head."

Lump sighed and said, "But she would never allow it, would she?"

"What? I would never dream of troubling so magnificent a sorceress with such a trivial task, such a *little* thing, you know, a few words said out of a book and it is done. Pfft! Why, *you* could do it."

"I could? But she says I have no talent for spells and such."

"Talent is hardly required, my lordling. One does not have to be a great cook to eat a meal nor be a great carpenter to use a table. It is all in the book. A few words . . ."

"What book?"

"The great, thick, old black volume your noble mother keeps on her shelf. Thirty-two pages from the beginning on the left side, there are words written in glowing red letters. You have the book, a candle, and a cup of water. You light the candle, you say the words, you toss the water on my cruel stone and snuff the candle. The stone breaks—I am free—I am your servant in all things. I fly at your enemies and fill them with terror. Ha-ha! Nothing could be easier, O my prince."

Lump hesitated. "My mother says—" he began.

But Bagordax, sensing his advantage, broke in, saying, "Yes, your mother, an estimable woman, a pearl, to be sure, but still . . . only a woman, and women have no sense of what is fair or honorable in these things. You have been hurt: you must repay in kind and more."

"But how will I get the book? Do you see? I cannot get the book, so . . ."

"Tonight, my treasure, my potentate," whispered the afreet. "They will be out tonight, and when they are out at midnight, you will get the book and the candle and the water, and it will be done; and in the morning there will be no sign, except the wailing in the camp of your enemies."

And so by this and like arguments Bagordax brought Lump to where he was able to say, yes, why not? Weak in spirit and body, bitter about what he thought of as betrayal by his mother, angry about the destruction of his little conceits, he succumbed to the kind of self-pity which, as much as the more famous deadly sins, causes the evils that afflict the world. And he *did* so want to participate in some magical act.

That night while the woman and the cat were out and about (for witchcraft is practiced largely during the hours of darkness) and Ysul snored wetly on her sofa, Lump crept into his mother's room and slid the heavy volume from its shelf.

It was black, as foretold, and the leather of the binding was curiously warm and yielding, as if it still contained a living body. He brought it with the candle and the cup of water to the schoolroom. He lit the candle and opened the volume to the proper page. The red letters seemed to move like sparks in a living fire. Bagordax crouched over his stone, and his features seemed to swim in the dim glow, like flames, too.

Lump intoned the words without understanding

their meaning. They seemed to hum in the room, not dissipating like ordinary sounds. The hum grew louder. Lump tossed the water at the stone; steam and dust rose from its surface. The vibration now shook the walls of the schoolroom. Bits of the ceiling were falling. Lump suddenly grew afraid. He felt as if he were a chip in a torrent.

"Snuff the candle," said a voice, a deep voice, not at all like Bagordax's voice, though it came from where the tutor was sitting. It was a voice that could not be denied; as if in a dream, Lump pinched out the tiny flame.

To his surprise, the room did not go dark. Instead it was filled with corruscating bands of blue and orange light around the figure of Bagordax, which grew, which touched the ceiling, which pushed at the walls. With a sharp noise and a stench the imprisoning stone exploded. Lump covered his head and made himself as small as possible under a table. Then there was a greater explosion, as the ceiling and the walls of the room shattered. An immense laughter, loud beyond bearing, rang out, hurting his ears. Peeking out from under his table, Lump beheld for the first time the afreet Bagordax unleashed, in his native shape. He fainted.

When he awakened, he was high in the air, lying in the center of an orange hand the size of a millstone, surrounded by eight fingers, each armed with a steel talon as long as his arm. He looked into a face that was all flashing, whirling eyes; tusks; snicking blue tongues; roiling pits; and mouths writhing with fangs dripping thick ichor, all set in a blue beard writhing like a nest of snakes.

From this horror came the great, booming voice: "Farewell, little worm, my little goblin boy. You have the gratitude of Bagordax the afreet, terror of the Seven Worlds, prince of Sheol. And for my liberation I grant you the boon you sought—the destruction of your enemies—for we of the tribe of Shaitan always keep our word, when it suits us and in our own fashion. And bid good-bye to your mother for me; I hope to meet her again amid more favorable circumstances. Ha-ha-ha-ha!"

With that, he placed the shivering boy on the floor of the ruined schoolroom and departed in a fiery cloud.

When Lump could stand again, he staggered into his bedroom, the nursery that Bagordax had constructed years ago. Here he found Ysul crouched in a corner, her fur on end, her eyes wild, snarling at shadows.

The room, he saw, was dissolving. Already starlight shone through gaps in the ceiling, and the walls were flaking into pieces and floating away on the breeze. Only the magic windows seemed to be steady, shining with a light that came from the far side of the world. But now they, too, shivered and started to dissolve. Before they vanished, Lump saw the Caravanserai of the Three Palms raided by bandits on black camels and Djer and his sisters carried off weeping, and he saw a great typhoon sweep over the Lagoon of Pearls, smashing Pa'aili's village into flinders, swamping the girl's canoe under a huge green wave. Then the windows went dark and blew away in a wind that sounded like the heavy laughter of the afreet.

"Oh, child, what has happened?" Ysul moaned. "Whatever will your mother say when she returns?"

To this Lump gave no answer but buried his face in his nurse's thick warm fur, and slipped from consciousness again.

The woman, when she returned a little after midnight, had no doubt about what had happened. There was the book and the ruin, and no Bagordax. Through much cajoling and the consumption of comforting tea, the boy was at last induced to speak and to confirm what she already knew.

"But *why*, Lump?" she asked. "Whatever possessed you to release Bagordax?"

"It is your fault," he wailed. "You wouldn't do anything to those people who hurt me, and Bagordax said he would teach them a lesson, and so I let him go. I didn't know that he would get huge and wreck everything."

The woman went pale and stood up. "Oh, child," she said in a hopeless voice, "what have you done?" Then she dashed out of doors and took two skipping steps down the garden path and a third step, leaping into the air, and from this last she did not descend, but there was a shimmering in the air, and an owl flapped upward from where the woman had been and glided away on noiseless wings.

When, after half an hour, she came back into the room, her face was bleak.

"What is it, lady?" asked the cat, who had never seen her look so.

"All destroyed!" she cried. "The family and the workmen slain and burned and torn to pieces, and the buildings smashed, and the wreckage arranged to form an arrow, pointing here. The villages are already raised, torches in the streets. Oh, clever Bagordax!"

"He is a demon, after all; it is what we might expect," said the cat with a calm he did not feel. "We are ruined here, at any rate. What shall we do?"

To his surprise, the woman fell to her knees before him and touched his face. "Oh, Falance, I must ask you a great favor. The mob will be here soon and we must escape with the boy while we still have the dark. I need the help of hands and the boy is too weak and distraught, and therefore, my dear cat, of your courtesy, will you allow me to turn you into a man?"

Falance felt a powerful urge to wash, but stifled it. He said, "Surely, you need not ask, madam."

"Oh, but I must, Falance. I have not the time to do it in your despite, and Falance . . . I must tell you that I may not be able to turn you back."

The cat swallowed and thought of what life would be like as a great, clumsy, dirty thing, with half his senses cut away, but only briefly, and said, "I am content, lady. For your succor I would be a turnip."

At this she smiled, which was something they rarely saw, and it warmed even Lump, who was in the depth of utter misery and shock. She ran into her workroom, from which they heard clattering and muttering, and she ran back out with a small stone bottle and a saucer. She poured the contents of the bottle, a milky liquid, into the saucer and bade the cat drink it, which he did, grimacing. Then she tossed some powders into the hearth, where they flared and yielded a plume of yellowish greasy smoke, which curled like a thick serpent into the room. Now she took up a finger drum and beat a rhythm out on it and sang the enchantment, as the smoke curled around the cat, covering him where he lay.

In a short time that seemed like forever it was over. The smoke crept back into the fire, and there, lying on the floor, dazed, was a thin, lithe man, dressed in the buff coat and breeches of a footman, with silver-buckled shoes on his feet. He had a flat, clever face, with a thin silver mustache on it, and his speckled grayish hair was long and tied back with a ribbon. He blinked his large green eyes and rose uncertainly to his feet. He flexed his fingers, staring in wonder at his hands.

"Falance, quickly now!" said the woman. "I need a pumpkin, as big as you can find, and two large rats. Bring it all to the side garden. Ysul, watch the boy and keep guard, that we are not surprised!"

She ran out to the garden to a place where the

ground had been dug up for a late crop. There she tread out a space seven paces by seven and made it smooth. Then she took a long white stick and traced a design in the earth, chanting all the while. From a pouch she carried she brought forth magical objects: a small blue stone, a brass figure, a dried bunch of flowers, a mass of hair, liquids in vials and powders in jars. These she arranged at the proper points in the design, which now began to glow with a soft white light.

"I can still catch rats, I am happy to say," said Falance from behind her. "Here are two stout fellows. The pumpkins are quite small. Will a muskmelon do?"

"Yes. Give the rats to me."

She spoke to the little creatures briefly and then placed them on the diagram, tying scarlet cords from their necks to the melon, which sat by itself in the center of the magic space. The glow increased. The woman pricked her finger with a little knife she wore about her neck, and tossed seven drops of blood in precise places. The glow leaped up and blotted out all sight. There was a roaring noise and the earth trembled. Then it was dark again. They all blinked, and when their vision cleared, they saw that in the magical space sat a little closed wagon, colored green and gold, hitched with red leather harnesses to a pair of skinny black nags.

"Very well thus," said the woman. "I name you Duty and Desire," she said to the horses, "and may you pull well and together. Now we need food and drink for a journey of several days, bedding for us and the boy, pots and such. Attend to that Falance, while I gather some things from my workroom. Boy, gather any small things you want to take with you, for we shall not return here."

Lump stood by the garden's edge, confused and close to tears. "But why must we leave? Can't you stop them with your power? Or make us invisible to them?"

The witch paused and was about to speak sharply to him, but he looked so woeful that she could not. "Child, you have not ever understood the limits of my art, and I have no leisure to explain now. You say, can't I stop them? Of course I can, but can and may are two different things. The Pattern has been smashed here, by deaths that were not fated in this line of the world, and I am responsible. Therefore I must pay the penalty before the courts of the Wise."

"But you were *not* responsible!" the boy protested. "It was not you who released the demon." Here the child felt the stirrings of remorse but suppressed them, preferring to think instead of unfairness and his own discomfort, and to dwell on his fear.

She sighed. "Yet another thing I have failed to teach you: I am responsible for *everything*. That is my fate on the common earth, or was. Ah, but there is no longer time for teaching or talk. Ysul! The boy to the cart! Quickly! They are coming!"

Indeed, the far woods were shining red with the reflection of many torches; and when the wind blew fair, they could hear a low, frightening mutter, as from scores of angry voices.

At last they were loaded. Falance sprang effortlessly up onto the wagon, the boy crouched miserably on the bedding within, and the woman laid her hand on Ysul's head.

"My brave bear! You must slow them down until we are deep in the woods where they cannot follow. Escape afterward if you can," she added, knowing well there would be no escape. The bear nodded and said, "I understand, madam. Allow me to say what a pleasure it has been to serve you."

Then the woman put her foot on the wagon wheel, but paused and returned to the cottage and plucked a red rose from the wall and put it in her hair, and left her home. Nor did she look back at it as she urged her horses into the night.

From the rear window of the wagon, Lump could not but look back, and so he saw the mob come through the garden, ripping and tearing, saw them fire the thatch, saw Ysul charge out roaring, saw them fall back in dismay, saw the billhooks and ropes they used to drag her down at last, and then the wagon was into the woods, rushing along the trails, while the briars and vines leaped from their path and the roots of the trees writhed themselves out of place to lift the wagon's wheels.

Name

Once it was clear that no one was actively pursuing them, the woman slowed the horses to a walk. They moved deeper into the forest. It was utterly dark under the trees, but there seemed to be no doubt about their direction; a path opened up before them in the underbrush, and the horses trod it as easily as if they were following a well-known way home. Neither the woman nor Falance spoke of Ysul.

"You have done this before, this trick with the melon and the rats," observed Falance after a long silence. "I noticed that you did not need the book."

"Yes, once before. It is a spell strong enough to furrow the mind forever, and so it came easily. I had the necessaries, too, put aside in a particular place."

He could not see her in the dark, which disturbed him, for with his cat's eyes she would have been visible. Yet he wanted the comfort of her voice and so he said, "It must have been before we came together, yes?"

"Yes," she replied, "it was long ago and in a far country. I was very young. I had just . . . let us say, left my mistress to make my own life, and ignorant as I was of the world's ways, I got into trouble with the authorities. I was to be burned for curing too many people. There was a judge there, an upright and noble man, who interceded, and I was freed. We became friends. He was interested in our art. I spent many evenings with him talking, something that was very strange to me—I mean conversation with a man. He was married, too, to a sweet and delicate woman, whom he loved deeply, and she him. Their one sadness was that they had no children. I was able to help in this, and they had a daughter. He insisted that I be godmother to her."

"What, *you*!" exclaimed Falance.

"Yes. It *is* unusual but not unprecedented. In any case, the holy water did not boil in the stoup, nor did the nave of the church collapse. They named her Eyella. After that I traveled much, as you know, and some years later I returned to his city. I found all changed. The judge's wife had died, and after a period of mourning, he had married his housekeeper, a respectable widow with two daughters of her own. Eyella was by then a well-grown child of about ten, beautiful as the dawn but oddly contorted in her faculties. She would have nothing whatever to do with her stepmother, despite the woman's kind intentions, and also she had developed a peculiar and irritating trait: nothing was ever clean enough for her. She washed her hands until they bled; she changed her clothing ten times a day; a cinder could not pop onto the hearthrug but she must leap up and scrub the spot.

"The judge consulted me, but, as you know, such cases are difficult and refractory to the healing arts. I advised him to let time work on her until the shock of her mother's death might dissipate. Alas, for him there was no time! There arrived turmoils in the state; the judge fell from favor and was dispatched to a distant province on some mission from which he did not return. The family was much reduced. The stepmother, now twice a widow, struggled to keep the family fed and clothed. Eyella, of course, was quite distracted now, and her phantasms grew worse. She imagined that her stepmother was interfering with a romance she had conceived, in the darkness of her mind, with the prince of that realm. Nothing would do but she had to attend balls where she could meet with her supposed lover. The stepmother came to me in despair. How could they afford to send Eyella to balls? I visited my goddaughter, and I saw clearly that she was in a world of her own. Her scrubbing fancy was worse, and she swore if she could not wed the prince, she would perish."

"Remarkable!" said Falance. "I suppose this is where the pumpkin comes in."

"Yes. The family still had a perfectly adequate chaise, but only a coach and four would do. I used mice, and rats for the footmen and driver. The spells are quite similar. The stepmother and the two sisters did up a ball gown, which Eyella cruelly rejected. I turned it into something quite different, which satisfied the poor thing. It was blue, I recall, with little dyed fur slippers. So she went to the ball. Oh, yes, and I cast a glamour on her that would have felled a regiment of princes."

"The prince saw her and loved her, then?"

"Yes, naturally, but the mad girl happened to spill some wine on her slipper, and so was not perfect. She fell into a rage and threw the thing into a bush and ran away weeping, hopping on one foot. But he found her, and married her at last, and so there was peace in the house of my old friend.

"I fear I must sleep now, Falance. Are you tired at all? Can you take the reins?"

"I am fine. I will take a catnap later. And did they all live happily ever after?"

"Well, they lived. The trouble with glamours is that however strong at first, they all will wear off, and there you are with just your character. In any case, Eyella and her prince had a great number of children, and I suppose however happy they were or not, they were at least very *clean* children. As for the stepmother, the girl never spoke to her again nor to her stepsisters, nor did she help them, although they had little enough. The plight of stepmothers is ever hard."

"And of foster mothers, too," said Falance softly, as the woman fell into exhausted sleep. "But at least she had peace in the end. And you, my lady, when will you have peace again?"

The dawn reached them thinly through the heavy foliage of the heart of the forest. The horses stopped of their own accord by a little stream, and Falance jumped down from the box and unhitched them. He discovered he knew how to do that. He thought he could also fix a wheel if one should come off the wagon or sew a button on his coat. Apparently, these skills came with his new body. There was a dagger on a belt at his waist. He drew it and made a pass or two; not nearly as handy as claws, but he could use it. He led the horses to graze the stream bank and drink from the water, wondering whether they liked being horses as little as he liked being a man.

Falance knelt down and lapped the cool water. Then he squatted on the bank and gingerly dipped his hand in the water and washed his face, dabbing moisture here and there. It was not a satisfactory wash at all. He was trying to get at the back of his neck when he heard a stifled laugh behind him.

It was Lump. "You are doing that all wrong," the boy said. "That is not the way people wash." The boy went down on his knees beside the stream and splashed water on his face and head, scooping with both hands. "See?" he said, dripping and looking back at the former cat, whose face bore an expression of the utmost distaste.

"Ah, well, I suppose I must." Falance sighed, splashed himself, too, and shuddered.

"But what of the rest?" he asked after vainly trying to stretch himself so as to inspect the small of his back.

"Oh, you must take off your clothes and leap into the water, and rub yourself all over with clean sand or soap, if you have it."

"You are not serious!" said Falance, aghast.

"I am," said Lump. "You have seen me bathe in the kitchen copper a thousand times."

"If I saw, I did not take notice," said the other, looking with horror at the bubbling water. "Well, perhaps another time." They rose and walked back toward the wagon.

"Look, there is a wolf!" cried Lump. "And he has something in his mouth. Oh! It's a hare."

"The red wolves offer this gift to the lady," said the wolf, then trotted off into the dark woods.

Falance picked up the hare, sniffed it, and said, "Fresh! We will have it for breakfast."

He knelt and drew his blade and skinned and cleaned the hare, while the boy watched. "Have you done this before, Falance?"

"Skin and gut a hare? Oh, many times, but it is odd, I admit, using my front legs to open it and having only one blade instead of ten. It is done, however, and now we must see if your lady mother is awake."

The woman was awake, stretching and yawning. She had not been refreshed by her brief slumber on the wagon bench.

"Mother, the red wolves have brought us a hare for breakfast!" shouted Lump.

She looked at the dressed carcass sourly. "And when the gray wolves hear of it, they will drag in an elk so as not to be outdone, and the foxes with bring ten brace of pigeons till the wagon stinks like a butcher's shop, and the bears will bombard us with honeycombs with the bees still on the sting."

"We are not cheerful this morning, my lady, I find," said Falance.

"We are not, Falance," she said and stomped off.

"My lady!" called the cat man. "We must cook this."

"Oh, yes, yes!" she said testily, and without breaking stride she called over her shoulder, "Fire, be!" and made a gesture. Instantly, blue and yellow flames erupted out of the greensward, although the grass was not scorched.

On this fire, Falance stewed the hare in a kettle with cabbage, onions, carrots, garlic, and thyme, all gathered from the wild by Lump.

"This is very good, Falance," said the woman as they sat around the fire and ate. Washed, rested, and fed, she was in better countenance. "I was not aware that you could cook."

"No more was I, madam," replied the cat, "but after all, I am a domestic animal." He licked his plate and set it aside. "So, there is breakfast down, and, if I may inquire, lady, what are our plans?"

"My only plan is that at the next full moon, which is three days hence, I will draw down Lump his Name. Beyond that, it is out of my hands. I expect I will be punished."

"Punished!" exclaimed Falance. "But you are without blame."

"Am I? That is not the way it will be seen, I'm afraid. I was guardian of the Pattern in our forest and the Pattern is broken. Had I been up to my work, as I had been for so many years, those people would never have come to the forest; I would never have left a child and a bear alone with that demon; I would have raised the child so that he was proof against Bagordax's wiles. No, I have failed. Mothering was simply more difficult than ever I imagined. I scanted my true work because of it, nor was I as good a mother as I had thought, and so we are come to this."

As she spoke, Lump was shriveling inside. He felt disgraced beyond any power of forgiveness. They were at this pass because of him. He thought of their cozy home, lost forever, burned and ruined, and he struggled to keep from wailing out loud.

The woman looked at him as if sensing his thoughts. "You are not to blame yourself, Lump," she said kindly. "I should have warned you; I should have seen what you would feel about what those people did to you; I should have put Bagordax's *head* into the stone. But I did none of these things. You are only a little boy and he is a demon prince; what could I have expected?"

While perfectly true, this was not what Lump wished to hear. Tact was never high among the woman's skills. The boy shivered and, after a pause, asked, "What will happen to you?"

"That I cannot tell. But," she added in a brighter tone, "perhaps it will not be so very bad. I have done good service; and I have friends among the Wise. Also, if I have erred, it was in the cause of love and nurture, and perhaps She will take that into account." The woman rose and brushed off her skirt. "In any case, the sooner we arrive, the sooner we shall know."

With that they packed the wagon, hitched up the horses, and continued down the trail, which still opened before them, although they saw no movement of the vegetation, then closed after them, forming an impenetrable tangle of briars and undergrowth.

Lump sat on the box next to his mother, saying little. The woman drove the horses, although they hardly needed any driving, while Falance stretched full-length on the wagon's roof and slipped into the relaxed, yet ever alert, doze of cats.

The forest grew darker and thicker. The trees— gigantic oaks, beeches, and chestnuts—were larger than any Lump had ever seen; they seemed ancient and their bark was green with mosses. It was quieter, too, than the woodland he knew, with only the occasional invisible warbler or the crash of a larger animal breaking the heavy silence.

Two days passed thus. Each morning, they found provisions left them by the animals and birds: no elks but little piles of nuts; a brace of fat partridges; a haunch of deer; and once, a large loaf of bread filched from some housewife's windowsill by a raven. Early on the third day, the woman said, "Falance, today you must drive. I must spend some time inside, alone, to prepare."

Now Lump and Falance sat together on the box as

the trees moved past, the boy silent and lost in his own unhappy musings, while from behind them came the sound of chanting and the beat of a tiny drum. Every so often there was a faint breeze from nowhere, laden with sweet, improbable scents.

At last Lump could contain his curiosity no longer and asked, "Falance, what is she doing in there?"

The cat replied, "Oh, I suppose she is traveling to and fro among the worlds, speaking to this one and that one, recalling favors done, trading this and that. . . ."

"Trading?"

"Oh, yes, there is a trade in the magic arts. Certain amulets and spells can be used by only one person at a time, and your mother has many of these. She is pawning them, I imagine. And also she is strengthening her soul for what must come. Look, there is a fog coming in."

The path was now slanting downward, and the air grew cooler and damper. Tendrils of mist slipped through the great trunks and piled up in thick banks that soon obscured all but the nearest. Soon, these, too, were gone into whiteness, then the ground was lost as well, then everything but the tails of their horses. They plodded onward, enveloped in dampness as impenetrable as wool. Lump no longer heard any sound from the interior of the wagon except perhaps a low whispering hum, hardly distinguishable from the pounding of the blood in his ears.

Then the horses stopped. Falance got down from the box to see what was the matter, and the fog swallowed him up instantly. Some time elapsed. Lump writhed against the urge to call out, the urge to run screaming into the wagon and bury his face in his mother's skirt. These he resisted, but still he jumped and let out a little cry when Falance reappeared suddenly, right at Lump's elbow, and said, "The path has disappeared. We are in a small clearing and are obviously meant to stop and wait."

"Wait for what?"

"For whatever will come, obviously," said Falance. Then he stretched, yawned, slumped in his seat, and fell asleep.

Lump did not sleep. He sat shivering and peering into the fog, and seeing things that were not there and also things that were there but not believable. This is common enough in an ordinary fog; however, this was clearly a magical one and far richer in phantasms. There were sounds, too, groanings and crashes, that seemed to come from but a few paces away; and these kept Lump jumping at intervals. Falance slept through it all, and Lump thought that he would rather die and be eaten than awaken his companion.

Some hours—days, Lump would have said—passed in this manner. The fog grew brighter by degrees. The air turned warmer; a breeze sprang up that shredded the mist like a rotted banner. The wagon stood in a clearing not more than thirty paces in width; and there was sunlight again, a quite different sunlight. It was thick and yellow and warm, and the air was thick and scented and soft, and the grass was so green that it hurt Lump's eyes to stare at it.

Falance awakened, stretched, looked about him, nodded, cleared his throat, and said without preamble, "There is your mother."

A figure had emerged from the woods on the far side of the clearing, walking toward them. At first Lump did not recognize her, but as she came closer, he saw that it was her and that she had changed. Instead of her usual gray and brown costume, she was clothed now in dark brocade, embroidered stiff with silver figures and runes and studded with pearls and shining jewels. More remarkable still was her face, which seemed to glow with its own light, as when on an over-cast day the sun breaks through for an instant and sends a shaft of brilliance across a valley to turn some tree into a bright torch.

Falance, with a single sinuous motion, took up his old place on the roof. Lump noticed that Falance, too, seemed to glow and that his buff coat now shone with gold braid and jeweled buttons. He looked down and found that his own plain shirt was run through with silver threads and worked designs. The woman swung easily onto the box, clucked at the horses, and they were away.

A broad avenue covered in short grass had opened out of the clearing. As they entered, a flock of singing birds with long iridescent tails flew overhead. Colors—violet, scarlet, and gold—flashed intermittently in the shadows of the trees. Lump turned to the woman.

"Mother, this is the same as that time we saw the troll, isn't it? We are in the unseen world."

"In a way," she answered and then held her hands before her with the fingers interlocked. "As I've explained, the unseen world touches and joins with the common earth at many places but, so to speak, only at its edges." She touched her breast. "But now we are at its very heart. This is Faeryland, my dear, or as some say Tir Nan Og, or Avalon. Or also the Country of a Thousand Years."

"Why do they call it so?"

"Because it is thought that only once in so often is a mortal allowed to come this far over its borders. Or it may be that, once here, he is made to stay so long before returning to the common earth."

Lump was staring wide-eyed around him, his former misery dispelled. She touched his hand, and when he looked up, she said gravely, "Yes, it is a place of delight, true, but also of the most deadly danger; and the most dangerous is often the most delightful. You must stay awake, my boy, if you wish ever to cross the border again into the world of men."

Lump nodded, not comprehending her meaning, until somewhat later a leaf fluttered down from a tree and landed in his lap. He picked it up and examined it. It was the palest green imaginable with silvery veins running through it in the most interesting pattern, which glowed with a rosy light. The pattern curved around on itself, and as he traced it with his eye the leaf seemed to get thicker—no, *deeper*—in some odd way that revealed even more of the branching passages, and then he fancied that he could almost leave his body and go trotting down those shining corridors at the end of which he knew waited some unimaginable delight. . . .

Suddenly the leaf was snatched away; Lump felt for an instant an insane rage and grabbed for it. His mother tossed it away, saying angrily, "Didn't you hear what I said? I said *stay awake*! Everything in this country is a trap for a mortal such as you—every leaf, every pebble, every glimmer on the water. You must keep your eyes moving at all times; do not become interested in anything for more than a few heartbeats or you are lost."

Lump shuddered and tried to do as she said, and indeed there was so much to see and absorb that his gaze leaped willingly from one marvel to the next: a party of fauns; a one-eyed ogre with a knobbed club shuffling off their path; overhead, glimpsed briefly, a bird the size of an elephant, a roc; something shining bronze in the distant woods that clanked and wafted an odor of hot metal.

"Oh, Mother, is that a dragon?" he asked excitedly.

"No, dear, only a firedrake, a small one. Dragons do not dwell in these precincts, not on the surface at least. Look, there! A pair of gryphons."

The wagon was crossing a wide, shallow stream,

and the beasts were disporting themselves in the water, splashing and leaping and calling out in voices that were part eagle's scream and part lion's roar. They were bathing, or perhaps fishing; Lump could not make out which, for as soon as they spied the wagon, the gryphons gave a frightened screech and fled, bounding from one slick boulder to another until they had enough speed to take to the air.

The woman watched them turn into specks and vanish in the metal-blue sky of Faery, and sighed. "They are glorious, aren't they, my dear?"

"Yes, Mother, but why do all the creatures of this land flee from us as if they were frightened?"

"Why, they *are* frightened. What would you have them do? What would a herd of sheep or of men do if a hippogriff or a troop of elves came into their midst? They would flee screaming, too."

"Yes, but those creatures have magic powers, of which the beings of the common earth have reason to be afraid."

"That's true, but you must understand that as they are to us in our world, so are we to them in theirs. We are strange and uncanny and full of magic to them."

"But the folk of the common earth, most of us,

have no magic," Lump protested.

"Do we not? We have birth and death, sorrow and joy. We have art and industry; we have poetry and love. We have pity and we have mercy. They have none here; and therefore, these I have named are as baffling to the folk of this world, and as frightening, as spells and shape changing would be to a shepherd or a shopkeeper. Believe me, the stoutest knight of Faery would run mad with terror at the sight of a windmill. In the world of men it is remarkable that a cat turns into a man; here it is just as remarkable for a kitten to turn into a cat. Magic is but a word for an art beyond our descry or a happening that fails of easy explanation."

"But you've warned me that this world wants to ensnare the folk of common earth. Why?"

"All things seek to control or destroy what they cannot understand," the woman answered sadly. "In the common earth men use the pyre and the rack against such as I am; here madness and dissolution serve the same purpose."

"But you—witches, I mean—you are part of both worlds. How can you survive?"

She laughed. "We barely do," she said, and then more gravely, "and, indeed, I may not for much longer.

Look here," she said, fingering the embroidered edge of her sleeve, "there is a lifetime of study in this matter, but I will try to explain. You see that each side of the embroidered cloth has a different appearance. They are opposites, in fact, yet both sides are made of the very same threads and, moreover, are both tied to the same fabric. This side, all glittering, is what we know as Faery; this side, duller but more honest, showing the knots, is the common earth. Both sides, with the fabric between, is what we call the Pattern, which the Wise study. We cross over, and perhaps we help to heal the breach between the two, for it is a cause of much evil, and She suffers much pain from it."

"But who is this She that you talk of all the time?"

The woman waited for a moment before speaking. "She is the First Made Thing, and each thing She makes, and each thing destroys. She is the Pattern and the Pattern is Her." The woman made a gesture with her hand.

Lump thought about this for a long minute and then he asked, "But if She was the First Made Thing, who made Her?"

"That is a matter of some debate on the common earth," said the woman curtly. "There is much argument about it and even wars. But we do not discuss it here, in Her place."

"And are you to visit Her? To be judged, you said."

"Yes, but it is not a matter of being judged. It is hard to explain. The important thing is to correct the Pattern."

After that, she would say no more, but drove along, alone in her thoughts. The yellow sun moved as the ordinary sun did, but, it seemed, more slowly; the shadows gathered, violet and umber, and the sky turned the ineffable deep lavender of twilight in Faeryland. Gradually the path widened, and the trees thinned at the same time as they grew straighter and thicker and taller. The landscape now resembled the park of a royal estate but far more grand and noble. At last they came to a wide flat meadow and halted. Lump gasped. In the center of the meadow, by itself, was a tree the size of a mountain.

"What kind of tree is that, Mother?"

"It is not a kind of tree, dear. It is The *Tree*. All the trees in both worlds—and worlds beyond these, if any there are—are all the merest reflection of this, their model and guide. Its roots go down to hell and its branches rise to heaven and it holds the Pattern together. Now, we must hurry and prepare, for all must be ready by the rising of the moon."

"Does Faeryland have a moon, too, like we do?"

"Oh, yes, and such a moon! As you will see, its light is thick and rich as cream, and it seems as if you might scrape it from the ground. It tingles on the skin, like a breeze. Do not stare at it, mind, when it rises!"

Falance had awakened, as he always did the moment the wagon halted. He jumped down and conversed with the woman for some time, while Lump walked around on the soft, soft grass, casting careful glances at the Tree and wondering how long it would take to walk around it. Its top was quite lost in the purpling sky; Lump did not even consider what it would be like to climb it.

The woman and Falance drew a complex design on the ground with colored powders, and lit at precise points on it fat candles, whose flames did not flicker and each of which sent out a different scent. They made Lump lie down in the center of the design, and the woman knelt and spoke to him softly.

"In a moment the moon will rise above the trees. You must not move or speak, and keep your eyes shut if you can. When I draw down your Name, I will come and give it to you. Now, this is very important. A true Name cannot be said in human speech, and thus I must blow it into your soul direct; but in order for it to work in you it carries with it a *sigil*, or place name, which can be heard and spoken, and this I will whisper into your ear. This is the first and the last time that the sigil name may be spoken aloud. Do you hear me, Lump? You must not speak it aloud, even when you believe you are entirely alone, for should it ever be voiced by another tongue, then all the ills that have ever befallen you will be as nothing to the ill that will come on that voice. I know you have disobeyed me before now, but here you must not disobey, or answer for it at your grave peril, against which I shall be helpless. Do you understand this?"

"Yes, Mother," said Lump from a mouth gone dry as flour.

She rose. "Very well, then. Here is the moon. We begin."

Of the ceremony that followed, Lump could remember little. He heard the drum and the chanting, and it sometimes seemed that there was more than one voice in it. There were deep uncanny sounds, as if the earth were creaking on its spindle. He felt the moonlight of the faery moon plucking at his neck; and once, when a particularly loud noise made him blink his eyes open, he saw the rich whiteness flowing over the grass like a living thing. At last, he felt his mother draw near. She put her face close to his. It was shining like the moon itself, and her eyes were dark as the night sky, and like the sky, they showed stars flaming within their blackness. She blew a breath into his nostrils, an air scented with the whole of the earth: cold rock and damp sap and hot blood. He felt Something flood into him, but what exactly it was he could not have said. Then she placed her lips by his ear and gave him the word that stood for his Name.

After that, they slept long and woke with the sun high in the day. They did not take breakfast, for they were not hungry but full of ease and a bouncing energy.

"I must go now," said the woman to the boy and Falance. She was dressed in a long green robe picked out with silver moons and stars and leaves, scattered with sparkling colored stones; and on her head she wore a wreath of holly. Her face shone with an expression that was at once terribly sad and full of joy. Lump had never seen the like and he stared at her, almost stupefied.

"Falance, should I not return," she continued, "I lay it upon you to carry the boy back to the common earth. I do not think any will stop you, for I will have paid your fee. But you must take care." Then she kissed both of them, and without a further word she strode directly to the Tree. They saw her flash green against its gray bark for a moment, and then she was gone.

"Oh, Falance! What shall we do?" cried the boy.

Falance smiled and replied, "Well, you know, I have always wanted to play cards, which I could not easily do in my old form of a cat. I believe there is a deck in the wagon. Let us try while we wait."

So they played as the hours dragged on: gammon, wands, and catch the knave, each trying not to glance too often out the open rear door of the wagon and losing track of the count and the cards and having to start over again.

Then, in the midst of a deal, Falance suddenly stood up, scattering the cards. "She is back!" he declared and ran outside. Lump followed.

The woman was walking slowly across the greensward.

"I am glad to see you," said Falance when she had come near. "How did you fare in the courts of the Wise?"

"Well enough," said the woman lightly. "I am not a tree. Or a frog. I am no more a witch. I am exiled; the unseen world is barred to me henceforward, from sundown today."

"But there is still your lore," said Falance desperately. "You still have your enchantments."

"No. All spent. Oh, perhaps I have kept back a few homely remedies against dire need, but aside from that I am stripped quite naked." Her tone was so cheerful that Falance looked at her askance.

"You said 'spent.' On what, madam, if I may inquire?"

"On favors and fines. And on this," she said, holding out her hand. In her palm was a little ball no larger than a pea which glowed with mottled green and blue lights.

Falance stared at it and his jaw dropped. "By my tail!" he exclaimed. "That is an earth klaver. I have never seen one before, save in pictures in books."

"I am not surprised," she said. "There were ever only three, and one is lost."

"What is it for, Mother?" asked Lump, peering at the little thing.

"It is for swimming through the earth, my dear.

One who commands this need never fear capture or abuse, bars, walls, or pursuit. It is a most puissant charm and it is for you. I promised I would name you, and that you would do feats of magic, and now it has come true. You will be the only magic in our family now, I think. Are you not pleased, my child?"

Lump looked up at his mother's face, and his vision began to blur with tears. This was the moment when he should have fallen on his knees and cried that he was sorry, that he knew that his pride and disobedience had brought them all to this ruin and that he loved her and was grateful for her immense sacrifice. If he had done that, they might have talked seriously about what lay between them for the first time in their lives, and something new and better might have come out of it. But such sacrifices are often unbearable for the young to contemplate, and so it was with Lump. He suppressed his tears; his eyes cleared, but the unshed tears fell inward, as such tears always do, and turned to ice and froze his heart.

He answered as a prince does when given a bauble by a courtier: "Yes, I am pleased, Mother."

"That is well," she answered, after a long, uncomfortable silence. "And now you must swallow it, and when we are out of Faery, I will show you its use."

Lump took the ball and tossed it into his mouth. For a moment he felt dizzy and his knees bent, as if he suddenly weighed as much as a hill, but this quickly passed, and he felt no different than before. He noticed Falance staring at him with what seemed a bitter look. The cat is jealous of me, Lump thought; at last he knows whom she loves the best. *He* did not get a magical prize!

There was a sudden movement below the trees on one side of the glade, and they all turned to watch. A troop of cavalry emerged from the wood, riding in a column of fours; but what cavalry! They were dressed in uniforms that glimmered and changed color when the sun struck them, and they had helmets and breastplates made of what appeared to be solid moonlight, hard, white, and gleaming. They bore aloft lances tipped with diamond points and pennons that writhed like colored flames. Long, furled wings grew from their shoulders and trailed past the flanks of their steeds, who were the color of clouds, and winged as well. They approached slowly, without the slightest sound.

"Who are they, Mother?" asked Lump in a breathless voice.

"They are the household cavalry of Faery, my love," said the woman. "I expect they are our escort from this place."

The faery at the head of the troop now broke from his fellows and trotted across to them. Ten paces away he stopped and dismounted, leaned his lance against his saddle, and then walked the last few yards. He gave the woman a graceful, ironic bow. He was so beautiful that to look at him was like a heavy blow to the chest. His eyes were violet, not the weak purply-blue called violet in human eyes, but the dense, deep violet of the actual flower, with very little white showing around the iris.

She returned a correct curtsey. "Good morrow, Huon," she said.

"Good morrow, Elisande," said the fairy, smiling, showing slightly pointed shining teeth. "This is ill met. What a lot of trouble for a human child! We arrange such things more conveniently in Faery, as you know. This is the person, I presume?"

"Yes," said the woman. "He is called Lump. Lump, make your bow to Captain Huon."

Lump stepped forward and bobbed. He looked into Huon's face, into those eyes like blooms. They were the most marvelous things he had ever seen, he thought, and then he thought, Oh, if I could just go with this creature all my troubles would be over. I would be happy forever, just to be with him, to look into, to drown, in those eyes. A scent like lilies tickled his nose, delightful and pure! He felt warm, and a hum like distant music filled his ears, and he wanted to find it, to follow . . .

"*Huon, stop that!*"

His mother's voice cut through the delight like the clang of a brass pot. Huon let out a musical sound like a laugh, but it had no humor in it. Lump gasped. He felt as if he had been gutted; sweat broke out over his face.

"That is how it is done with these creatures, my girl," said Huon, "since you have forgotten."

"And you have forgotten that it is not my way, and you have also forgotten what happened to you the last time you tried your tricks around me and mine," said the woman sweetly.

The fairy's exquisite face stiffened and he said, "Well, madam, this has been pleasant, but I am here to tell you that when the sun tangles in the lowest bough of the Tree you are to be gone, and we with you, to see you do not lose your way. In the meanwhile, we have prepared a modest entertainment to while away the time."

Huon made a gesture with his hand. Behind him the troop dismounted and came forward, forming a line as they did so. Huon bowed again, took up his lance and reins, and strode lightly back to his troop.

"Is he a friend of yours, Mother?" asked Lump.

"One is not friends with faeries, dear. With the Good People one may help or be helped, hinder or be hindered, but 'friend' does not figure in their vocabulary, no."

The faery lancers had formed a ring, in the center of which there were some with instruments—horns, pipes, and drums.

"What is happening, Mother?" asked the boy.

"Oh, the fay are preparing to dance."

"Do they dance to honor you, then?"

"Oh, no," she said. "It is part of my punishment. They mean to make my exile more bitter, that I shall never more see the fay dance. Now, as for you, you must not on any account see it. Go now into the wagon, and on my shelf of simples you will find a red clay jar, and in it you will find soft beeswax. Use bits of it to stop up your ears."

"But why?" cried Lump, gravely disappointed. "Why must I not see the dance nor hear the music of the fay?"

"Oh, child, I am experienced here, and Falance is an animal, so we are safe; but should you but once see this dance, no sight of common earth would ever again give you pleasure—not the face of a beloved, nor that of your own dear child, but you would lust after a lost perfection. And as for the music: once in a rare while a person of the common earth hears, as from a great distance, the horns of Faery, and then they run mad or become great poets or both together. To hear them at this slight remove and so clear would be the end of you, from the pure deadly joy of it. Go quickly now! They will soon begin."

Lump scurried into the wagon and stopped his ears and sat on his cot. And as he sat there, the thought of being denied even one look at the dance grew intolerable to him, as he had almost no experience of denying himself things, and the glamour of Huon's look was still upon him, distracting his senses. He crept to the front of the wagon and pulled aside the leather curtain that separated the cabin from the driving seat.

He saw the fay dancing. Their wings were spread

wide as they trod a measure in the air. As he was not a great musician, he was never able to describe what he saw, for no human words can comprehend that concentrated essence of loveliness—beauty as terrible as a bomb. All we know of beauty on earth is but its muddy shadow; music alone can remind us of its glory.

And his heart—that poor thing that had been broken by the wicked children in the cellar and frozen by his mother's sacrifice—twisted in his bosom, and he fell back in a faint, as if shot by a poisoned arrow.

Earth

The cavalry of Faery drove them all night at break-neck speed, while goblins howled and the heavens cracked flame; and in the morning they found themselves alone in a sodden field under a gray sky, the sky of the common earth. The horses were covered with foam, and they drooped their heads as Falance rubbed them down. The woman sat silently on the seat, her face in her hands.

"What now, my lady?" asked Falance, when the silence had gone on a worrying length of time. "Where are we bound? There is no road here and—"

"Oh, leave me be, Falance!" she snapped. "I am all a-jangle and cannot think. I must rest for a while."

To his immense surprise, Falance saw that the woman was weeping, had long been weeping, and that her gray eyes were rimmed with red. He had never seen this before, as witches do not weep—it is one of the things they surrender when they become witches, and these tears were the best evidence that the woman was a witch no longer.

"Then go inside and rest, my lady," said the cat kindly, overcoming his dismay. "I will gather some fire-wood and build a fire. It is cold and damp, isn't it, for summer?"

"We have no idea if it is still summer. It may be early spring a hundred years after we first set out. You know well that time does not flow the same there as here. Have some sense!" She climbed down from the seat and sank into the mud. "In any case, here we are and here we must make our way." She looked at him curiously. "Can you make a fire in fact? Without the help of magic?"

"I believe so, my lady. There is a tinderbox in my coat pocket, and its use seems to be in my head."

"Well, then, proceed," she said and clumped to the rear door of the wagon. "Some food also would not be amiss, though where we will get it I cannot think. I will be more intelligent after I sleep, I hope."

The woman slept long. She was awakened by hunger and by a delicious odor coming through the door. She rose and went to her boy's cot. She was stunned at the sight of him, for his feet hung over the edge of it and his shoulders were almost as broad as a man's. He seemed to have aged half a dozen years during the night. She gently roused him. He was sluggish and irritable, and when at last he was on his feet, she explained to him what had happened, reminding him about the strangeness of time in Faery. He examined himself in her glass and snorted. "I have not improved with age, I see. Robbed of a few years of life, am I? Well, no matter; I wish the rest of it would fly as fast!"

She was dismayed to see the coldness in his eyes, almost as if, in gaining those years, he had been transformed into another person. It is just the shock of Faery and the moving, she told herself. It requires but time to repair.

"Is that a rabbit, Falance?" she exclaimed when she came to the fire, the boy slumping along behind her. "How extremely clever of you! And this nice fire, too! I am surprised."

"Perhaps not as surprised as the rabbit was, my lady. It had no notion of being run to earth by a creature of my form; this body retains something of the nimbleness of my previous one, I find, and a good thing, too. While there is game, we will not absolutely starve. But I must tell you: the woods hereabout say it is not spring nor yet summer but autumn. Winter will be upon us shortly, and what then shall we do?"

"I will tell you, brave Falance," answered the woman, whose humor had much improved with the warm meat. "You have given me an idea, with your talk of nimbleness. Magic is denied us, true, yet we are not without skills. I have my herb lore and healing and my legerdemain, and I can pretend to tell fortunes. You can leap about and climb poles and walk on ropes well enough to amaze any crowd of folk. We will be mountebanks, in short, and travel in our wagon from town to town and to the fairs, and have a merry life."

Falance nodded, his practical nature satisfied by this plan. He inclined his head toward Lump. "And the boy?"

"By 'r Lady!" the woman cried, and snapped her fingers. "But he is our prize act, of course! No magic? What was I thinking of? He is the boy who cannot be held by any prison cell or bond, however strong. They will shower money on us. Come, my Lump! I must teach you the art of it this instant."

At this, Lump threw off his sulk and brightened, and she led him to a place a short distance from the wagon.

"Now, Lump," she said, "this is simplicity itself. Mind the tune! The cantrip is: *'Earth into water; fire into light; air with me; away down!'* When you sing these words, this solid earth will become for you like a great sea. All heavy things, walls and chains, will be as vapors that you can float through. The ordinary rocks will flow about your body like water. Only the very hardest crystals will be solid and the pure metals, so you must glide between them, as a fish around a water weed."

"But how will I see beneath the earth, where no light is?"

"By the heat. It is hot beneath the earth, and the deeper you go, the brighter it will seem. Do not be afraid; while your Name is safe and you hold the klaver in your body, no harm can befall you. To return, say the words backward, and you will return to the surface and be as you were before." The boy hesitated, although it was not for the reason she thought. She said, "Come now—there is nothing to fear."

"I am not afraid," said Lump coldly, and he repeated the cantrip.

But for one moment he was in deep terror, as the sun and everything he knew vanished. The muddy soil slipped by his face like froth, and the clay beneath it. He felt as if he were plunging through dark waters. And then, slowly, his heart and breathing steadied, and he began to swim through the living rock.

It was like passing through a sea of infinite depth, with the light—a strange ruddy glow like that of a setting sun—coming not from above but from below. The rock waters were not of one color but were arranged in layers and immense cliffs and chasms, all still and silent. Among these, in glittering masses, lay the crystals, in all colors, but mostly pale and white like trees and bushes and rivers in their different growths. Here and there he saw solid metallic pools, shining glossy black and red, white and yellow in the dull light.

He swam until his arms and legs were tired; but his mind was not tired, because of the fascination of the place, the queer sights and the smells, too; for each sort of rock had to him a different perfume and a different feeling on his skin. And he was all alone in this world, or so it seemed; it belonged to him, he was its emperor. And as he thought this, the thought struck him that for practical purposes he was all-powerful on the surface, too, for what puissance could harm him or say him nay? He could do anything he wished.

The woman and the man-cat were waiting, sitting companionably together and talking when they saw Lump pop breathless out of the ground, naked as the day he was born, for, of course, he had fallen right through his clothes. These he found and put on and walked toward the wagon, his face bearing an odd expression: triumph mixed with unease.

"How fared you, Lump?" asked the woman brightly.

"Well enough. The thing seems to work, at any rate."

"Oh, but tell us!" she said, smiling. "What did you see and what was it like?"

Lump said, "It was like nothing in particular, except that I was alone and no one to ask me questions, which was the best part of it. I am tired and am going to lie down. Wake me when there is something else to eat. And . . . do not think that I will join your show. I would rather starve and die in a ditch than to show my hideous face to some herd of stupid people for their mocks and howls. And you cannot make me."

With that, he strode off and vanished inside the wagon.

Falance spat twice and snarled, "That lad wants a good dozen hard bats with the claws half out. How dare he speak to you that way!"

The woman could not contain a long sigh, but in the next moment she smiled and patted Falance on the knee.

"My dear friend," she remarked. "You hurt for me, and I love you for it. But these are my deserts, which I must endure. He is cruel and ungrateful, as I was negligent and unfeeling. Cuff and cuddle, you used to say; oh, had I possessed the sense to listen! But now he is too big to cuff, and he will not have a cuddle to save his soul."

"Yet don't you hate him for it? Why, see what you have given up for him!"

"Given up? I suppose it seems that way. But look you: as you know well, a life in magic is perilous, and I have been at it for a long, long time. The powers may take as much as they give—more, sometimes. There are women older than I in our sisterhood whom I would not wish to be for a moment. The common folk have their legends of evil witches, and indeed there are such, those who have allowed power to corrupt their reverence, their humanity. Perhaps I was becoming so."

"You? Never!"

"No, I could feel it, Falance, a hand of ice fumbling

at my heart's gate, and perhaps this is why I began the long chain of actions that has brought us to this muddy place, beginning with the day I picked up Lump in his basket. There are no accidents, you know. So, in some way, it may be for the best. I am a plain woman again and will be evermore. For, truly, you would not want me to end up like Huon, would you?"

At this, the woman contorted her face into a cold and inhuman mask, a remarkable mimicry of the fairy's look. Falance gaped and exploded in a laugh. As everyone knows, it is exceedingly difficult to make a cat laugh, but, one laugh let out, others followed, most heartily, and the woman joined in.

Within the wagon, Lump imagined they were laughing at him, and pulled a blanket over his head, and thought dreadful thoughts.

When the two friends had recovered their breath and wiped their streaming eyes, the woman said, "Well, admit it, Falance, we did not do much of that when I was the all-powerful Quiet Woman, so there is something to the good. As for the boy, all we can do is be ourselves and endure, and seek what is over the next hill." So saying, she mounted the box. Falance leaped up beside her, and she snapped the reins, calling, "Ho!

Duty and Desire, you noble rats, you demihorses, pull together, pull away!" And off they went, tossing mud behind them.

Not over the next hill, or the sixth even, but after much slogging on rough tracks—for now the roots and stones did not leap from their path, but made their wheels slip and balk—they came to a broad king's highway and took it gladly up.

The road was busy with traveling folk. Draymen shouted and whipped their horses; the coaches of the wealthy, with gilded postilions and liveried servants, jostled for place with men driving flocks of sheep, and herds of cattle and swine, and country girls with their gaggles of geese. Every so often all were driven into ditches by the trumpets of royal messengers pelting hell-for-leather with the mails, scattering mire equally over draymen and coaches, sheep and geese.

Lump had never seen so many people, and not the deepest sulk could overcome his natural and still strong curiosity. He sat at the open rear door of the wagon as the long dusty day passed, wearing a hooded cloak to conceal his looks, and stared and filled his mind with incomprehensible impressions. Why, he wondered, did these people flog their beasts when a word would have done all? But they never seemed to speak to their animals, except sometimes to their horses, yet the horses never spoke back. It was possible that here in the wide world, animals did not choose to converse with men, or men could not hear them when they did, or perhaps it had something to do with the fading of magic that his mother and Falance were always talking about, something to do with too much iron.

A sudden disturbance down the road, and here was iron for you! A battery of artillery—four black cannons—with six black horses to each, sweating and straining, with troopers riding them bareback and snapping whips or astride the limbers, their faces covered with the spatters of the road and calling out jokes to the goose girls as they passed.

Once again the wagon was forced off the road. This time the woman did not steer it back, but continued past the ditch to a small clearing already inhabited by an odd lot of weary travelers.

"The sun is nearly down and this looks a good place to rest," she said. "There is water nearby."

They settled in. Falance built a fire and cooked the remains of their game and wild vegetables, and the woman watered the horses. Later she and the cat walked into the woods and cut down three tall straight birches and spent some time forming them into poles. These they lashed to the top of the wagon.

They were sitting around the fire after supper when a tattered man in a worn soldier's coat and cap came over and begged a light for his pipe. The man, Lump observed with interest, wore a black patch covering one eye and most of one side of his face. As he was puffing off a lit twig, Falance remarked, "But there you have a fine tinderbox at your belt, sir. You have no need to beg fire."

"Oh, that!" said the veteran, looking oddly over his shoulder. " 'Tis no use for a light, that one. It's got dogs in it. Big dogs, eyes like millstones, eyes like round towers. A nuisance. Still I keeps it, for, you know, we poor old soldiers keeps all manner of tack in hopes it will come useful one day."

"Why is that black thing on your face?" asked Lump suddenly.

"Lump! Your manners!" said the woman.

"Oh, that's all right, ma'am," said the veteran, grinning horribly. "I don't mind. 'Twas at a fierce mighty battle in High Barbary, me boy. A corsair's saber sliced away me eye and near half me face, so I wears this here patch so as not to frighten folks, so horrid do I look in the light of day. Well, I thank 'ee kindly for the light. Good evening to you all."

He hobbled away from the fire, and straightaway Lump said, "That is what I must have, but over the whole of my face."

"What!" she cried. "Your whole face in a black mask? You would look like the hangman."

"Better than looking like a goblin," Lump replied, and would not be argued out of it, except to agree that they would wait until they came to a town.

This they did the next morning. It was a small place of not more than two thousand souls, ringed by crumbling ocher stone walls, with grass and trees growing out of the battlements and white-and-brown goats to browse it. Past the wall there were narrow, smelly streets faced with overhanging buildings. The twisted way led eventually to a small cobbled square with a church on one side and taverns and stables on all the others. The keep of an old castle loomed over all.

When the woman had stopped in the square, Falance took the poles they had cut and made them into a tall tripod, and ran a rope from the top of this to a hook at the corner of the wagon. Then he leaped for the rope, swung up upon it, and began to dance along its length, cutting capers, standing on his hands, and performing back flips. A crowd of idlers and people passing gathered around the wagon. The woman stepped out and made little leather balls appear in her hands and disappear; she pulled scarves from her ears and mouth, and juggled four balls and four flaming brands.

Lump watched this from the wagon. He was filled with shame and excited at the same time. Finally, he could watch no longer and slipped away below into the earth.

The woman and Falance gave their best, but the crowd was thin and never grew larger; and the only ones who applauded were two young children, richly dressed, who were in the company of their servant, and a man with a twisted back and a remarkably long nose, who stood foremost in the throng and watched all with an avid eye.

When the people had drifted away, the woman inspected what had been dropped in the brass pot she had set out on the ground.

"Hmm—I have not had much to do with money," she said, "but this appears to be four brass groats and a clipped penny. Mountebanks must be thin folk with these wages. It is scarce the price of a small loaf."

"You must cry the show," said a voice.

The crook-backed man stepped forward. A bit past middle age, with a snapping bright eye, he was decently dressed, if threadbare, in a yellow coat and a peaked velvet hat with a brim; and he leaned on a short, stout stick.

"You must have a boy go about the town," he said, "dressed in motley with a drum, and—if you have two boys—a pipe or trumpet, and cry the show. That will bring all the people to you, do you see, and not just the idlers in the square and people who are on errands and cannot stop. And also, you must deck your poles and yourselves with bright ribands and glittering spangles, to delight the eye. Then you must bravo the act: say what crowned heads you have amazed, the prizes you have won, and so forth, so that folk will think they are lucky to see you."

"You speak knowingly of these things, sir," said the woman. "Are you perhaps a mountebank yourself?"

"Was, good lady, was. Allow me to present myself. You see before you Pinocchio, if I may say it, the greatest tightrope and trapeze performer of this age, late of Balducci's Exposition. You have, of course, heard of it."

"I am afraid not. We are from an isolated district. We are just starting out as mountebanks, as I suppose is all too plain."

"Well, well," said the cripple, grinning around his long nose. "As far as strict talent, you are fine as you are. Your man there on the slack rope—Balducci would give his remaining ear for one such as that. How sprightly! What grace! He is very like a cat."

"Thank you, sir," said Falance.

"Yes, and you, mistress: what flashing fingers! I was quite amazed. But, as I say, sadly, mere skill is not enough. Cry and bravo is the game, with us artistes—a word, by the way, we much prefer to mountebank."

"I beg your pardon," said the woman, "but am I to understand that you are no longer a—an artiste?"

The man indicated his hump with a twist of his head. "Yes, a broken bird am I. Not five years ago in this very spot I was attempting to walk between yon church spire and the top of the castle keep, when a wind sprang up and I was o'erthrown and crashed to earth, with the result you see—a sad twisted thing. The Exposition left without me, and here I stay."

"How dreadful!" said the woman. "But, sir, Pinocchio, you have given us good counsel, and in fair

exchange would you allow me the exercise of my healing arts on your poor frame? I have skill in such matters."

After some persuasion, she led him into the wagon
and had him stretch on a cot, first removing his upper
garments. She prodded and kneaded and rubbed in a
salve made from bitter bugle, black samphire, elf gen-
tian, and the forefeet of young basilisks. While she
rubbed he told her a little of his life as an acrobat, how
he had been the child of a poor cabinetmaker who
wanted him to go to school, how he had run away with
the circus and never looked back, although he regretted
having to dissemble to his poor da, who still believed he
was a deacon.

"Why, why, this is colossal!" cried Pinocchio, when
she had done. "The pain is quite vanished and I feel
supple again, far less a block of wood than before.
Hooray!"

Though he was still bent, he was clearly less bent
than before and easier in his motions. The woman
smiled at him and said, "I am happy you're better, and
you should continue to improve with time. And I hope
you'll continue to favor us with your good advice."

"Oh, more than that, my good lady, more than

that," said Pinocchio. "I will *devote* myself to your success. First, if you are to be, as we may say, mountebanks, then you must have a *bank* to *mount* on, do you see? A bench or little stage, which we usually arrange on the side of the wagon, hinged, so that it can drop down when you perform. Otherwise the people in the back of the throng cannot see you and will offer nought. I have a friend, a wainwright, who will do one up for you. Next, you require colors—"

"But, sir, we have no money!" cried Falance.

"Tut! Think nothing of that! My wainwright has a rash and his child a croup that will not mend. Do for him what you did for me and he is yours, and his whole shop, too. The same with the other merchants we will patronize. Health is a coin beyond compare." Pinocchio lowered his voice and looked sideways. "And it may be that you are skilled in other matters? Love philters? Potions to discomfort a rival?"

"No," said the woman curtly. "I am a healer and, as you say, an artiste and no more. So—it is late in the day and we are all hungry. Perhaps there is a cookshop nearby whose master has a wen or a sore toe."

There was, and over the next few days the woman and Falance were made free of the town and its goods.

The grateful craftsman constructed a stage. A gouty draper contributed brightly colored stuffs, and a gilder traded a box of shining bangles for the relief of his dropsy. They took their meals in a bakeshop whose owner's daughter was no longer deaf. The sergeant of the town guard was relieved of a boil, for which he gladly relinquished an almost-new drum and a fife.

Lump they rarely saw, as he preferred to spend his days in the secret spaces of the earth, emerging at night, ravenous and with little to say. The woman thought this skulking was no way for the boy to live, and she resolved to do something.

She thereupon went again to the wainwright and obtained from him a piece of thin veneer, white boxwood with just a blush of pink and without flaw. A potter produced, in exchange for a cure for his warts, a head of a handsome youth in clay. With this in hand, it was an easy matter to soften the veneer in steam and press it over the head, so it conformed to the fine features. The eyes and mouth cut out, a little paint, some ribbon, and there was a mask, as lifelike as any mask could be. She placed it on his cot.

The next morning the three of them were in the wagon; rain beat on the roof and the town square was swept with squalls of wind, and so there was no show. Lump fingered the mask. In fact, he was delighted with the thing, but he was of an age and disposition that forbade expressing delight of any kind to his mother. Instead, he tossed it lightly aside, saying, "I suppose you expect me to wear this so that I can troop about with the drum."

"That would be a great help to us," the woman said. "I can heal here and there, but done too much it draws the sort of attention it is well to avoid. I would rather not end my days tied to a stake. And I thought you would enjoy it. I had always heard that boys like to bang on drums and be the center of all eyes."

"But I am not like other boys, Mother," Lump retorted. "I do not wish to be stared at, mask or no."

At this, Falance could not contain himself. "Nor did your mother wish to be a mountebank juggling for small coins where once she was the great enchantress of the world, but she surrendered that for your sake. And do you now refuse this favor, this trifle—"

"Please, Falance . . ." said the woman, moving to stand between them. Falance was crouched with his hair standing up about his face and his eyes sparking.

"I'm not afraid of you," said the boy.

"Oh, stop it, the two of you!" cried the woman. "Go sit down, Falance! Lump, have some sense! We are a family and we must earn our bread together. A boy we require, and you are that boy. I do not speak of compulsion, but I should think that you would not wish to play the layabout and merely take, while Falance and I work. So, what is it to be, my son?"

Lump was not so inhuman that he did not show a blush of shame at this, and he grunted an assent. Thereafter, the troupe did better. Lump cried the show through the town, dressed in a red and white striped cloak and a broad black hat with a red plume, beating on his drum (which he rather enjoyed, but little did he admit it) and wearing his mask. People smiled at him, which was a new experience; and after a few days he thought a mountebank's life was a bearable misery.

The show itself was much improved. With Pinocchio's advice and active help (for his back was now nearly straight and he was lively with it) the wagon and its appurtenances were tricked out with everything gaudy appropriate to such a conveyance: spangles, bits of colored glass, bright paint, ribbons, and furbelows. Falance had a tight yellow and white costume, with bells sewn on it that jangled merrily when he made his leaps on the rope. And he learned to caterwaul on the fife. The woman had a handsome red dress with sequins. Now she made appear and vanish not only balls and scarves but doves, hens, live frogs, and, for the finale, a small, beribboned piglet. The coins showered in.

But soon, all who had interest, leisure, and spare coins in the place had seen the show, and Pinocchio gave them intelligence of the Cold Fair that was to be held outside the great city of the land. There they might be sure of gaining enough to see them through the winter indoors.

"And besides," said the former acrobat, "you will be in the neighborhood of that immense town, the marvel of the world, whose streets flow with gold. Many a troupe of artistes does it support, and well, too. This is my advice: go there and prosper!"

"So we will," agreed the woman, "and many thanks for your good counsel."

"I have one more," said Pinocchio. "Your equipage lacks but one essential, and that is a name. For there are many shows, and you must distinguish yours from the rest, so that patrons will know to look for you. It should be painted on all sides of your wagon, in red letters, picked out with best gold leaf."

"That is sensible," agreed the woman, "but what should the name be?"

"It should be grand," said their adviser. "For instance, 'The Magnificoes' or 'The Gorgeous Attraction.'"

But these were in current use, and they had to scratch their heads for a better. The woman suggested 'A Woman, a Cat, and a Boy,' as being honest and plain, but Pinocchio said it sounded like a mere inventory. Falance came up with a few that demonstrated (as if any more proof were needed) that cats have no imagination at all. Finally, Lump, who had been sitting silently behind his mask, said, "Why not say what is the truth? We are nothing but outcasts from Faeryland."

At this Falance snarled, and Pinocchio looked confused, but the woman laughed and said, "Just so, Lump! That is true and that is what we shall be called."

And they had the man who painted signs for inns and such paint THE FAERYLAND OUTCASTS on the sides of the wagon, and he threw in several pictures of royal faeries looking grim; grim they were but not in the least like true faeries. And so they left the town.

*   *   *

They reached the great fair at sundown on the third day of their travel, and although the sky's light was fading, the glow of the gathering could be seen from miles off. Ten thousand torches and tapers and colored lanterns were abroad, set out by those who had goods on offer or purveyors of entertainments of every imaginable kind—dances and theater shows, with bright and prancing players; religious processions, pompous and grave, shedding incense on the evening air; gambling dens packed with glittering and avid dandies and their gorgeous consorts; taverns and beer gardens, shaking with light and noise and music.

As they drove through the narrow lanes, Lump sat in the open back door with his feet hanging down and observed all this from behind his mask and was not impressed or excited as an ordinary boy would have been, for the blight of Faery held him in thrall. The lights, noise, and amusements were to him mere pathetic shadows of the true joys and beauty to be found in that land, and he regarded with cold contempt those who were so easily satisfied.

A space was found beside a pavilion devoted to gambling. They hobbled and fed the horses, and bought pies and ale from a stall and ate. Then Falance built a fire in a brazier and erected his poles and ropes. Lump had just begun to beat on his drum when a large man wearing royal livery and bearing splendid mustaches on his wide, florid face stepped up and said that he was a fair marshal. The fee for mountebanks was declared at two pennies, which the woman paid him. Taking it, he said, "For another penny I have tickets for tomorrow morning."

"And what is to be then?" asked the woman.

"We are burning a dozen or so heretics and witches near the river docks. If you wait til then, I warn you, good places will be impossible to find."

"I think we must decline, thank you very much," said the woman after a pause. "Is there much burning of witches hereabouts?"

"Oh, certes," said the marshal. "We are in the fore-front of nations in this, as the king's majesty, whom God preserve, is much against their vile tricks and weird conniptions. Some places merely brand and whip them nowadays, but we don't waste time with that. No, burning is sure, and makes a splendid show and a warning to foolish women. Do you not agree?"

"Oh, yes," replied the woman. "An effective warning to women indeed."

The marshal bustled off, and Lump began his cry to the drumbeat: "Hola! Hola! Hola! The show of the Faeryland Outcasts is about to begin, an amazement and a delight for all ages and conditions! You will not believe your eyes, my lords and ladies! Come all, come all!"

When a sufficient crowd had gathered, Falance leaped up on his slack rope and began to juggle three lit candles. On the wagon stage the woman pulled burning lamps from her sleeves and drew live doves from her mouth.

Their location proved to be a fortunate one, since the crowd going into the gaming pavilion was a rich one; and so little knots of splendidly dressed courtiers and merchants and their fine ladies were pausing to view the antics of Falance and the woman. They gasped, they clapped, they laughed and moved on, and coins glinted in the firelight as they rained down, clinking, upon the stage.

"This is very well," said the woman, when they were all assembled around the wagon's tiny table after the show. "How much do you count, there, Lump?"

Lump had become the treasurer of the company, by default. No cat can count above ten, and the woman, who could compass a spell of two hundred verses with perfect ease, was thrown off in her figures by the slightest distraction.

"I make it sixty-two pence, half penny," replied Lump, "with six groats and two of these, which we have never had before."

Two small circles glinted yellow on the table. "They are gold, if real," he said and picked one up. "They count as twenty pennies, I am told. There is the head of the king stamped upon them and his name, Magnus the Second."

"He looks a grim fellow," said Falance, peering close. "What is on the back?"

"Words in an old language they used to use hereabouts," replied Lump. "I asked one of the people here, and he said that it means 'Come back to me!' for the king, they say, loves gold above all other things." He tossed the gold clinking onto the little pile. "Well," Lump said, without enthusiasm, "if the rest of the fair goes as well as tonight, we should make what we need to pass the winter indoors, with food enough. And then in spring another round of this mumchance life, I suppose." He put on his mask and cloak and took two pennies from the pile. "Let this be my night's wage.

Perhaps I will find something to amuse me, doubtful as that may be."

Saying nothing else, he left.

"You are growling, Falance," said the woman, after a silence.

"Was I? I was not aware of it. Yet I cannot help but become angry when he acts that way. No courtesy, no 'Mother, permit me, and I will take my leave.' I would not treat a dog the way he treats you."

The woman chuckled, saying, "From you those are strong words. But come, what he is cannot be helped by our moping here. We are at the fair, hi-ho! And there is music and there are what passes for rare sights on this common earth. Give me your arm, Falance, and we will promenade."

So they went out. On the far side of the way there was a banner that read CAPTAIN JOHANNES—MASTER OF THE BLADE. LESSONS AND EQUIPAGE FOR THE DUELLO.

Set up under this sign was a little booth selling edged steel—rapiers, sabers, and poinards, stilettos and misericords—with a light-haired, plump woman attending its counter, a woman just past the bloom of youth with a plain but pleasant visage. Beyond, there was a ring marked off with colored ropes, in the center of which stood a strong-looking, lithe man, somewhat older than the counter-woman, dressed in old-fashioned doublet, hose, and cape, and brandishing a rapier and a long, straight dagger. In a loud, clear voice he declared, "A challenge to you gallants and bravos from Captain Johannes, myself the greatest swordsman of this or any previous age, late in service to the Grand Turk, to the emperor, and the several palatines, to duel in the Spanish fashion. A gold magnus awaits him who can pink me with either sword or dagger before I have him at my mercy, and only a penny to play. Come, come! A penny against a magnus! For shame, gentlemen! No one? Ah, here is a fine, brave fellow!"

A richly dressed youth had stepped forward, half pushed by his laughing friends and their ladies. He was somewhat in his cups, but he drew his steel and waved it about with many a flourish, and gave his coin to the young woman in the booth. Then the two men crossed blades under the blazing torches.

The woman and Falance watched this new thing with interest. In a while, Falance remarked, "He is toying with the mark, lady, to draw out the show and attract others. Look, there! The popinjay was a dead man just then, quite helpless against a return from the left side."

"What, Falance! Are you a swordsman as well as an acrobat?"

"No, lady, not I. Yet I once used near a score of blades at once, you know, and this play with only two seems no great accomplishment. Let me but watch a few more bouts and perhaps I will risk one of our pennies, with your kind leave."

Captain Johannes disarmed the lad, amid great laughter from the sidelines, and then three of his companions tried, whose laughter soon turned to groans as they lost their silver, bout upon bout. Falance watched carefully, and at last he stepped to the booth and laid a penny on the counter.

"Mistress, if you would give me the use of a long blade? I have a short one already."

The woman measured him with an expert eye and handed him a rapier from the rack behind her. "Good luck," she said, smiling pleasantly.

Instantly their blades crossed, Johannes found, to his surprise, that he was facing an opponent of more than usual quality. Back and forth across the ring they dashed, and the metal rang. Johannes was tired from his previous bouts, but still he ought to have been able to overcome this strange, swift person with ease, for the man clearly had little technical skill. Yet he could not; again and again the fencing master cornered Falance against the barrier ropes, and ever he slipped away with prodigious darts and leaps. At last, Johannes used a trick he ordinarily only brought forth in deadly combat: he pretended to stumble, and when Falance's sword point came in at him, he caught it with his hand wrapped in a thickness of cloak and yanked it forward, so that it was planted into the sand, immobilizing his opponent for a heartbeat, which was all that was needed. His own sword point flicked up and touched Falance's throat. Then he laughed.

"Ha-ha! Splendid! Who are you, fellow? Why don't I know you already? You are a soldier, yes? A guardsman, perhaps?"

"My name is Falance and I am no soldier. I am a cat," said Falance, breathing not at all heavily.

"Ha-ha! Of course you are! By my hilt, man, you use your sword like a broom, of course, but what legs, what wrists! A month with me and you could claim a place as captain of the guard in any realm from Cathay to the Western Isles."

"I thank you, sir. In exchange I could teach you to climb walls."

"Oh, no, not I! Two feet on the earth for Hans. But, come, this was thirsty work. I will buy you a stein of beer and we can exchange lies. You and your wife, of course," indicating with a nod the woman standing there.

"She is not my wife; I am her servant."

"Your pardon, then," Johannes said and shouted out, "Gretl! Shut up the stall and come! Enough for tonight. Let us drink and be at our ease." The young woman did so.

"Your wife helps you at your work, I see," said Falance.

"Oh, no! She is a rare judge of blades, Gretl, to be sure, but she is my sister."

The former witch was introduced to the pair as Mrs. Forest, a name she had decided was fitting for her new life in the cities of men. The four of them went to a nearby beer garden, a place of rough trestle tables under an arbor of autumn leaves and blossoms hung with colored lanterns, where harried barmaids ran to and fro with ten foaming mugs in each hand and the patrons shouting and pounding on the tables.

Johannes ordered steins around and sausage rolls and herrings and paid the score, in recompense, he said, for the best fight he had had in many a year. They were served, and between quaffs and gobbles, Johannes spoke freely of life in the king's city, to which Falance and the woman listened with great interest. Magnus was a stern ruler but fair, all agreed. He would have every groat of his due, but not a groat more. Johannes had a little school of arms in the upper part of the town and Gretl bought and sold weapons in the same establishment. Many merchants were waxing rich on the city's trade and the king's fair dealing; they wished to ape the nobles and for this some sword skill was necessary, and so Johannes prospered. The young woman was quieter than her brother, but she often finished his sentences for him, and always he looked toward her to confirm what he said.

The woman thought, They seem a happy couple, if "couple" is the correct word. She sensed that the two had lived a hard life, in which their devotion to each other had been the only fair thing. She thought, Perhaps Falance and I are becoming thus, and the thought amused her.

The woman and the cat, for their part, said little, content to let the light talk of the siblings wash over them. They were unused to socializing, having lived so long outside the compass of society, except the society of witches and beasts, which is not at all the same thing. Falance had scarcely spoken at length to any people at all in his whole life.

The sound of a mandolin caught their attention and they looked to where a strolling player had appeared at the gate. This player, a Gypsy, had a little girl with him, and he hoisted her up on a table. She was a dark, ragged, starved-looking thing, but when she gave voice, the beer garden fell silent; for her singing was as pure and lovely as a linnet's. She sang the old ballad about the young man who falls in love with a cruel mistress, who asks him, as a token of his love, to kill his mother and cut out her heart and bring it to her that she might eat it. This the youth does, kills his mother and cuts her heart out, but, as he runs back with the heart dripping in his hands, he stumbles and falls, and the heart drops to the street and speaks in his mother's voice, saying, "Oh, my darling child, have you hurt yourself?" That is the chorus of the song, and the child sang it most plaintively.

There was a hush when the song was over, and then a great pulse of applause, and the coins flew. Falance was not surprised to see that his mistress was crying; it is a song always affecting to mothers, and then he saw with dismay (in one of those coincidences on which stories are constructed but which, despite that, are hardly unknown in real life), that Lump was standing beside the next table, masked, watching them.

The woman saw him, too, in that moment, and hastily brushed her eyes with her sleeve and beckoned him over, smiling. He stood still for a moment, with his arms folded, and then sauntered over and sat down on a stool.

The woman made the introductions. Johannes looked the boy over and said lightly, "It is after hours for all us mountebanks, lad. You may take your mask off."

"May I?" answered Lump. "Perhaps you will take yours off, too, you and your sister. Yours are made of flesh and mine of wood and paint, but we do cling to them, do we not?"

Johannes's smile became uncertain and he looked at the woman in puzzlement. She asked her son with a calm she did not feel, "What have you been doing this fine night, dear?"

"Oh, me? Going to and fro on the earth and under it, Mother. What else would I do? Two pence will not buy me admission to the king's ball; and, you know, it is not a masked ball."

"You seem to have spent your two pence on drink," said Falance, with an edge to his voice.

"Yes," said Lump, "the strongest I could get. I wanted to see if I could make the world less ugly, but, no—it is still as ugly as me. We are a pair. You should see your face, Falance—if you were still a cat, you would spit. And you have still not learned to bathe—I can smell your cat stink from over here."

The woman moved presciently: before Falance could make the violent lunge he had intended, her hand gripped his arm tightly. He fell back in his seat, growling, and Lump giggled. "Poor kitty," he mocked, "save your claws. You know I am beyond your grasp. I am the magic one now; it is I who have the earth kl—"

He stopped. He could not breathe. His mother's hand held his collar with an iron grip, twisting it, cutting off his air. He had not known she could move as fast as that or that she had the strength of old briars in her thin arms. Her face was pressed up against his mask and her eyes looked like a storm at sea, black-gray, shot with lightnings.

"Be silent, you lout!" she said in a hissing undertone. "How dare you disgrace yourself and me and place all of us in danger! Don't you know how this realm fears witches and all magic? Do you hate us so much that you want to see us staked and boiling in our own fat?"

She released him, and he fell backward off his stool, gasping and speechless. The woman rose and addressed Johannes and his sister. "Thank you kindly for a pleasant evening. I regret this disturbance, but the boy is not used to strong spirits. Forgive him. And now I think we shall return to our wagon. Falance?"

Without another word, nor sparing a glance at the boy on the ground, she swept out of the place like a duchess, with her servant at heel.

Gretl rose and helped the boy to his feet and sat him on the bench beside her. Johannes seemed embarrassed and stared into his mug. Gretl pressed a maidservant to bring a jug of water, from which the boy gratefully drank, until his throat and stomach felt less outraged.

"You know," said Gretl in her gentle voice, "it is really not well to behave so before your mother."

Without thinking, Lump blurted out, "She is not my mother; she is a witch!" And then he gasped and looked instantly around him to see if anyone had over-heard and then realized that these two had of course heard it, and he turned pale. He was not really an evil child, and certainly did not want anything evil to befall the woman; but he was confused in his feelings, both because of his age, which was common, and because of what had happened to him in Faery, which was as far from common as may be imagined.

To his vast surprise, Gretl was not at all shocked at hearing this, but nodded and said, "I rather thought she was; our own dear stepmother was a witch, too, and had something of the same manner. Did she not, Hansl?"

"Yes, very like, dear," the man agreed. "I remarked it especially around the eyes. Needless to say, we will keep it dark as dark. And do you as well, my boy!"

"You were raised by a witch?" asked Lump in a hoarse whisper, astounded.

"Oh, yes," said Gretl. "We ran from our parents, you see, into the dark forest, and she took us in."

"Why ever did you do that? You are both comely."

"Why, thank you, sir," said Gretl, laughing, "but had we been as fair as the Fair Folk, still it would have done us no good."

"It was our father," said Johannes. "A country nobleman of good lineage but foul temper. He conceived a hatred of Gretl, and treated her most cruelly and me also, when I took her part."

"Our mother, poor thing, was vain, greedy, and weak," added Gretl.

"Never did she stand in his way," said Johannes, indignation rising in his voice, "though he beat Gretl savagely, and she only a little mite. Many is the night she crept into my bed, weeping, with the blood running off her. Then, one day— Oh, Gretl, you must tell it, for it makes my blood boil still, although many years have passed."

Gretl held her brother's hand and stroked it and said, "Our father was a great horseman, and one day he came in sweaty from the breaking of them and called for wine. It was my duty to bring him his cup, which I did, but then he shouted at me so that I spilled a drop. He cursed me and struck at me with his great horse whip. I fell to the ground, near senseless with pain. Then Hansl came dashing forth, brandishing his little dirk, and attacked our father with it, stabbing him in the leg. At this, our father dashed the knife from his hand, for Hansl was but a boy of eight at the time, and savaged him with the whip and locked him in a room in the tower, swearing he would hang him with his own hands on the morrow. But I stole the key while he slept his wine off, and released Hansl, and then we fled to the forest wild.

"How many days we wandered, lost and freezing, I know not, for it was a cold spring when we escaped, and no food at all on bush or trees. The little bread and cheese I had thought to take was soon gone and we starved."

"Then we found the bread crumbs," said Johannes.

"Yes, dear, the bread crumbs. We heard a twittering one morning and saw a long avenue of birds feeding on crumbs. We fell on our knees and lapped them up, we were so hungry, and then my clever Hansl killed a thrush with a stone. We tore it apart and ate it raw. The trail of crumbs soon disappeared, but by then we were close enough to smell the gingerbread baking, and we followed our noses to the little house. That is where we found Mother Green."

"That was the witch," Johannes put in.

"Yes, and she took us in and fed us, and we told her our story, and she said we could stay with her as long as we liked."

"She was very old and nearly blind," said Johannes.

"Yes, and that was the reason for the bread crumbs. When she went out to gather herbs and berries, she left the crumbs so that the birds would guide her home. And so we stayed . . ."

"Until our father came looking for us . . ."

"With his hounds he tracked us. These he tied and he waited until Mother Green was gone out, for he feared all things magical. I was outside when I saw him . . ."

"And you gave a great shout, saying 'Hansl, hide yourself!' "

"That I did, and you ran into the cottage and hid within the oven, which had a heavy iron door of the kind fitted with a counterweight, so it could be lifted easily with one finger . . ."

"So our father pursued me and reached into the oven, trying to catch me, and I climbed up into the chimney, being at that time so thin, and you, my clever sister, ran forth . . ."

"And with a little knife, I cut through the rope that held the counterweight, and the iron door crashed down upon his back." She smiled at her brother.

"Was he killed?" asked Lump, wide-eyed at the tale.

"Oh, no, only stunned and trapped," answered Gretl. "There he stayed until the witch came home, and we told her what had passed. She spoke a mighty spell and turned him into a pig. A boar hog."

"We ate off him all winter," said Johannes. "And grew back our weight. There we rested many years, until at last the old woman died, leaving us a little store of pennies, and we went out, the two of us, into the wide world, and I took up the trade of weapons because we no longer had friends nor family, and, you know, a fellow must protect the honor of his sister or die. And there! That is our story. Will you not tell us yours?"

Now feelings made war in Lump's breast at this invitation. He longed to open himself to this kind woman and frank, admirable man, to make friends with them, to slake a thirst that had tormented him nearly his whole life. And yet he feared them—what would they say if they saw his face? Would they not recoil in horror? Moreover, the blight of Faery still gripped his heart, lashing him to seek an impossible grace and perfection. He found himself thinking: These were after all not particularly interesting people, not even very good-looking, and who knows what they might want of him? Better to slip away.

A sigh tried to escape his lips through the stiff wood of his mask, but he stifled it. He said coldly, "I have no story of any interest to you. Good evening to you both." And he turned away from their surprised faces.

He walked rapidly from the beer garden, and he found his footsteps leading him again to the royal pavilion, a huge scarlet tent spangled with gold stars, out from which a ball sent its merry tunes. There was a lane made of scented bark all around this tent, and along it at intervals were posted royal guardsmen with halberds to keep back the throng of ordinary people who wished to feast their eyes on the persons and dress of the realm's magnificoes.

Lump pushed his way to the front of this crowd. He had discovered that he loved display and fine clothes and the glint of jewels in the hair of lovely women and music and fine scents. All these recalled, in a way he could not fully describe, the vacant ache that was all that remained of his glance at the faery dancing. He sought such sights out now as one may suck on a rotten tooth, so that the sharpness of the pain seems to relieve the constant dull ache.

He watched the coaches and carriages arrive and

the fine people step down, showing silks and plumes, and wafting perfumes over the mob. Now came a coach even more ornate than the others, its panels dripping gilded figures, with six matched steeds white as linen, and the drivers and footmen all in green velvet with silvered facings and frogs. One of these leaped down and flung open the door, from which descended a large man got up like a wedding cake with layer upon layer of fine stuffs and gold lace; his hat was decked with a white plume so long it nearly touched the ground. He had a rosy, wide, proud, satisfied face, and his sausage fingers sparkled with rings. He turned to hand from the coach someone within.

Lump saw a flash of white like foam—her dress—and a flash of golden light—her hair—and she looked directly at him with eyes as dark blue as the evening when the stars are just about to come. The faery ice rattled in his heart. Then she turned and was gone on the man's arm.

The stricken boy turned to his neighbor. "Who was that?" he demanded.

"That? Why, the miller Vandy, the richest man in the town, it is said."

"No, that girl—who was she?"

The man grinned and replied. "Why, that is the miller's daughter."

"And her name? Do you know it?" Lump waited, and the name fell upon his ear like a faint, last echo of those enchanted horns.

"Aude."

Power

The winter came and it was a fell one, with snow blocking the streets, the river freezing solid, and the wind down from the mountains blowing icy and long. The Faeryland Outcasts were, however, snug enough for the while. They were installed in a lodging near Johannes's school of arms, a cozy apartment with three rooms and the use of the kitchen in the back, stabling for the two horses included next door; and besides that they had employment. An impresario, Krupska by name, had seen them at the fair and engaged them for the winter season at his Colossal Circus of Joy, which was held in a large hall known as the Bear Garden. The circus went on to fill the intervals between the actual bearbaiting and bullbaiting that were the usual winter pastimes of the people of the royal city.

Falance and the woman proved a popular turn. The cat's antics on the very much higher ropes of the Bear Garden were as animated as those he had performed at the fair, and much more thrilling. His specialty was falling, seemingly out of control, from the highest rope, down, down, while the crowd shrieked and covered their eyes, only to catch himself on the lowest rope, landing, needless to say, on his feet. There was, of course, no net. The woman did her illusions calmly and gravely, and added card tricks to her repertoire, calling members of the audience up to pick and choose and be baffled, to the delight of all. Silently, each evening, the woman asked the forgiveness of the tormented animals.

They gained a mild notoriety in the city. Although the woman changed as soon as she could out of her red spangles and dressed soberly in stone gray and sparrow brown, Falance with his strange boneless walk and his long fluffy hair was hard to mistake. Children often followed them in the street until bought off with small coins; and several times they received invitations to galas in the palazzos of the rich, which they politely declined, much to Lump's ire, for he loved wealth and display more than ever. They found that they rather enjoyed the camaraderie of the performers, the woman especially: she had not realized how much she had missed the closeness of the sisterhood from which she was now barred. Johannes and his sister became their dear friends; they alone in the city were privy to the secret of the origins of the three Faeryland Outcasts.

With this charming life Lump had little to do. No boy was needed to cry the show now, and aside from his slight duties as treasurer, he was free to wander as he wished. What he wished to do most of all that winter, naturally, was to spy upon the miller's daughter.

His powers made this simplicity itself, especially as these were increasing with experience. It had always been an inconvenience that he fell through his clothes when he invoked the magic. Through practice, he found that he could extend the magic influence to include his clothes, his mask, and what small objects he chose to carry on his person. He was also learning more about the mysteries of the under earth. He found he could ride the waves of pressure and heat beneath the earth and be carried much farther than his arms and legs could have taken him. To Lump, a great mass of volcanic basalt or porphyry bulging through a layer of limestone was like a wave in the sea on whose face he could travel, with the sea taste of the limestone on one side of him and the dark stink of the volcanic rock on the other. When he was on the surface, usually at night, he would study the stones used in building, the frozen forms of the sea he played in; and he found he could divine the inner qualities of these blocks from their surfaces, just as a skilled jeweler can see the invisible fire dwelling in the uncut diamond. During this time, he acquired the habit of bringing back bits of colored rock and metal lumps from deep in the earth. These he kept in a leather bag in his room, and would take them out and play with the trinkets, enjoying the shine and light of them, and cherishing them as symbols of his power. He almost felt pleasure at this mastery, but the full feeling was stalled by the faery coldness in his heart; and even his most fascinating expeditions left him with a sense of hollow futility.

His major study, in any case, was Aude. The miller kept her closely guarded in his great mansion, second in grandeur only to the royal palace itself. Yet the corps of green-liveried servants was no barrier to one who could pass through walls and rise through marble floors. Lump had learned to control the magic bubble so that it floated in the midst of the stone walls of the miller's palace, walls that were to him as insubstantial as mist.

Thus he could study the beauty at every moment of her day: when she rose with a delicious stretch and yawn in her perfumed bed; when she was served her chocolate in bed; in her bath carved from a solid block of lapis lazuli; as she chose her morning costume; as she beat her maid for not polishing her silver buckles; as she descended the broad alabaster stairs to the breakfast terrace; as she cursed the cook and flung a silver teapot at her head because the eggs were not perfectly done, neither too moist nor too dry; as she quarreled with her older brother, Mostin, about who would use the great coach that day; as she cozened and caressed her father so that he would let her use the coach; as she played by the fountain in the courtyard with her six little dogs; as she went out with her maid and guards to the shops.

On the streets it was impossible to pursue her, yet twice each week he was able to see her as a natural boy might see a girl, for the miller was avid to pass as a gentleman and had become a pupil of Johannes at the fencing school. He brought his son and his daughter along to admire his skill, which was, in truth, not all that admirable. His gold was, however.

So Aude came and perched on a tufted chair in the *salle d'armes* and admired herself in the mirrors that ran along each wall and flirted with any young gentlemen who happened to be there (and there always were a good number, once it was discovered that Aude attended her father's lessons). Lump watched from the shadows and hated the young men with all his heart and loved Aude mutely from behind the false face.

And he was waiting for her when she returned, lying in her chamber's walls, watching her picking at her food—the most delicate morsels that the market offered—while she accepted the homage of the dinner guests, if any, or teased and enraged her brother if there were not. He watched her giggling with her maids and hired companions—for friends she had none—and ordering them about and making them cry. He watched her sleeping until he was near falling asleep himself and had to go home to his own bed.

After some months of this, he knew everything that could be known about Aude the miller's daughter, except that her beautiful golden head was as empty as a gourd and that her heart was full only of herself.

The spring arrived at last, in a rush of waters, the crack of breaking ice, squelching mud, and the woman saying, "Falance, my heart is sick with this place of stone, and iron, and senseless cruelties. I must be in the wild woods again, to smell the spring flowers, violet and dog rose, and hear the blackbird and the thrush under the sunny sky and the nightingale singing its heart out in the glades of the night. Therefore, let us gather our wagon and horses and take to the road. Lump, you will come with us and be our bravo boy again and do your escapes at last. It will do you good; I vow, you look as peaked as a starving rabbit."

At first Lump was about to refuse; the thought of passing a season without the daily sight of his beloved seemed intolerable. But then he thought that he had no way of earning his bread or paying for lodging in towns, so grumbling, he packed his rock collection and his drum and his few other possessions and climbed onto the wagon.

It was a rainy spring, which meant that they were covered in mud on the road and that when they did get to a town worthy of a show, people stayed indoors or hurried past with capes over their heads. The Faeryland Outcasts did not prosper. They had consumed their winter's earnings by the end of May and were reduced to living on what Falance could catch in the forests.

The woman was happy. She heard the song of the birds, she walked in the fresh rain with her face held up, she rolled in wet grass. She ran all night through the moonlit forest and bathed in mountain pools icy with snowmelt and returned in the morning with scratches on her face and body and joy in her eyes.

Falance was happy because the woman was, and Lump was unhappy because she was not. Her smiles, her humming a glad tune while it poured with rain irked him beyond endurance. One evening, after the third dinner in a row of stewed squirrel with wild carrots, Lump smacked his wooden spoon down on his plate and shoved it violently away.

"Too much salt?" asked Falance mildly.

"Too much squirrel," snarled Lump. He was thinking of the sort of dishes Aude and her family ate, like cock's combs in malmsey or larks in syrup, and was full of an irritable and hardly understood resentment.

"Surely you kept some little spell against need, Mother?" he asked sourly. "Something that would bring us a spread table of ever-flowing salvers. I am hungry, and tired of this wretched food, and tired of being poor. Can't your precious Goddess be convinced to make you a witch again?"

"You misapprehend the situation," said the woman coldly. "It was an inevitability, as was explained to me. A rock falls into a pool and the ripples spread. It is the case that I cannot be both a mother and a witch, or not the sort of witch I was. Were I to stop being your mother, I would again be what I was."

Lump's face grew white. "Don't blame me!" he cried. "Don't you dare blame me! I didn't ask for you to save me, did I? Go be a witch, why don't you! I don't need a mother!"

With that, he mumbled the magic words and vanished.

Falance remarked, "He has learned to carry his clothes with him. That must be helpful; I have observed that men set much store by proper clothing at all times. Do you suppose he will return this evening?"

"I doubt it," said the woman sadly. "He will not forgive me for saving him, and he will chew on it all night below the earth."

"In that case, I will help myself to his stew," said the cat, reaching.

"You know, I sometimes think that I would have been more successful with a girl," the woman mused. "Perhaps boys need the contact of men to learn how to comport themselves, and, really, he has never known a man."

"But I am a man, lady," said Falance.

"You are a cat in the shape of a man, Falance. It's not the same thing."

"No? Pray, wherein lies the difference?"

"I don't know. That's part of the problem, you see. I simply don't know enough about such things, as you have pointed out more than once." The woman finished her meal and mopped the last of the gravy with a piece of stale bread. Then she said, "But on the other hand, I suppose girls have their problems, too. Tell me, did you ever know Phyllis Hawklover? You would have been quite young, I think."

"A little dark woman. Lived in some sort of a tower?"

"Just so. She was not much of a witch, Phyllis, more what we call a spaewoman. A good heart, though. She lived in an old tower keep, and raised kestrels and merlins at the top, so Hawklover was her name. What happened was that one morning she came down and found a ragged tinker woman stealing greens from her little garden. The woman must have been deranged, because when she saw Phyllis she ran like a deer, leaving her bundle, and in the bundle there was a little fair-haired girl baby."

"I know this story," said Falance. "Phyllis gave her

some outlandish name and raised her as best she could, but the maiden she grew into was mad for boys. And there was something about her hair, too."

"Wouldn't have it cut or done up. She used to sit in the bird loft and call out to men riding by and let her hair down the tower walls, so it glinted gold. You could see it leagues away. And Phyllis would cry out, 'Oh, Rapunzel, pull up your hair!' but little did she mind her stepmother. And the men would climb the stairs. In the end she ran off with some knight or other, and never a look back or a further word, and broke poor Phyllis's heart."

"And is your heart broken, my dear lady?" asked Falance tenderly.

"Oh, my, yes!" said the woman, smiling broadly and blinking tears from her lashes. "But perhaps it will mend. In any case, we must plan out the rest of our season. I say we should complete our swing north and hope the weather improves, but then return in June for the Hot Fair in the city and see if we can recoup our fortunes. Lump needs some new shoes and clothing, and you are looking somewhat tatty yourself, Falance. Imagine! For the first time since I was a lass I will not be tending the sacred fires on Midsummer's Night but juggling for coins in a city. That will be queer."

It has been nothing *but* queer since you brought home that wretched basket, said Falance, but to himself.

The Hot Fair, when they came at last to it, proved to be nearly twice the size of the Cold Fair and richer, for it was in this season that the ships came from the East and the South, and sailors tanned on foreign seas came singing up the river in fleets heavy with silks and spices; gold and ivory; peacocks, pearls, wines, and perfumes.

Now the Faeryland Outcasts did not have to scuffle and bribe for a good place, for Krupska welcomed them back to his circus with many expostulations concerning how much they were missed. Awaiting them, too, was their apartment near the fencing school, whose master and his sister were likewise glad to welcome them back. From the window of this apartment the woman and her family and her friends watched the great procession that began the fair. First came squadrons of girls dressed in white, scattering rose petals; then jugglers and fire-eaters and men in fantastic costumes walking on stilts; then the blue-coated keepers of the royal beasts, leading lions and tigers and bears or carrying huge gyrfalcons and eagles on their fists; and then the procession of the Church, with the cardinal and his bishops in red and black, and long lines of white- and brown-robed monks, chanting and bearing holy images. Then the soldiers came, bands blaring martial airs, horse and foot, dragoons, hussars, lancers, grenadiers in tall hats, and light infantrymen in forest green with woven ivy around their heads. Last of the troops were the brigade of royal guards, all on matched white horses who pranced and curvetted, with their gilded armor and plumed helmets flashing in the sun. After them came the king.

He was in an open carriage pulled by six black horses, with his life guards clattering around him. All along the line of spectators, heads bowed like wheat under a breeze. The party in the window of the fencing school bowed, too, all except Falance, for a cat may look at a king. Falance stared; and saw a small well-knit man with dark hair and beard, dressed all in cloth of gold, with a gilded feather in his cap. He was alone in his carriage, for he was unmarried, the people said, because he had not found a princess rich enough to pay the dowry his greed demanded. This king looked right and left at his bowing subjects until his eye fell for an instant on Falance's green-eyed stare and he frowned, and then an instant later forgot it, perhaps thinking it a trick of the light. It was a glad day for him, for the fair would bring in great wealth.

Behind the king's carriage came those of his council, foremost among which was that of Vandy the miller, pulled by four bays with braided manes, a carriage only the slightest bit less gorgeous than the royal one. In it sat the miller, dressed in silver braid, and his son, Mostin, with black silk velvet on his back and a haughty sneer on his face, and the miller's daughter, the matchless Aude, caparisoned like a queen of the East, in gilt brocade so stiff she could barely move.

Lump saw her and gasped so loudly that his mother heard it and turned to glance at him and in that glance saw all, and was saddened by it.

Now the fair took over the life of the city. By day everywhere was trading and hard bargaining and the clink of coins on the bankers' benches and by night feasting and shows and illuminations and balls. Krupska had set up a temporary ring in the center of the fairgrounds, and there his circus performed until the small hours.

Lump spent his nights as before, spying on Aude.

Yet somehow this lurking pleased him ever less. He wanted beyond all things to have a conversation with the girl, to say, "A pleasant day, demoiselle, is it not?" and to hear her lovely lilting voice reply with, "Indeed, sir, but perhaps later it will rain."

Every other day, when the miller Vandy had his appointment at Johannes's school of arms, Lump resumed his attendance, in hopes that Aude would accompany her father. She often did, for she enjoyed the attentions of the bravos who idled about the academy and the bold looks of the itinerant mercenaries that Johannes hired to act as fencing partners for his students.

Thus Lump was there on the day that changed his life and the lives of all of them. He was in his usual place on a stool near the placid Gretl, in a lightless corner by the sword rack. Aude, in a deep-cut gown of palest blue, was sitting near the window, where the rich June sunlight could play with advantage on her shining hair. She was dallying with two young grandees, friends of her brother, who was also standing by, having just finished a bout with Johannes. They were all drinking yellow wine chilled with snow. The master was in the center of the room, walking among the half dozen pistes, on which his pupils were fencing to and fro. He called out corrections and encouragement as he passed. The miller Vandy, clothed in a white canvas tunic, was puffingly dueling a lean mercenary, a fox-faced man, with reddish short hair, recently hired. They were fencing in the French style, wielding rapiers tipped with cork buttons.

Then, in a moment when Johannes's back was turned, the cork button flew off the mercenary's sword and came bouncing across the floor to roll against Lump's stool. He looked up, startled, and, glancing away from Aude, saw the mercenary parry the miller's sword and drive his blade deep into the miller's breast. The miller gave a cry and dropped like a sack of his own flour.

A moment of horrified silence. Then Aude started to scream, a high, maddening sound. Her brother, Mostin, roared, "Seize him!"

But the mercenary was too quick or too ferocious to be easily stopped. In three great leaps he was at the door and down the stairs, sword in hand. Mostin ran to the window and shouted to his footmen standing by the coach, "Stop that man! He has stabbed my father!" Three of them hared off after the mercenary, who was, however, quickly lost in the fair-crowded street.

Aude was kneeling at her father's side, wailing. The miller's white tunic was dyed red with his heart's blood, and his silent face was as white as the tunic once had been. Mostin was crying for someone to call the city guard, to call a physician. The grandees and the other pupils had run off to join the pursuit. Johannes was standing as if paralyzed.

Lump alone moved to some purpose. With a calm that surprised him, he ran to Aude and said his first words to her, which were, "I will fetch my mother. She is a skilled healer." Aude looked up at him blankly, as if he had just fallen from the moon.

He dashed out and up to the apartment he shared with his mother and Falance. The woman was at the window seat, sewing some sequins onto her red dress. Falance was sitting at her feet, stone in hand, putting a razor edge on one of the knives he juggled. Lump burst in, breathless, with his mask askew.

"Oh, Mother!" he cried. "Come quickly to Hansl's! The miller has been stabbed in the heart. I think he may die."

Without a word, and with only the slightest hesitation, the woman rose, rushed to a small chest, took some items out and put them in a leather wallet. Then she followed her boy out of the room at a dash, with Falance behind.

She entered the fencing room with her smooth, swift, silent tread, a wren-brown figure, very erect, and approached the stricken miller, who was by then surrounded by a crowd of his servants, with some constables who had run in from the street. The man's son barred her way, his eyes wild.

"What is this! Who are you?"

"I am called Mrs. Forest," said the woman. "I am come to cure your father."

"You? What are you, some midwife? Get gone, you peasant trull, the king's own physician is sent for!"

The woman fixed his eye with her own and said, in a voice of steel, "Step from my way, child, unless you want your father dead."

Almost without knowing he did so, Mostin moved aside. The woman knelt by the miller, who had stopped breathing. She touched the weeping Aude on the arm, saying, "You must leave me, girl, and take your brother with you and the servants."

"No! Never!" cried both siblings in horror.

The woman shouted, "Hansl! Clear away all these people. I must have quiet and solitude to work."

Instantly, Johannes snapped out of his stupor, yanked a great cavalry saber from the rack, and, swinging it around his head as if it had been a rattan, until it sang, cried, "All out! All out! Let her work, or he dies!"

Thus he drove them all from the room and down into the street, and he stood guard at the door with the steel held erect and menacing.

An hour passed in this way. Aude and her brother sat in their carriage, she wailing, he screaming threats at the impassive fencing master. Lump and Falance leaned against the wall, and they both felt in the familiar thickening of the air and saw in the indescribable shimmer of the light that the fabric of common reality was being warped by heavy magic. The others did not notice.

"She did say she had kept something by against need," observed Falance, "and clearly this is a sample."

"But—but I supposed she could do no great magic anymore," said Lump in a low voice.

"Then you supposed wrong, didn't you? But now it is hard going with her. She is working like a cart horse."

"What do you mean?"

The cat looked sharply at the boy and replied, "I see you still don't understand who is your stepdam.

You didn't know her when she was young, at the height of her powers, before she tired of practicing the Great Art at its highest reaches and retired to our little cottage. Ah, she was . . . I have not the words . . . incomparable! Before she was twenty she was acknowledged the greatest enchantress since Morgan le Fay! They called her the Maiden Dire. Why, in those days, she would've had that fat man up and dancing jigs were he a moldering corpse, and that in a minute with a flick of her hand and a word."

Lump briefly recalled his sole experience of that lost enchantress in her naked power and just as quickly returned it to the cellar of his memory, with a chill racing down his spine.

At that moment, the door to the school of arms opened behind Johannes's broad back, and the woman stepped out. She looked pale and strained, and her hair was pasted to her forehead with sweat. The front of her brown apron was stained black with gore.

She walked to the carriage and said, "You may send to bring your father down now."

"He lives?" cried Mostin.

"Yes. Some weeks of rest and good nursing will see him right."

The miller's two children leaped from their carriage and rallied their footmen. In a few moments they had carried the miller down to the street and settled him in the carriage. He was unconscious, but he was breathing easily and his color was good.

"Home! And do not spare the whip!" Mostin ordered the driver.

"Wait, Mostin! The woman . . ." said Aude.

"Oh, yes—our thanks to you, woman. Here, take this." He proffered a heavy purse.

"I cannot take money; it is forbidden," said the woman. "You may give it as alms or what you like."

"Oh, well then . . ." said Mostin.

"Oh, but the boy who got her," said Aude, noticing Lump standing there. "A coin . . ."

The silver penny flashed in the sun and clinked at Lump's feet. With a crack of the whip and a rattle, the carriage leaped from the curb. Lump stared at the penny, his face burning under his mask. Then he spun on his heel and walked off, leaving it shining on the street.

"Did you observe, my lady, the son's face when he found out that his father yet lived?" asked Falance later that same day, when he and the woman were in a public house at their evening meal. Lump had not returned. The woman, having finished eating, was working at making the smoking crackers she used in her performances, filling little paper cylinders with incendiary powders from various copper flasks. She looked up from her work and replied, "Yes. It did not bear an expression of relief or filial love. Rage, rather. What did you make of that?"

"Of that I make perhaps an arrangement between the son and that fox-haired mercenary that no one ever saw in the district before Hansl engaged him. Murder, as they call it here. Odd, he has everything he might wish of the world's goods, yet he wishes even more, which he might have were his father to die. It is peculiar: we cats occasionally kill our fathers, you know, and far more often do our fathers kill us, but not for any cause other than meat or passion for a she-cat, and little is made of it among the cats. Yet, as I understand it, this is considered a grave offense by men, to kill your father."

"So I have heard," said the woman. "Although I have observed that the lives of the mothers are held cheap enough, which makes little sense to me. It is another puzzle for us, Falance. We are such kittens in these matters. But look—here is Hansl with Lump. What long faces you both have!"

The fencing master and the boy sat down at the table and Johannes called for beer. He said, "Do you wonder? My most famous and powerful client near killed in my rooms. We will be ruined. Poor Gretl has not ceased weeping. How could I have let it happen! I survey the blades and their corks every day." The beer came and he drank the stein off in a gulp and ordered another.

"We have just been discussing this," said Falance. "We think the son arranged the murder of his sire, under guise of a mischance at swordplay." And they explained why they thought so.

"The devil!" exclaimed Johannes. "Well, this is something else! It seems I am the dupe of a villain and not to blame as a careless teacher. I feel better, in any case. But look at Lump! I found him mooning about the streets, looking like a boy who has lost a silver penny. Why ever did you leave your tip lying there, sir? Money does not grow on trees, you know."

"I didn't want their tip," said Lump tightly. "I am not their lackey."

"He would not have refused a kiss from the miller's daughter, I believe," said Falance, with a cat's sure instinct for torture.

"Shut your mouth, Falance!" cried Lump.

Falance opened his mouth to say more, but merely yelped, as the woman's foot ground down upon his toe under the table.

Johannes let his second flagon thud down empty on the table and said, "Now, we mustn't bicker, friends. What we should do is to go out seeking pleasure, like all the other folk in the city. We will rouse poor Gretl and go to the theater. There is a new play, with music, at the Monarch, by the Bear Garden. I will pay the gate, for you have taken a great weight from my spirit, Mrs. Forest."

"Yes, let us go!" said the woman happily. "Neither Lump nor Falance has seen a play. Perhaps it will serve to wash this ill day from all our spirits."

So they went. Afterward, as they walked home through streets full of rollicking fairgoers, Gretl asked the woman how she had liked the play.

"The songs were merry enough, but the matter of it was absurd," she answered. "I never heard such nonsense."

"But it is an old story. Everyone knows it," said Gretl.

"That is as may be, but nonsense it remains. Look you: suppose there was such a witch as is seen in this play, and she had a stepdaughter. Of course she would have devoted herself to teaching her arts to the girl, if the girl had any talent at all; and if she had none, the witch would have raised her kindly, as I have done with Lump and your foster mother did with you. Never would she have been jealous of the girl's beauty, for what use to witches is beauty or other snares for men? Even worse, no true witch would have used so powerful a magic object as that speaking, far-seeing glass for so trivial a purpose. 'Who is fairest of all?' Piffle! As it happens, I know the woman who owns that mirror, and a very grave and learned dame she is. Chalphorna the Bright, she is called. You know her, Falance."

"Yes, a grave and learned dame, indeed, my lady," the cat agreed. "And uncommon ugly, too."

"Now, further, supposing a witch of that power wished to slay her daughter," the woman continued. "It would be the work of three minutes, with no nonsense about poisoned apples that fail to work. But the crowning nonsense is that the girl flees from this witch, her stepmother, and is taken in and cosseted by dwarves. By *dwarves*, for all love!"

"What is wrong with that?" asked Gretl.

"What is wrong . . . ! Have you ever *known* a dwarf, dear girl? I do not mean an unfortunate human whose bones are stunted, of course, but a *dwarf*. A kobold. A Nibelung. You have not? Fortunate person! I have, and let me tell you that any girl not deprived of her senses would have raced for shelter at the bosom of the blackest witch ever made rather than spend an hour with an actual dwarf, much less *seven* of the creatures. Seven dwarves? Where do they get these notions?"

The woman expatiated for some time upon the vices of the dwarves, by which time the party was shaking with mirth. Even Lump was smiling behind his mask. They passed a tavern, and Johannes suggested closing the evening with a round or two, but the woman and Falance cried off, saying they needed their rest, for Johannes rarely stopped with two. So they parted and the three proceeded alone to their lodging.

They entered the short, narrow, dark street on which it stood. It appeared quite deserted. But as they passed the little stable where, among others, the horses Duty and Desire had their dwelling, there was a sound, and Falance's keen ears picked it up: a creak and a jingle, a step in the darkness.

"Lady, hold!" he said. "There is something amiss."

Indeed there was. Lights appeared as the shutters came up on several dark lanterns. The street was full of men, troops of the city guard. A sergeant stepped forward, brandishing a mace and a paper. A trooper held a lantern over his shoulder and shone it on the woman.

"Are you Mrs. Forest?" the officer demanded.

"I am so called," said the woman. "What of it?"

The sergeant cleared his throat and read from the paper in one breath. "By this warrant issued this fourteenth day of June in the seventh year of the reign of our gracious sovereign Magnus second of that name by the grace of God king it is hereby ordered that the woman a sojourner in this city known as Mrs. Forest be seized by hand and foot and carried to a place close held by the king his officers and there put to the question whether or no she hath practiced the despicable and hideous arts of witchcraft most loathsome to the king's majesty and the sanctity of the Church and the accusation be this to wit she hath raised by means infernal and unholy a corpse from death and is thereby proved a cursed minion of the devil and all or any who dare resist this warrant its execution shall answer it at peril of the king's justice given under my seal Vashon Royal Magistrate God save the king."

He rolled up the paper and cried, "Seize her!"

Two guardsmen stepped forward to grasp the woman. Falance moved in a blur. There was a flash of steel, a cry, and a clatter, and both men were on the ground groaning. The woman's hand moved from her apron pocket; little sparking things flew through the gloom, and the street was instantly full of thick red smoke.

The guards hesitated, stunned. They had often come for witches—that is, they had arrested any number of harmless, deluded, or lunatic old women. The essential absurdity of this practice, the idea that someone who commanded the powers of darkness would let herself be meekly dragged away to torture and death, had never presented itself before to their minds, but now it dawned on them that witches might actually be dangerous.

So they quailed and drew back, and their sergeant cursed and beat on their backs with the butt of his mace, until a breeze dispersed the smoke, when they saw neither the woman they sought nor her companions but the two bleeding guards there on the paving stones.

"They are in their lodging, you fools!" the sergeant shouted. They tried the door. It was bolted from inside. An axe was found and they got to work.

Upstairs, the woman was calmly loading bottles and bags from her cases into a shawl and her leather wallet. Falance stood by the door with sword and dagger, listening to the crashing of the axe from below.

"Listen, Lump, Falance and I must go out the back, over the roof, and to the stable, and escape on the two horses. You have your own means, far better, to disappear. Our purse is light, alas. Take this money and what you can carry of your things. My love, I am sorry for this. You are a good boy at heart . . ."

Lump stared at his mother, frozen with fear, breathing in gasps, his mouth too dry to allow speech. How much there was that he wanted to tell her, now there was no time left!

"They are through the door, my lady," said Falance. "We must be off."

"Yes, Falance. You are a good boy at heart, my Lump, ah, but, love, you should not have watched the faeries dance. Yet all things change, and what was twisted may grow straight with time. This is why She made time. You are not as hideous as you believe. I will send word of where we cast up through Johannes or Krupska. Protect your Name. Farewell, my son." She raised his mask and kissed him on the cheek. Then she gathered up her burden and was gone from the room, in the steps of the cat.

Breaking wood, a cry, a neigh, and a clatter of hooves on stones. The sound of a careful tread on the stairs. Lump ran to his room and grabbed the bag that held his rock collection, feeling stupid as he did so, but he could think of nothing else to save.

He heard the sounds of booted feet. A guardsman came into the room, sword at the ready. The last thing Lump saw before he sank into the floor was the man's open mouth and bulging eyes, as for the first time in his life he saw witchcraft.

Gold

Lump spent a lonely, miserable night beneath the earth. When at last he emerged in the gray morning, he returned to the fencing school, to find it locked with a city guard at the door. At the nearby tavern, at which Johannes was wont to drink, he went in and inquired of the tapster what had become of Johannes and his sister.

"Oh, that's a bad business," said the man. "They are both taken up, but a few hours past, and accused of harboring a witch. Why, never did we suspect it: he seemed a fine brave fellow, and she was always a pleasant dame. Also, Krupska the circus master is likewise arrested, on the same charge, for he gave place to that wicked witch they were hunting, her and her man. It shows one can't be too careful nowadays—the vile creatures are everywhere."

The man looked closely at Lump, at his mask, and his eyes grew wide. "Why, but you are that witch's boy!" he exclaimed, and then shouted, "Ho! Call the guard! The witch's boy is here. Catch him!"

Lump was already running out of the tavern and whispering the cantrip. Once under the earth he rested until his chest ceased to heave and thought about his plight. He had no friends and no way to regain the company of his mother and Falance. Nor could he remain in the city without being constantly hounded. Although none could catch him for long, yet it would be a miserable life. How could he eat or rest?

So he drifted through the stone until after a while he felt the familiar salty chill of limestone; and he rose and saw the bed of a river floating like pale mist above him. Then he recalled that at the mouth of the river was a seaport, and he decided to go there. He could lose himself in so busy a place, where there might be strange people aplenty besides himself.

He did this, taking many days. For food, he stole, first from the cellars of peasant cottages, then from suburban villas, and finally from the shops and warehouses of the port itself. He took a tiny room over a dock, smelling of old fish and the tides, and tried to find some work, but was unsuccessful. What, after all, did he know how to do? In a week or so the money he had was all gone and he had to roam the streets. He would not starve, but within the bubble of magic he could neither sleep nor eat, and so he had to crouch in the corners of alleys, gnawing his cold bacon and bread. He grew dirty and ragged, and the paint on his mask chipped and cracked. He lodged in bushes in vacant lots, in common with the poor of the port city, who were numerous, loud, filthy, and raucous. His shoes were stolen, and he developed a thin, persistent cough.

He woke one morning to the sound of conversation in his ear. A whining voice said, "He is near dead anyway. Let us leap upon his throat and feast."

Another of the same sort replied, "That may be, yet he looks as if he might deliver a keen blow still, and my ribs are too tender to take another."

Lump opened his eyes and sat up. Two stray dogs were staring at him with yellow eyes, their tongues lolling out.

"Miserable hounds!" said Lump in their own language. "Come near and you will see what sort of blows I can deliver!" And he reached for a stone.

The dogs fled, more out of surprise than from any fear of the missile. There were not many left who could speak to animals, and they were not about to challenge one of these, perhaps a mage, who might turn them into cats, or worse.

Now, thought, Lump, the very dogs seek me as prey. I am dying and I must find work or begin a career as a thief of money, before I am too weak for either.

From time to time he had ventured into the commercial center of the town, so he could see gracious buildings and richly dressed men and women, which sight always gave him pleasure. He thought constantly of the miller's daughter, and longed to be rich and handsome or, failing that, rich only, for he had seen that wealth made toads lovely.

On this morning, his search for work having proved futile, and with theft becoming more attractive, he was lurking in an alley off the Street of the Jewelers, when a man walked up to a nearby shop, clearly a foreigner from his dress and queer way of speaking. The proprietor, whose name was Robard, if the sign above his head did not lie, greeted the outlander as a familiar; and, after a ritual cup of wine, the stranger pulled out a sack and spilled a pile of red pebbles on a black cloth the merchant laid over his counter.

Robard, who was a lean and sour-faced old fellow, mumbled and examined the stones with a lens; and then there began a period of strenuous bargaining. Lump was too far from them to hear what was said, but he watched the proceedings with great interest, because, if he did not mistake, he possessed several of those red stones, and far bigger ones, in the pouch at his belt that held his rock collection. The foreigner at last accepted a leather purse that clinked heavily, made his bow, and departed.

Lump stepped forward to the counter. The old man regarded him distastefully.

"What do you want?" said Robard. "Work? I already have a sweeper. Get gone!" And, in fact, Lump saw the back of a black-haired girl plying a broom in the shadows within the shop.

"I am not here to sweep, sir, but to sell," said Lump. He took three of his largest red stones from the pouch and laid them on the black cloth. The jeweler's eyebrow twitched and he licked his lips. He poked the largest stone with a skinny forefinger.

"Where did you get these, boy?"

"From my mother," said Lump, for he thought that if the man knew how easy these pebbles were to get, he would disdain them.

Who is she then, the empress? thought the man,

and aloud he said, "Well, well. These are not too bad. Perhaps I will give you ten, no twelve silver pence for them."

Lump was no fool. Immediately he said, "Nay, I will take not less than twenty pence."

They agreed on fifteen, and Lump walked away delighted. He could replace the stones as easily as children gather berries from roadside hedges, and so this meant he would have lodging, clothing, and food aplenty henceforward.

As he walked through the bustling marketplace, he heard light steps behind him and felt a tug on his sleeve. He turned. His mouth gaped.

"Pa'aili!" he cried.

The girl frowned. "Yes, Pa'aili is my name, sir, but how do you know it? We have never met to my recall."

"But how did you come here? I thought you were drowned in the great wave of the storm."

As he spoke these words, Lump saw fear enter the girl's eyes, and tears.

"Yes, there was a great storm, and I was blown far from the Lagoon of Pearls, my home. I clung to the wreck of my canoe, until a ship passed by and took me up. This was the ship of my master Robard, who was in those parts searching for precious gems and pearls. Since then I have been his slave, and he is a mean and hard man. When I saw him cheat you, I felt . . . I don't know what I felt, except that I thought that somehow I must help you, as if we had been friends, although perhaps only in the lands of dreaming."

"Yes, the lands of dreaming," repeated Lump. "But you say he cheated me—how so?"

"Those stones you sold him are worth far more than he gave you—worth gold, not silver. You must go to Odd John the goldsmith, at the corner of Jewel Street by the fish market. He will pay you the true worth of them, should you ever have others to sell. Now, farewell, boy in a mask: I must return or risk a beating."

She turned, and was gone; her step, and her grace in motion, so familiar, so fondly recalled that it would have made his heart leap had it not been frozen over. Instead, he shrugged and sought a dark alley where he descended into the earth. It was a matter of moments to locate the strongbox of the wicked Robard, extract the stones he had sold (they hung in the mist of the safe like apples on a tree), and return the pennies. Then he reappeared in the alley and followed his nose to the fish market.

The shop, when he found it, proved to be a tiny, disreputable-looking stall jammed between a warehouse selling nets and a fishmonger's. It was open, however, and at the counter sat an elderly man whose fine white hair spread in an aureole around the round black cap he wore in the center of his head. He had little square spectacles on, and was reading a book.

"Excuse me, sir," said Lump. "I am looking for Odd John the goldsmith."

"What d'you want with him?" asked the old man, not looking up from his reading.

"I wish to sell him some red stones, of which Robard tried to cheat me, but I have them back and I am told John the goldsmith is an honest man."

At this the man looked up, and when he saw Lump's appearance and his mask, his pale blue eyes widened with interest and he said, "He is. But are you? Why do you wear that mask?"

Lump considered several fanciful stories in the first instant, but the man's frank face dissuaded him from such invention. Instead, he replied, "The reason is, I am very ugly and also proud, and so do not desire to be made a mock of."

"Fair enough," said the man, and held out a

gnarled hand. "Jack's my name, and I am the goldsmith you seek, though some do call me Odd John." Lump took the proffered hand and said his name and then Jack said, "Let's see your stones.

"Hmm, hmm, hmm," he said as he examined them, and then, looking up, added, "very interesting. I'd like to see the rest of them that you've got there in that bag. But back in the shop, eh?"

Lump followed the man into the dimness. There were no windows to dilute the musty smell within, which did not improve when Jack lit a smoky lamp. Lump stared about him all agog at what the yellow glow revealed. Odd and mysterious objects filled the room. From the ceiling hung stuffed birds and bats and structures of wood and fabric that looked like artificial birds. One wall was taken up by a bench and shelves full of flasks and bottles, which glowed with their contents' colors—red, blue, green, purple, and all the shades in between. The next wall held hooks from which depended instruments and equipment of bronze, steel, brass, dark woods, and gleaming glass—astrolabes, compasses, dividers, dissection knives, limbecks, brass tubing in different lengths, glass rods, pestles, lenses, round mirrors, telescope tubes, sextants, gears and springs, orreries, and animal traps. At the base of this wall stood a small furnace. The third wall was all books, brown or black and dusty, more books than Lump had ever before seen in one place. The final wall contained shelves and cabinets displaying bird skins, skeletons of various small animals, rocks, pressed plants, and jars in which a staggering variety of creatures and parts of creatures bobbed in the brown murk of the preserving spirits of wine: two-headed babies, goiters and carbuncles, a five-legged piglet, and so on.

There was a table in the center of the room that bore the tools of the goldsmith's trade—scales, tongs, files, hammers, a little anvil. Jack cleared a place on it and laid down a dark cloth. Onto this Lump spilled his rock collection. The old man took up his tongs and looked at Lump with an appraising eye. "You don't know what any of this is, do you, boy?"

"No, sir. They are just what I picked up because I thought them pretty and interesting on my—my travels."

"Your travels. Bless me! Well, I expect you'd like to know, wouldn't you? Fine—I'm your man, then." He began to arrange the objects on the cloth, naming them as he did so. "Ruby, ruby; emerald, first quality; here's, oh, bless me, the largest, by'r Lady, great ruby I've ever seen in my life, the size of a hen's egg; another emerald, flawed. This is a precious garnet crystal in schist. This is a hexagonal mica crystal, worthless, but interesting; moonstone; white jade; topaz; another topaz; yet again ruby; a chunk of mere red carnelian. Now, here's rose quartz, very nice; this is iceland spar, of no great price but useful for philosophical purposes; this is, oh, my, no, it cannot possibly be a yellow diamond, not at that size!" The old man picked this last named up and used it to scratch a topaz. "Oh, look you," he exclaimed, "it marks true!" He weighed the stone. "A hundred ten carats, oh dear!"

His tongs probed again. "What is this? Merely an enormous great aquamarine? Into the trash with it, ha-ha! This bitty thing is an octohedral gold crystal, quite rare; and this is a gold nugget weighing, let us see . . . thirty-two ounces troy weight. This is sponge silver, hmm, twelve ounces. This is mere copper, fie upon it! Here's a piece of dogtooth calcite (God's breath, he picks up spar when he can pluck diamonds!). And this blue lump, my dear child, is only a star sapphire; it must be twice the size of my eyeball." The old man burst into laughter, leaped up, did a little jig around the table, and collapsed once more into his chair, wiping his streaming eyes.

"Why are you laughing?" asked Lump suspiciously.

"Why? Oh, why, indeed! Five and thirty years in the business, dealing in chips and odd lots, jet and jasper, and then one fine day, into my shop walks a blackguard boy with a mask on his face and the mogul's treasure in his wallet. What else to do but laugh! No, no, I see you are a serious fellow, so I will tell you how things stand. If these were honestly come by—"

"Oh, yes, sir," exclaimed Lump. "I would never be a thief."

"Oh, to be sure! I believe you, for jewels of this quality, if known to men, would have names and legends to them and I would know them as I know my own face. Well, to put a capper upon it, sir, you are rich! I am rich, too, by the mere commission on the sale of these pieces, but you, you are absolutely a magnate. If you can get more where these came from . . . where *did* they come from, by the way?"

This was asked casually, and just as casually, Lump ignored the question. Instead his gaze roamed around the room, and he asked, "Sir, are you by any chance a magician?"

"A magician! The farthest thing from it, in fact. I am a natural philosopher by avocation. There is no such thing as magic, you know."

"I am interested to hear it," said Lump. "But, pray, what is this natural philosophy?"

"Why, it is the study of the world, my son, the world and all that's in it. Everything, you see, must be taken apart, examined, and put back together according to a system. Then we will know what's what, and be rid forever of these old wives' tales and superstitions."

"And were you always a philosopher?"

"Nay, not I," said the old man with a chuckle. "When I was your age, I thought magic was the way to kingdoms and prizes. I once sold a cow in exchange for a handful of beans, because the sly fellow who sold them to me said they were magic. Ha-ha!"

"And what became of these beans?"

"Why, I planted them. And hoped they'd sprout up overnight into a vine I could climb into a magical world, there to seek treasure and my fortune."

"And did it so sprout?" asked Lump.

"Of course it did not!" exclaimed the goldsmith. "It grew tall, to be sure, exceeding tall, but after some weeks. And I never climbed it, although another tried. A great stupid lout, the tallest fellow in the district. He got so high and then fell and broke his crown."

"So that man cheated you, who traded for your cow."

"No! Not at all. For the beanstalk, d'you see, produced beans, great broad beans the size of your hand, and sweet and succulent they were, too. I took ten bushels to market and got a good price for them, and I used that money to buy me an apprenticeship in the goldsmiths. Alas, I did not prosper as a goldsmith, being too honest and no usurer, and also I was ever more interested in natural philosophy, the rocks, the stars in their courses, where the birds fly in winter, and so on. Not prosper until now, that is, my dear Lump, but now all will be made good."

"So you tell me," said Lump. He fingered the glowing mass that Jack had said was gold.

"But, Jack, is this gold the same as the gold in coins? The very same?"

"Aye, for gold is gold. The gold in coins comes from the deepest earth, or else mixed in sand from streambeds, and is hard to find and harder to wrest from its hidey holes. This is its appearance before it is minted as money. I am surprised you don't know this, for it is common knowledge among those with the meanest understanding. Who bred you in such ignorance, my lad?"

"Oh, just a stupid woman," said Lump angrily, for he was recalling all those nights spent on short rations, his belly rumbling, the days dressed in shoddy, ill-fitting clothes, when he was ashamed even to be seen by the rich girl he loved, when all the while in his wallet he had held in ignorance a great fortune. "A stupid woman, who knew nothing of natural philosophy. Now, Jack, let us go on, for I am impatient to be rich."

"I, too," agreed Jack, "but we must be careful. Here is my plan: we shall outfit you with a legend, for no one will believe that a ragged boy, and a masked one at that, could garner such wealth by fair means. Let me think—aha, I have it! See what you think of this. . . ."

Three years had passed when at the time of the Christmas revels held by King Magnus in his royal city, an enormous gilded barge rowed by fifty oarsmen approached the king's docks there. At the center of the barge was a pavilion made of cloth of gold, and supported by posts of solid silver elaborately chased with the figures of tritons and mermaids. At the center of this pavilion was set a gold-leafed throne studded with gems, and on it sat a young man dressed in a black silk costume picked out in crimson. On his face he wore a golden mask with matched sapphires outlining the eyes and matched rubies outlining the mouth.

There was a crowd of people waiting at the dock, all richly dressed, officials of the city and of the court, chief among whom was Vandy the miller, fatter and richer than ever and now King Magnus's chancellor. His daughter, Aude, grown even more beautiful, was in attendance, dressed in a gown of blue velvet. And beyond this gorgeous circle a troop of dragoons held back a vast throng, for everyone wanted to see the man on the barge.

They had heard with increasing fascination over the past three years how a prince of far-off Cathay, heir to the mighty emperor of that land, had been dispossessed by a scheming brother but had managed to avoid the assassins, while escaping with a thousand soldiers, each bent double under a sack of imperial treasure, each sack holding enough to buy a province, and further, how the usurper had sworn to pursue Lum-po (for that was given out as the prince's name) to the ends of the earth and slay him. For which reason the prince wore a golden mask, so that none of the legion of murderers sent by the foul brother could see his face and be sure it was indeed him and not one of the dozens of masked duplicates he employed.

The barge landed, the royal trumpets blew a fanfare, and Lump stepped out onto the crimson carpet that covered the dock. The chancellor, Vandy, greeted him with an effusive speech. But Lump did not look at the fat miller; his eyes were fixed on Aude, who stood next to and a little to the rear of him. And the eyes, the sea-blue eyes, of Aude were fixed on Lump, glowing with delight.

This was what Lump had worked for these three long years; the gold to win his way into the heart of Aude. Under the tutelage of Jack the goldsmith, he had learned that gold breeds gold, even faster than a boy can pick it up from inside the earth, and moreover that once the veins of gold and gems are located, it is more convenient to hire men to tear up the skin of the earth and delve for them. So Lump soon had mines and workshops and argosies to all the seas, and banks and warehouses, for having an unlimited supply of gold and jewels is a great aid to success in business, and even more is the ability to spy without detection upon rivals. Lump became a magnate indeed, and it had been all for this, this melting look from the lovely Aude, beneath which he now basked.

He gave orders; from the hold of the barge appeared a coach that put to shame the gilded coach of Vandy. It was inlaid with lapis and carnelian and rare woods and was drawn by six matchless black horses. The coach-man was a dark youth dressed in flowing white. This was Djer, the boy from the Caravanserai of the Three Palms, for after Lump had found Pa'aili he thought that perhaps the other distant acquaintance of his childhood had similarly survived, and being rich, Lump had hired minions to search the land for Djer, and they had found him enslaved to a hostler in the south. He was now ensconced as coachman and master of horse to the strange young man who seemed to know much about him. Lump also had ruined the jeweler Robard and bought up Pa'aili in the bankrupt's sale; she was now his housekeeper. Lump treated them both kindly, but not as the friends he had once imagined that they might be. He liked seeing them around his palaces, as a wealthy man will keep the rag dolls he played with as a child dis-played upon his shelves for sentimental reasons.

The coach ready, Lump invited Vandy and Aude to ride with him to the palazzo he had leased in the best quarter of the city, hard by Vandy's own great house. The brother, Mostin, he did not invite; and that proud personage had to stand, enraged, in the dust as the great coach and its liveried escort left the dockyard.

There was a ball that night in Lump's marble rooms. His servants had planned it brilliantly: the music was the sweetest, the viands and punches were of the richest and tastiest varieties, the wines came from the most famous vineyards, the walls were hung with brilliant silks and paintings, and the guests were the wealthiest, the most highborn and fashionable of the kingdom. The king himself attended. Lump was presented to the monarch in his disguise as Lum-po, prince of Cathay; and the king called him "cousin" and treated him with all grace. Their conversation was of taxes, mines, ships, trade, tariffs, and fees. The king left the party with a pleasant sense of having added another fat sheep to his flock: a good fellow, this Lum-po, despite his outlandish look. His gold was real enough, and that was what counted.

Lump claimed every dance from the fair Aude, and she seemed more than willing, her eyes bright, her smile unfailing, her laughter tinkling as she responded to Lump's charm and wit. Was it the conversation she found charming or the golden mask? Since it was Aude, perhaps there was no difference at all. He let the music carry them into a secluded corner, overlooking a snow-filled garden upon which a white moon shone like a bone afire. He reached into his sleeve and drew out a little box, placing it in her graceful hand.

"Oooh, sir! Is it for me?" she squealed, and opened it. Moonlight shot from a hundred facets of the great white jewel in the ring.

"I have loved you from the moment when first I saw you," said Lump. "I want you to be my wife."

"But, sir, you have never seen me before today," said Aude, her eyes riveted by the diamond.

"Not so. When first I came into this country I went in disguise as a poor boy, to ferret out the plots of my enemies. There I saw you in your splendid coach, with your gorgeous entourage, and then I vowed you would one day be mine. And that day has come."

Aude blushed, her mind groping. The ring she must have, come what may. Marriage to an odd masked foreigner did not, however, figure in her plans, nor in those of her father.

She affected a confused stammer. "I . . . I hardly know what to say, sir. We do not know you; I have never seen your face. Perhaps you are terrible to look at."

"You see the face of gold, at least," said Lump coldly. "And gold is without guile and free of confusion, which the faces of men rarely are. Also, gold is far from terrible to look at, and I have often noticed that it enhances wonderfully the appearance of faces made of flesh and bone. There are a dozen men at this ball who are ugly, yet their consorts are as lovely as can be. Save your father, and the king, I am the richest man in this kingdom, and I will have the loveliest maiden. Thus the world is arranged. Come, put on the ring, and we'll see what your father has to say."

Her father said little, except to temporize, although he was ardent enough in his admiration for the immense diamond. But there was the dowry to consider. . . .

"I require no dowry," said Lump.

"No dowry!" cried the miller. "My dear sir, what are you saying? My daughter to leave my hearth with no dowry? What would people think? No, no, sir: impetuous youth, passionate youth! Ha-ha! How well I remember! But these details are best left to wiser and more experienced heads. The negotiations can begin directly these holidays and revels are concluded. You have my word on that. In the meantime, you may, of course, call upon my daughter."

With this Lump had to be content, with that and the radiant smile Aude conferred upon him as she stepped into her coach at the end of the ball.

Yet smiles were few around the miller's family hearth the next day. Mostin was enraged that his sister had accepted a ring, however precious, from the mysterious stranger.

"We know nothing of him, father!" the young man complained, pacing to and fro in front of a fireplace that might have roasted an ox whole, stepping around the four huge Circassian mutes who had served his father as bodyguards ever since the attempt on his life and who never left his presence. "We cannot even see his face. How could you have allowed her—"

"We *do* know who he is: he is a prince of Cathay," responded his father.

"By his own report! He could be anybody."

"Not anybody, my son. Anybody does not pay taxes of eight hundred thousand magnus, as I have found. His royal highness is much pleased and wishes his court to show the new prince every favor."

"Including the hand of Aude?"

"Not necessarily," said the miller. "You know well what we have long planned for Aude."

Aude, who was playing with her little dogs by the fire, spoke up. "I am to be queen."

"So you are, my dear," said the miller fondly, and then, to Mostin, "but not at the price of a dowry so immense as to ruin us, which his majesty demands. My thought is, let us keep this foreigner giving gifts. Perhaps he will pay the royal dowry, ha-ha! And let us think of a way to satisfy the king's greed."

"And when I am queen," said Aude, "Lum-po will not dare to ask for his gifts back, and so I will keep all the pretty things."

Thus the winter passed. Each day, Lump arrived at the miller's estate to call upon Aude, and each day he brought a gift that surpassed all that he had given before. There were necklaces of emeralds and pearls, jeweled clocks that spoke the hour, and golden birds that sang a different song each day. And still Aude would not give him the answer, would she marry him or no.

Bets were placed throughout the highest society on this subject, for Lump and Aude were everywhere to be seen: at all the balls and parties and at court, where

Lump was much caressed by royalty. Where they chose to go they were the object of envious glances, Aude for her beauty and sumptuous apparel, Lump for his wealth and his mystery.

Aude loved the circus above all other shows, and so they often went to the Bear Garden, to Lump's discomfort, for he feared recognition by his former colleagues, nor did he much like frequenting the precincts where once he had lived in what then seemed snug comfort but which he now saw as mere squalor.

One evening, they alighted from their coach before the circus, and Aude shrilled, "Oh, look, my prince: a bear keeper!"

Lump shifted his gaze idly to where she pointed. There was an ill-favored, burly man there, and he had a muzzled bear on a chain.

"Give him a coin," said Aude. "I wish to see it dance."

Lump tossed a penny to the fellow, who caught it out of the air and bowed obsequiously. Then he hauled cruelly on the chain and cracked his whip. The bear rose slowly to its hind feet and the man snapped the whip against these to make it shuffle to the dull tune he played upon a tin whistle. It was an old bear. Its coat was falling out and its ribs stared from ill feeding and it had sores all over.

"Is that all it does, fellow?" asked Aude curtly. "Can it not caper?"

The bear keeper plied his whip more vigorously, but the bear just trod the same measure, around and around in a small circle.

"This is poor stuff, don't you think?" said the beauty, with a little sniff. "It bores me. Let us go in to the show."

"Yes, to the show!" Lump cried, and they turned away.

At that moment Lump heard a familiar voice, which said, "Lump, my dear child, my sweet nursling, don't you know me? I am Ysul, who loved you of old."

Aude giggled. "Now the bear is trying to sing. La! It does so as poorly as it dances." She laughed and stepped toward the entrance and Lump turned his back on Ysul, and without a word followed his beloved inside.

Rage

In the spring, when the ice had melted off the river, a ship arrived bearing an embassy from the emperor, offering the hand of his eldest daughter to King Magnus, together with a dowry that would have bought any kingdom in the world twice over. The king considered this with his council.

"This makes sense," he said, looking at the portrait of the imperial princess, which the embassy had brought, "for the girl is so ugly, I can understand why the emperor would pay so much just to rid his house of her. Why, with a face like that, had she not been an imperial princess, she would never find a husband unless she could spin straw into gold."

At this the council laughed most heartily, but the chancellor, Vandy, did not laugh, and spoke privily to his son. "This confounds our plans; what is your advice?"

The son whispered briefly in his father's ear, and

then the chancellor stood and spoke, saying, "Your Majesty, you need not seek an ugly woman if you want someone who can spin straw into gold. My daughter, Aude, the fairest in the land, has that art."

"What!" cried the king. "Do you mean it? How can this be? Vandy, say you have not been trafficking with witches!"

At this Vandy trembled, for he knew well how the king hated witchcraft.

"No, never, sire," he said. "It is a blessed gift from heaven above, for my girl has a golden heart, and this is how God rewards her."

So the king sent the imperial ambassadors back home with their portrait and their dowry, and soon it was announced that the king would wed the chancellor's daughter, Aude.

When Lump heard this, he flew into a black rage and rode in his coach to the miller's palace. But they would not let him in. Nor would they return his gifts. He heard the footmen snickering as he left.

So Lump had to watch as the royal wedding progressed with great pomp and watch as the cardinal archbishop placed the royal crown on Aude's shining head. And his heart was wracked with pain and anger, and he thought only of revenge.

That night, Aude was decked in the finest silks and laces by her ladies-in-waiting and placed in a gilded bed to await her new husband. In he came, together with a troop of his guards, one bearing a spinning wheel and the others massive bales of straw.

"Why, what is this, my husband?" asked Aude.

"It is straw, my wife, and a spinning wheel," said the king. "Your father assured me you could spin straw into gold, and here is a good batch of it. Sit you down and begin!"

"But, my lord, I cannot spin straw into gold," said Aude. Then her heart trembled in her bosom as she saw the black ire build in the king's face. Yet even if she was not clever, still she knew enough to fashion an excuse, and continued. "That is, when anyone is about. I must be alone, all alone."

"Very well," said the king, still suspicious. "Alone you shall be until the morning. And listen: if there is not gold here where there is now straw, your pretty head will be forfeit, and that of your father, too. There is still time to recall the imperial emissaries." And he left the chamber, locking the door behind him.

At this moment, in his own richly appointed

bedroom, Lump could find no rest. He tossed and scattered the covers, called for wine, drank, paced the floor, smashed the wineglass. Just past midnight, he shed his mask, dressed in his old ragged black clothes, and sank through the floor.

He was not, of course, thinking clearly; notions of slaying the king and stealing Aude flitted through his mind as he sped through the earth and the misty walls of the royal palace. Just short of the new queen's bedchamber he paused and listened. He heard sounds of weeping and was gladdened: she was not, at least, happy in her marriage.

But a surprising sight met his eyes when he emerged in a darkened corner of the chamber. There was Aude, sobbing her heart out, crouched amid a great quantity of straw. Curious, Lump stepped from the shadows. Disguising his voice by affecting a low growl, he said, "Why are you crying, fair lady?"

She started, and her eyes went wide with horror. "How did you get in here? Who—who are you?"

Lump enjoyed her fright. He stepped closer and answered, "I go where I please; walls and doors are nothing to me. As for who I am, let us say I am a friend."

He kicked at the straw. "What is all this? I did not

expect a queen to spend her wedding night amid the bedding of cattle."

At this, Aude began to weep again, and the whole story of her father's boast emerged, amid unattractive gurgles and snorts.

"Spinning straw into gold, eh?" mused Lump, when he had heard her out. "That is why the king chose you, I see. But why did you choose the king over, what's his name? That prince in the mask who was courting you? Surely you felt something for him?"

"Felt? Why, surely I loved his jewels and rich presents, but the king is richer by far, and I kept the presents. Besides, who knew what was behind the mask? Why, he might have been as ugly as, as ugly as . . ." Here she looked Lump in the face and was about to say *as you*, but thought better of it.

"As a toad," she finished, weakly.

"Indeed," said Lump, who was not deceived. "And here you are, amid straw, married on a lie for which you and your dear father will pay on the scaffold. A pretty story!"

"Oh, pity me, stranger!" Aude cried in desperation. "You who can pass through walls, can you not help me escape?"

"That I cannot," said Lump. "However, were the price right, I might help you with your spinning."

"*You* can spin straw into gold?"

"Oh, yes, but this is not the right kind of wheel nor the right straw," said Lump lightly. "Nevertheless, I can fill this room with gold in a night, which will satisfy the king. But what will you give me in return?" Here Lump looked so avidly at her that she blanched.

"Anything! Anything you desire that is in my gift."

Now Lump paused for a moment and thought of what he might ask for that would do her the most hurt, her and the king. And presently, amid this vile thinking, a new and powerful desire broke in, one that had struggled long in his breast for expression and only came out now, when his fond hopes had been dashed and he had to content himself with the rich but bitter brew of revenge. A vision passed through his mind, a vision as fanciful as those he had entertained of winning the esteem of friends or the love of Aude: he would raise a child! This child would make good all his own failures. It would be as beautiful as he himself was hideous, of course, and brilliant, lacking nothing that great wealth could supply, an ornament and a delight. And it would call him daddy and love him with all its heart.

So he said to the trembling girl, "If I save you, you must give me, one year from now, your firstborn babe."

Aude sighed with relief, for what to her was a phantom baby in a year compared to her own neck on the morrow? "My babe? Of course, yes! I promise!" she cried.

"Very well, my lady. You must toss all this straw in the fire, and I will return with the gold." And with that, he sank into the floor before her eyes.

Lump, of course, had gold aplenty in his cellars. He filled two great sacks full, clutched these to his breast, staggering beneath their weight, and traveled through the earth to the queen's apartment, where he scattered the gold—bricks, wire, lumps, and coins—around the spinning wheel, and burned the sacks and the remains of the straw.

"All looks well, my lady," he said. "The illusion is complete, save for one little thing." At this, he caught her right hand and dragged her over to the spinning wheel. "This hand has never done work harder than lifting a teacup. It must look as if it had spun all night." Then he pressed her fingers cruelly down on the point of the spindle, until they were pierced and dripping blood. And in that blood, he made her write out a contract binding her to her promise. Then, with a last mocking bow, he vanished.

In the morning, early, the king unlocked his lady's chamber and goggled at the piles of shining gold.

"By my beard." He laughed. "It is true! The girl can do it! I hardly believed it, but here is the proof!"

But if Aude thought she was over the worst of her trials, she was mistaken, for the king ordered twice as much straw as on the first night, saying, "You have done well, madam, but not well enough. I will have twice, nay thrice, what the emperor offered, to recompense me for the shame of marrying a mere miller's daughter, when I might have had an imperial princess. Get you now to work—spin away, straw into gold! And the forfeit be the same if you fail."

Five nights did Aude weep atop piles of straw, and five nights did she receive her strange visitor, who brought, as agreed, sack upon sack of gold. In fact, Lump had to sell off much that he possessed for ready bullion, and the drain was such that the price of the metal rose on the market, so that his fine palace, barge, coach, and horses all went to pay for it.

At last, even the king's vast greed was satisfied, and he thought to look at his bride, at her poor ravaged hands (for you may be sure that Lump made them bleed afresh each night); and for the first time he realized what a creature he had married and his thoughts turned for the moment away from getting money, and he took her in his arms.

Lump left the royal city after that, by night, in a hired boat, taking only Pa'aili and Djer with him, and returned to the port town where first he had made his fortune, there to wait out the year until he could claim his fee from the queen.

It was not a pleasant year for Lump, nor for those around him. His life, formerly sober, became madcap and hectic. He fell in with a crowd of rich idlers; he gambled and drank, as if trying to escape some dreadful nemesis. He quarreled with all the merchants with whom he traded, took wild ventures on mad argosies, and lost heavily. Although he could visit the interior of the earth in search of treasure, yet even the earth cannot compete with all the gaming tables, and he had to swim ever farther in search of rich lodes. He abused Pa'aili and Djer until they nearly wished for their former employment as slaves. He slept uneasily and often woke shouting in the night. Jack the goldsmith, once his friend, quite gave him up.

The only constant thing in his life now was that once a week he was waiting at the printers when the court circular came out, and he snatched it with the ink still wet from the journeyman's hands. And finding no notice of a royal birth, he uttered a vile curse and flung the paper from him or tore it into shreds. Then he returned to his mansion and ordered yet another improvement on the nursery he had built—another toy or ruffle or painted scene. He spent most of his time in this room nowadays, cooing to his future child while his servants exchanged dark looks and shook their heads.

At last came the day when, instead of this, he clutched the paper to his bosom and shouted with glee. Indeed, all the church bells of the port soon echoed his joy, for it was known that the queen had been brought to bed of a son, and the kingdom had an heir.

Now Lump cast off his wicked companions and labored to bring his affairs into a better order, and sober he went early to bed.

Queen Aude, as may be imagined, had quite put from her mind the bargain she had made. In any case, she had no intention of keeping it, for although she liked the baby well enough, and would have been sad to give him up, the king doted upon his son and loved him nearly as much as he loved his treasury. If he had known of her bargain with the ugly man or, worse, should she actually keep it and surrender the babe, her lovely head would have decorated the palace battlements within the day.

So it was a great shock to her when, upon a morning when she was alone in the nursery with the child, she saw Lump walk out of a wall and over to the cradle. He studied the baby for some minutes and then looked up at Aude, smiling, showing long, yellow, snaggled teeth. "I am come to collect what is owed me, your majesty," he said.

"No!" cried the queen. She dashed to the cradle and snatched up the infant, who, unaccustomed to his mother's clumsy grip, began to fret.

"But I must, dear lady," said Lump. "We must all keep our bargains."

"What—what will you do with him?" she asked in a quavering voice.

"Why, I suppose I will eat him. Isn't that what monsters do? And am I not a monster? But I am not certain yet whether I shall have him fried or baked. Now, give it over!"

The queen began to weep and to grip the baby more tightly, which made him wail. Lump chuckled at this scene, as it afforded him the keenest pleasure; for while we may hope that those who have been tormented will become sympathetic to the torments of others, such is hardly ever the case. In fact, the opposite is more often true. The tormented ones become the worst bullies of all, and so it was with Lump.

Lump had no doubt that he could snatch the child from his mother and disappear with him clutched to his breast, but he hesitated. If he left now, this fun would be concluded; and the queen had shown, by her surprise, that she had not been dreading his reappearance: no, she had forgotten him entirely. He considered how to magnify her pain. An idea swam into his head, and part of him, the prudent part, rejected it immediately. But that part had long since been banished to the cellars of his mind.

"I tell you what, queen," Lump said. "I am not unmoved by your motherly devotion. I, too, had a mother, you know. I will be back on the morrow at this time, and at the same time on the two days after that. If you can guess my name before the third time, in three guesses each time, I will relent. But if you fail, I will surely take the babe on the third day." With that, he vanished, leaving the queen and her son weeping on the floor.

As soon as Lump was gone, Queen Aude rang for the child's nurse, as she could not stand it when her baby cried. The nurse came, settled the baby, and observed the agitation of her mistress closely. That was part of her job, since she had been suborned by Aude's brother, Mostin, to spy on the queen. Alerted by the baby's wails, she had had her eye long enough at the nursery keyhole to observe the interview between the strange man and the queen.

That evening, as the queen entered her bedchamber, she found her brother waiting, grinning at her.

"What are you doing here, Mostin?" she asked testily.

"Why I am here to help you, dear sister, and myself, of course. Have you thought up any names yet for the little sorcerer?"

The queen gasped.

"Yes, I know all," said Mostin easily, throwing himself down on a sofa. He took a gold piece out of his pocket and flipped it into the air, so that it spun and shone in the light of the candles.

"It was the gold, wasn't it? I thought Father had sunk himself for certain with that idiotic promise to our lord and master that got you your crown. Now you know and I know that little, pretty Aude cannot spin straw into gold. Your only knowledge of gold, dear girl, is how to spend it. But somehow you produced the gold. So I suspected some sorcery from the first. I wonder what the king would say if he knew his gold came not from his lovely wife but from an ugly little goblin sorcerer."

"You spied on me!" cried Aude.

"Ah, she finally comprehends. Of course, I spy on you, dear. I knew that such a nincompoop as you are would ruin yourself in a twelvemonth, and the family with you, if I did not watch out for your interests. So you promised him the prince and heir for the gold. I think even Magnus would not approve of that bargain." He laughed and spun his coin, so that it rang.

"Oh, stop your jesting and think!" said his sister. "What am I to do? He walks through walls, Mostin!"

"As to that, clearly you must find out his name, which will not be easy, as I understand that sorcerers are careful with their names. To find the name, we must find the man. We cannot track him through the earth, so we must consider what we know of him. He can make gold; therefore a rich man. He wants a child; therefore an unmarried man, probably one who cannot marry, because . . . well, leave that for the nonce. Finally, one who hates you and wishes you to suffer greatly. Hm, something is nibbling at my mind, Aude, but I cannot bring it forth." He wrinkled his handsome brow in deep concentration, still flipping his coin.

"I have obtained a book of names from the royal library . . ." said Aude, but her brother cut her off with a curse.

"Numbskull!" he snarled. "What good will that do, when there are thousands of names? How do you imagine we will pick the right one when we have but nine guesses?" This distraction made him miss his catch, and the coin flew in a long arc across the room, to land jingling on the wooden floor.

Mostin let out a whoop and snapped his fingers. "That is it! I have him! It is that witch's boy, the one in the mask. I threw him a coin and he did not pick it up. You recall! That day when Father was stabbed and died, and the witch brought him back to life . . ."

"Yes, and then you set the authorities on her."

"Of course! We cannot have witches, after all! The

boy in the mask. He looked at you with such longing, Aude. And who else do we know who wears a mask? Who is larger than that boy, having grown somewhat but surely has the same big-shouldered, long-armed look. And who is very, very rich. And who loved you passionately. And whom you betrayed . . ."

"Not Lum-po?"

"*Of course*, Lum-po, who is surely no more from Cathay than I am. He is that witch's boy. They are one and the same."

"I will have him arrested!" exclaimed the queen.

Mostin groaned. "Have you not the tiniest lick of sense, sister? Arrest a man who can pass through stone? No, I must travel to the port, where he now lives, and spy upon him and learn his name. I will leave now, as we have but three days." He grinned and picked up his coin. "This one I shall never spend, but wear it around my neck as a charm." He resumed his seat. "Or, you know, maybe it would be more amusing to see what the king does when his beloved heir vanishes."

"Oh, Mostin, don't! You must help me!"

"Must I? Well, perhaps. But then our lovely queen, my sister, will surely do me a favor. Or two."

And he told her what he wanted.

*   *   *

It is odd that Lump, who was the greatest of spies, had no fear of being spied upon, but such was the case. Mostin had no difficulty penetrating his household. The coachman, Djer, was approached at a tavern, and he poured into the sympathetic ear of the wealthy stranger his sad story of slavery past and ill treatment now. He had no compunction about introducing his new friend to the housekeeper, Pa'aili, who also had a story of abuse, and, more significantly, had the keys to every room in the house. Gold changed hands, and Mostin was made free of a little closet that gave on the master's bed chamber.

In the meanwhile, Lump made his first two visits, and affirmed that his name was not John, James, or Stephen, nor yet Amelidoch, Mekiziclade, or Ximiphane. While he was gone on these missions, Mostin rifled his papers but could find no name mentioned save Lum-po or sometimes merely Lump. He waited in his hiding hole for the master of the house to return from this second night's travel. Fascinated, he watched the goblin return, rising slowly up through the floor like a bubble in a basin. The creature left the room for a moment and then returned, carrying an ornate cradle. This he placed on the floor, looking at it strangely, his eyes gleaming.

"No, no, my baby," Mostin heard him mutter, "no frying for you, no baking, but love, love and care, love and care, and the best of everything." Then he laughed and began to skip around the cradle, crooning, for now he was quite out of his wits:

> *"I shall not fry,*
> *Nor shall I bake,*
> *But tomorrow the Queen's own child I take.*
> *For little knows the royal dame*
> *That Rumplestiltskin is my name."*

At that moment, Lump stopped short, for as he gave voice to this sigil of his True Name, which he never had spoken before, a deep chill went through him, as the mighty Name his mother had given him vibrated in his breast. His vision swam, and for a moment his mother's face was clearly in his mind's eye, as it had not been for many long months. She seemed to be saying something to him, but he could not make out what it was. He staggered and collided with the cradle and barked his shin, and then the vision was gone and he was back in his madness. Tenderly, he set the cradle upright, patted its silken pillow, and murmured sweet endearments to the imaginary child lying in it.

Mostin writhed impatiently while this was going on and considered dashing out with his dagger drawn, but thought better of it; for who knew what wards a sorcerer might possess against such attacks? Eventually, however, the goblin slept, and Mostin could slip from his hiding place, take the swift horse that Djer provided from the stables, and gallop off into the night.

The next afternoon, Mostin was waiting in the royal nursery, dirty and unshaven, having ridden without halt through the night. Lump appeared on schedule, smiling broadly. His smile faded when he saw Mostin; and when he saw the confident look on the queen's face, he frowned.

"Well, madam, get on with it!" Lump commanded. "This is your last chance. Guess away!"

The queen said, "Is your name Lum-po?"

"No," Lump said, but his stomach roiled. How had they found him out?

"Then perhaps it is Lump. Is it Lump?"

"No," said Lump again. A pounding had started in his temples.

"Then it must be . . . *Rumpelstiltskin*!" she shouted.

At the instant this name flew into the air, Lump felt something burst inside him, and he felt as he had when grasped in the hand of Bagordax—a dismantling terror that shook his limbs and turned his innards to ice water. He fell to the ground, his sight grown dark. As from a distance he heard the whoops of triumph coming from the brother and the sister. She kicked at him and so did he, but Lump barely felt the blows of her silk slipper and his muddy boot. Somewhere a baby was screaming.

He bit his lip until blood spurted, struggling to control his jerking body. Desperately he gasped out the cantrip and sank into the floor.

But there was no feeling of freedom now, no mastery of the under earth. Now he felt trapped in a thickening slurry that closed damply, darkly around his face. He gasped for breath as he sank, while pain shot through his limbs, fiery and violent.

He fell through blackness for a time that seemed to have no end. At last he stopped. He could not move. Unyielding stone pressed in on him, grinding on his every pore, and filled the portals of his body.

I am dead, he thought. This is death, and no one will need to bury me, for I am buried already. And then, after a while, he thought, No, I am not dead, for this is worse than death. I have been flung outside the Pattern entirely. I have become a ghost.

Ghosts are not happy beings, Lump discovered. He was chained to a body that did not breathe, thirst, or hunger, that had, in fact, no mortal pangs at all. Yet he found his spirit was consumed by hatred, and that his lust for revenge was unslaked. And this ire was not directed at Aude or Mostin chiefly, but at his mother. No wonder they call witches wicked, he cried in the silence of his mind. Wicked woman, it is your doing I am in this tomb. Who asked you to give me a Name! Who asked you to bewitch me so that I could dive beneath the earth? All I ever wanted was an ordinary mother, who would rock me and tend my hurts and feed me soup and tell me stories and say I was a gallant fellow when the world turned against me. Cats and dogs in the street are better mothers than you! Spiders who eat their young are more tenderhearted, oh, cruel, vain, wicked woman!

And more of this, endlessly repeated until, if a mind could have grown hoarse with shouting, Lump's would have been red raw. After that, he struggled to insert his being back into the still carcass his flesh had become, madly thinking that he could struggle free of the enclosing rock. In this he was unsuccessful. I am a lump now in fact, he thought; oh, mother, you named me well! Did you plot that I would end this way? Did your cruelty really have no bounds?

After this came a kind of cringing self-pity. Surely no one had ever suffered like this for as little cause; surely there was some power he could call upon that would free him. Was there no mercy left in the world?

Lump had never learned to pray; for witches, although they are deeply reverent, do not pray. She whom they reverence is not interested in prayers but only in the working of the Pattern. But now he uttered what he imagined was prayer, begging the various saints and deities he had heard about on his travels to help him, promising service, devotions, canticles, cathedrals, if only they or He would reach down and pluck him out. But there was only a vast, heavy silence for answer; and for this silence, too, Lump blamed his mother.

Now there are tides in the earth as in the sea, but they are slow, slow, and generations may rise and fall between their ebb and flood. On such a ponderous tide Lump now floated. He saw his body moving, as from a distance. His mind, which had raced until exhausted like a rat in a tiny cage, now lay in stuporous despair.

Gradually, he became aware of a change. There was a faint light where there had been utter darkness, and a vacancy where there had been solid rock. Although still detached from his body, Lump now realized that this body had partially emerged from its stony prison. He was in a cave, low ceilinged and twice wider than his outstretched arms might have spanned. Only his head had emerged from the rock, he discovered; the rest remained clutched in its unyielding grip.

There was a sound; whether he heard it with his ears of flesh or through some magical intercession Lump did not know, but he welcomed it as presaging some change in the intolerable sameness of his existence. A slow, shuffling sort of sound it was, as if something were dragging across a rough floor. It drew closer. A shadow obscured an arc of the dull light. It was a bear.

It was a he-bear, a very old one. Lump could hear its wheezing, ragged breath and see that many of its teeth were missing and that one of its eyes was a cloudy disk. It collapsed with a thump on the rock floor and sighed, not an arm's reach from Lump's face.

Some hours passed. The bear's flanks heaved; its breath gurgled in and out. Lump watched the bear breathe. It was the most marvelous thing he had ever seen, he thought, this flow of air in and out of a warm body. He was content to watch it indefinitely, so grateful was he to be even a little out of the silent, clinging dark.

Then the bear shifted and its good eye came around and he saw Lump.

"I thought I smelled something," said the bear, "and I was right. It is hard to tell what's real and what's not, at my age. No, there are not many left in the Club of Twenty-six."

Lump found that he could talk, after a fashion, although the blue-tinged lips of his still face did not move. "That is very old for a bear," he said.

"This is odd," the bear said. "I have felt so queer all day and now I am talking with a man. Or the head of a man. Yes, it is very old for a bear. However did you learn to speak with bears?"

"A bear was my nurse when I was small," said Lump.

"Ah, you are *that* one," said the bear.

"You know of me?" asked Lump in wonder.

"Of course. There are few enough of men nursed by bears. The tale of Ysul and Lump is a famous one among us. I had it from my dam when I was small. Three times did Ysul save him—once from bear and twice from men—yet he would not save her even once, and so in misery she died, and he was buried in the earth for punishment. It is a very sad tale, to be sure."

"But wait," Lump objected, "that cannot be. When you were cubbed, I was not yet born. How could you have been told my tale?"

"I don't know, but many are the things kept in mystery from the bears. Although, now that you mention it, I have felt time behaving queerly of late. Just yesterday I was at my mother's milk, being only a thing as long as my claw, and then later that same day, I was a Three, on a spring day, just out of winter sleep, fighting with a big, red Five. How he did maul me!"

"That is against natural philosophy," said Lump. "Time does not behave so. You are old and becoming disturbed in your thinking, is all."

"That's possible," said the bear. "Or perhaps it is that I'm dying, and for the dying the doors of the past and future are opened. I am dying or, it may be, already dead; you yourself are hung between life and death, you know, and trapped in rock besides. In any case, here we are and must wait for what will come. How is your mother, by the way?"

"I neither know nor care," said Lump. "To her disregard and foolish cantrips I owe my present state."

"You owe your life to her as well," replied the bear, "and to a choice she made with her mind and heart, with no tie of unthinking flesh."

"I did not ask her to!"

"No, you did not. Nor did you ask for the sun to shine upon you, nor earth to nourish you, nor water to quench your thirst, but all these were given to you freely. And so you are at last free of all of them: you are quits with everything—neither mother nor sun nor food nor water have you now. You owe nothing at all, and how do you like it? *How do you like it?*"

"She did not love me!" shouted Lump at the bear.

"Yes, that is a good excuse for any ill thing. You were not loved enough. No, not enough. In the troll's cave that time, when she said she would give her life to save you, and you *knew* it was so, that was not enough. And when through your stupidity and pride you destroyed her place, and she saved you and brought you back to life, that was not enough. Nor was it enough that she sacrificed her art and all her treasures, the earnings of a long lifetime—no, not enough."

"You are not a bear," whispered Lump, and indeed the snuffling sound of the bear's breathing had ceased. It was dead. But the voice went on.

"And when she danced and conjured for gaping fools to earn the bread you ate, that was not enough. So what is enough, little Lump? If she brought you the whole world on a plate so you could devour it, would that be enough at last?"

"Stop!" Lump cried, "It is too much! I cannot ever pay—"

"Foolish child! More foolish man! Of course you can never pay! But no payment is required. Look at you, latched by hard stone, caught, crushed! But I say to you, this stone is butter compared to the stone in your breast, which catches you in a far crueler grip. Unlatch your heart, Rumpelstiltskin! Let the pain of the world flow in!"

"I cannot. I will die!"

"Yes, indeed, you may die, and become fully a corpse, as you are half a corpse now. Or you may stay as you are and sink once again into the unforgiving stone. Or you may wake at last and be alive. I think you have no other choices."

"Who are you?" Lump shouted, and "who are you" echoed and reechoed through the cave. There came no answer. Lump realized, and the knowledge racked his spirit, that the tormenting voice had been his own.

After that, there was only silence and the distant drip of water. Lump felt balanced on a needle over a void, afraid to think or feel.

Then came a scraping of claws, a pattering of feet. A pack of jackals entered the cave, laughing and sporting, attracted by the smell of the bear's carcass. They rent it and butchered it and carried away chunks of meat. Maggots feasted, too, and yielded a vast progeny of great green flies. Shoals of these rested on Lump's exposed face, but they did not eat of him, for he was not dead, not yet. Then came the carrion crows and the ravens, flying in low on stiffened wings, to tear away yet more flesh, until the white bones stared. The birds gone, it was the turn of the rats, hordes of them skittering and chattering, gnawing bone and sinew, burrowing into the naked skull, and when the rats had stuffed themselves, the beetles came in their thousands, and the ants in their tens of thousands, to polish the bones into whiteness.

Then silence again, and after a while the buzz of a single bee, a scout, who settled on the rib cage of the bear and found it good, and soon thereafter there was a mighty droning as the bee horde arrived with a new queen, and in the arched cathedral of the bear's bones they built their combs and bred their generations.

All this Lump closely observed; there was nothing else to do and it distracted him from his barrenness, all that pulsing life, and he longed to be part of it again, to be a rat, a beetle even, anything but the frozen soul he was.

And then came another bear, a young one this time, tracking snow into the cave. It was a female, Lump saw. There was a raging of bees as the bear ate huge chunks of honeycomb, and then, sated, she lay down and bore two cubs. Lump watched as the tiny creatures burrowed upward to the source of life and drank and grew fat and furry through the winter, and watched as the mother bear woke from her fitful winter's sleep to lick them and sing to them the deep-throated lullabies of the bears.

These Lump remembered well, and he felt pressing

in on his heart the weight of shame and regret, heavier and rougher than the shafts of granite that bound his frame. This must cease, he thought; live or die, this must cease. That poor bear, he thought, that poor woman! And for the first time since that night when the children tortured him, he wept and let the feelings pierce his heart.

In an instant, he was back in his body, tears pouring from his eyes, cutting through the heavy dust that covered his face. He took a great breath, another, and the most dreadful pain tore through his imprisoned limbs. He laughed through the crying and the pain, for the agony, great as it was, was the sign of life.

A rumbling arose that grew to a roar. The bear awakened and fled, with her two cubs at her tail. The floor of the cave split open and, with a last exquisite pang, one that seemed to tear him in two, the earth klaver leaped up from his belly and out of his mouth, throwing green fire, to vanish into the depths of the chasm. Then came water in a great gush, warm and muddy. It filled the cave. Lump held his breath and waited for the end. I have only one sadness, he thought, that I cannot see Ysul and my mother again, to throw my arms around them both and say that I love them.

But, much to his surprise, the rock that held him shattered in a thousand fragments, and he was free in the murky stream, swimming, borne up with dizzying speed through narrow channels until at last the earth spat him out, gasping, onto its sunlit surface. He was on wet paving stones, he found, at the lip of a well, surrounded by a garden whose bright flowers were tossed by the light and scented breeze of spring.

From a distance there came the sound of a lute.

Lump lay prone in the sun, letting it dry his hair and the few rags of clothing that still clung to his body. He found his legs much wasted, and when at last he stood, he staggered. He was ravenous, light-headed, bruised, and absurdly happy.

He looked about him and discovered he was in an oblong garden of beautifully tended plants, all sweet-smelling varieties: lavender, violets, many different sorts of roses, irises, and lilies, the beds cut through with little mazy paths. It must be high spring, he thought, perhaps early May; and he wondered how long he had been under earth. This garden was rimmed with high walls of dark stone, battlemented in the old style. At one end he could discern, past a row of miniature flowering orange trees, the delicate stone arches of a cloister. It was from there that the music came.

Cautiously and on unsteady legs, Lump moved toward the sound of the lute. At the end of his path there was a planter thick with jasmine, and he peered through its leaves.

In the shadow of the cloister there sat a young woman on a wooden bench, playing. She was very thin and pale, yet she did not seem sickly but had a kind of lithe, coiled energy, like a leopard barred in a cage too small. Her hair was soot black, with bluey lights where the dappled sun struck it. He could not see her eyes, for her head was bent over the strings of her instrument, but he could see the long, graceful line of her neck where her hair fell away, and it made him catch his breath, it was that lovely.

An oriole flew down from one of the trees and perched on a peg of the lute and startled her, so that she missed her chord, and she laughed out loud, a surprisingly hearty laugh from one so thin. She reached a bit of cut orange from a plate and held it up, still smiling, and the bird took it from her fingers and flew off. She sighed then, and adjusted her strings, and began once more to play, but now sang, too, in a low, sweet voice. Lump started, for it was a song he knew well.

> *"I was born of high and royal breeding,*
> *And at my birth, the king my father said,*

'Let all the fair folk that dwell within my kingdom
Come and lay their faery blessings 'round her little
      bed.'

"And so they came, and twelve they were in
      number.
They brought their gifts: first beauty, then a
      pleasant voice to sing,
Then charm, a kindly manner, grace to tread a
      lively measure,
And all else meet to wed some rich and handsome
      king.

"But now the thirteenth faery entered,
And wroth was she and bleak of bone.
Cried she, 'These gifts you gave are for delight
      of others.
You give the baby nothing for herself alone.

" 'So listen well: upon her eighteenth birthday
She'll have my gift, a present that is just for her.
Upon a spindle she shall prick her little finger
And fall asleep, and nevermore shall stir.'

"Thus did it pass, as she had spoken.
Although my father banished spindles from
      the land,
Yet one survived, kept secretly. I found it
And spun the wheel and pierced my little hand.

"Thus did I fall into the land of dreaming,
A land I loved, so beautiful and free.
Oh, you who sleep but hours, how can you
      imagine
The dreams of years? Do you not envy me?

"But then from paradise I was awakened
By th' prince's kiss, for which I did not ask,
Woke me to love and pain and loss and childbirth
And tears and weary years and many a heavy task.

"And now my beauty all has faded
That in my dreams I could forever keep.
I curse the prince whose selfish kiss awakened
Me. I bless the faery sent me to that sleep.

"I am the girl called Sleeping Beauty.
I never answer to that name,

For I am slave to love and duty.
It was the kiss that brought the chain."

The song pierced Lump to the heart, his fresh and newly tender heart, for it was a song his mother had often sung, and, made careless by the perfume of the jasmine and his delight in the music, he gave voice at the last line of the chorus. Immediately the young woman stopped playing and looked directly at where Lump hid. Agate, was his first thought when he saw her eyes, banded agate, or maybe chalcedony, a rich, shining yellow brown.

"Who is there?" asked the girl uncertainly. "Is that you, Jelny? Otho?"

She is blind, thought Lump, and he stepped forward from behind the jasmine, saying, "I am a stranger and I have strayed into your garden. I beg your pardon if I startled you."

"A stranger? That is odd! No one comes to visit us. However did you get into the garden?"

Here Lump thought he might dissemble, but the woman's face was so frank and sweet that he could not, and so he said, "My lady, it is a long, long tale, and tedious, I am sure, but the short of it is, I came up through your well, from within the belly of the earth, where I lay enchanted for I do not know how long."

The woman clapped her hands. "Oh, but this is marvelous!" She laughed. "Here I sit, alone and lonely, and up from the well comes an enchanted prince. It is like the ballads and stories. You are an enchanted prince, of course?"

"No, my lady, more of an enchanted pauper, I am afraid. I have but the rags I stand in, as far as I know. But tell me—do you by any chance know the year?"

"Yes. This is the twenty-first year of our king, Magnus II, whom God preserve."

"What! Twenty-one! By my tail! I have been under earth for near ten years. Yet aside from this beard I seem unchanged."

"Like Sleeping Beauty," said the woman. "It is to be expected in enchantments. And do you in fact have the tail you swear by?"

Lump laughed. "Oh, no, not I, but I had a—or rather my mother had a friend who was a cat, and he often swore so."

"Do you say swearing cats? My word, this is ever queerer! I suppose your mother was a witch?"

"Yes, she was," said Lump, surprised at the way the

conversation was going but content to chatter in this shady arcade with this charming lady for as long as she would allow. He had no pressing appointments.

The woman cocked her head and frowned. "Sir, do you make sport of me? How could your mother be a witch? It is well known that witches are cruel and eat babies. I was speaking but lightly."

"I do not sport, miss. But it is the case that my mother was a witch, and, as far as I know, she did not dine on babies. She enjoyed a nice salad and a roasted fowl or a grilled rabbit with rosemary dressing."

"Sir, you amaze me! And did she cosset you with magical favors and sing you witch lullabies?"

"Sometimes, but not as often as I would have liked. She was a very busy woman. I had a nurse."

"A faery, perhaps?"

"No," said Lump seriously. "A faery would make a very poor nurse. It was a bear."

At this, the woman gave a laugh and clapped her hands again, but Lump did not laugh along with her. Instead he thought of Ysul and how he had left her. He felt his eyes brim with tears; a sob burst from his throat.

"Oh, you are sad," said the woman. "You are crying. How cruel of me to laugh!"

"No, it is nothing, just that I thought of my old nurse and what became of her."

The woman grew sober. "This is all true, isn't it? Unless you are mad, which I doubt, for you have not the tone of a madman, or a teller of tales, which I also doubt, for we who cannot see can hear the truth more clearly than those who can. Thus you really are what you say you are—an enchanted man from under the earth, with a witch for a mother and a talking cat and a bear as a nurse. This is the most remarkable thing that has ever happened to me. What is that sound? You are hungry, I think!"

Embarrassed, Lump admitted that he was starving. The woman rang a little bell, and shortly a heavy-browed, strong-looking serving maid appeared, who cast a suspicious glance at Lump, but listened as the young woman gave her orders for a meal, a *large* meal, for "my guest." A silent serving man brought out a table. And servants quickly set it with a joint of veal; two fish pies; a roast hen; a brown loaf; and a cool, sweating pitcher of some light, bubbly wine. Lump fell to, trying not to gobble, and between mouthfuls told as much of his story as he thought proper for the young woman to hear.

When the meal was over, and the table borne silently away by the servants, Lump said, "I thank you most heartily, my lady. That was worth starving ten years for. But here I have taken your bread and wine, but I know not what house I am in nor who my hostess is. May I know where I am and to whom I owe my full belly?"

"Why, sir, you must be a stranger indeed. Everyone knows this place. You are in Bluebeard's castle. And I am Bluebeard's daughter. Nuala is my name."

She held out her hand, and he grasped it. It lay soft and warm in his palm, like a sleeping bird, and he said that he was called Lump.

"That is an odd name," she said. "Are you lumpish?"

"Extremely so," said Lump, and wondered that he could speak so lightly about his appearance, which had been for so long a torment to him; and then he thought, I am only brave because she cannot see me. It made him sad. "But," he continued, "Bluebeard is also a strange name. I knew a creature once with a blue beard, blue as the sky. Is your father's beard really blue like that? Oh, but I am so sorry! You could never have seen it."

"I have seen it many times. I was ill when I was five, a violent fever, and when I woke I was as you see me now. As for his beard, it was not blue as the sky is, but so black it shone blue, like my own hair."

"It is lovely hair," said Lump, somewhat to his own surprise. "It is raven colored, but soft looking, like a marten's fur."

Nuala's pale cheeks colored. "Thank you. I have never had a compliment from a man before, save from my father, which does not count. So, with everything else, this bids fair to be quite the most interesting day I can remember. I will return the compliment: you have a very gentle voice, Lump, and mellow. And your smell is very pleasant—not unlike a damp rock with mosses."

"I thank you," said Lump. "Nor have I had one from a girl. My own mother was scant with her praise, and I never had a father. What is he like, your father?"

"Was. He is dead. Well, not to bandy words, he was a monster, although he was kind to me and I loved him. He would marry a woman and go off on a journey, leaving the keys with her and an admonition not to open a certain door on pain of death; and she would, of course, always open the door and he would slay her on his return and put her body in that very room."

"And your mother?"

"She never opened the door. My mother has no imagination or curiosity at all. I believe I take more after my father in that respect, as I have much of both of these qualities, and perhaps I would be bloodthirsty, too, if I could see. In any case, she would not open it, and would not open it, however many voyages he made, and he grew ever angrier; and she met his anger with a calm smile and a psalm, for she is very devout, and at last his brain burst and he died."

"I am sorry," said Lump.

"And I, too, but, you know, I think that, though he loved me, he would have in the end set a trap for me, too, and I would have fallen into it, and he would have slain me. He had just that one curious vice; otherwise, he was as brave, strong, and kind a father as one could wish. Now it is just we two; my mother would be happy for me to enter a convent, but I do not think convent life would suit me."

"Why not?"

"Because I long for a man," she answered, and then her hand flew to her mouth and crimson bars appeared on each cheek. "My goodness, I cannot believe I said that! I must be losing my wits at last. What I meant to say was that when I was a little girl I dreamed of being married and, though the dream is now impossible—for who would marry me?—yet I cling to it."

After this, they were silent for a long while, in their own thoughts, he watching the afternoon turn into purple evening and the shadows of the walls move across the garden, winking out the brightness of the blooms, she sensing the cooling of the breeze and the growing quiet of the birds and beasts at the close of the day.

"You will stay for supper," she said abruptly. "I will order another place set, and for the night, too. I will have Margareta make up a room. We have dozens."

So it happened, although Lump protested (feebly enough) against this generosity. A butler laid out a suit of clothes for Lump, all black silk, and the supper was eaten in silence off sumptuous plate, with Nuala's mother at the head of the table. She was a severe-looking dame, dressed in black bedecked with many a holy medallion and cross, and she spoke but once to Lump, inquiring as to his religion, and, receiving what seemed to be an inappropriate answer, behaved thereafter as if he did not exist. But Nuala reached under the table and touched his hand lightly, and so he was content.

That night, Lump lay awake for some time watching the moonlight creep across the ceiling and thinking that but yesterday he was dead and buried and now he slept on a feather bed, watching the moon, breathing air scented by jasmine and roses, with a belly full of fine food. What next? And there was also the lady Nuala.

By my tail! he thought. I am falling in love again, and this time it is the love of an open heart. When I was in love with Aude, I felt overheated, sweaty, ashamed, afraid, furtive, driven. In a way it was much like being trapped in the earth, for I knew that she did not love me, and never would love me. But this, this is as it was when I was a boy, the woods and fields, those *feelings* . . . before everything became horrible. It is like eating a crisp apple on a windy hill. Because I am sure she likes me—those blushes, her kind words! Shall I tell her I love her? No, it is too soon; she would be frightened. I will wait a day or two. And thinking these and other pleasant thoughts, Lump fell into a deep and restful slumber.

But in the morning, at breakfast, Nuala seemed pinched and strained; and when Lump asked her what was the matter, she answered, "My mother says you are not fit company for me, for you are poor and have no family and are not churched in our way, and, my Lord! I did not tell her anything about the witch part, or she would have called for the guards—but, anyway, she says you must leave today." At this the young woman burst into tears.

Almost before he knew it, Lump had come around the table and lifted Nuala from her chair and enfolded her in his arms, where she sobbed and did not pull away.

He said, "Listen to me, Nuala. Your mother is right, you know, about all those things; but there are things that you do not yet know about me, and, if you will, I will tell you them and one other thing besides, which you may be happy to know. Let us go and sit on that bench in your garden where we first met."

So they did, and Lump told her his whole story, the bad with the good.

When he was done, she said, "It is hard to believe I am sitting on my little garden bench with someone who has danced with Queen Aude. Is she truly as beautiful as everyone says?"

"She is, and more," said Lump, "but, Nuala, it is a hollow beauty that does not touch her heart. As a woman, she is not fit to carry your bathwater."

"She can, at least, see," said Nuala in a small voice.

"Yes, but she is blind as a mole to anything but her

own glory, ease, and pleasure. You see more, and more important things, with your good heart than ever she can see with her perfect eyes."

When she heard these words, Nuala sighed and turned her head away, and said, "But it must have been fine to be at court and attend balls and pageants, to have seen the old chancellor, Vandy, before his fall—"

"His fall?"

"Yes, it was a great scandal. He was convicted of corruption on evidence brought by the queen, his own daughter, and went to the scaffold. His son, Mostin, is the chancellor now, and a very great man, they say."

"Yes, he must be, and I hope he is happy with it. I was great once, as I said, and was miserable. There may be some who have the art of being great and happy together, but apparently I am not one of them." He took her hand in his and continued, "So, now you know all my life's story, and, you recall, I said I would tell you that and one thing more, and this it is: I love you, Nuala, and wish I could spend my life with you and be your husband. Will you be my wife?"

"Oh!" cried Nuala, growing pale. "I don't know what to say. This is like a faery tale."

"It is not in the least like a faery tale," said Lump,

but kindly. "There are no faeries in it—and a good thing, too, as you would agree, if you had ever met any of the Undying Race. And I am not a handsome prince but only an ugly mountebank's assistant. Save my heart, which cannot be worth much, I have nothing to bestow upon a lady with a castle. My wallet is empty . . ." Here he turned the little pouch inside out to demonstrate its vacuity, and something small popped out and fell with a tiny clatter to the flagstones.

"What was that falling?" she asked, for her ears were most acute.

Lump went down on his knees to search, and found it, and whistled.

"What have you found?" asked Nuala.

"It is a little diamond," said Lump, marveling. "Blue white, about three carats. It must have stuck in my pouch when I was out a-gathering jewels by the bushel in the under earth. Well, here is the prettiest omen imaginable. It is enough to buy us a little house and feed us until I can find some way of earning our living. Now you *must* tell me yes."

"Oh, I do, Lump, with all my heart," she cried, "and I would have even without the jewel, for I have so long wished to be free of this great barn, full of nothing but death and devotion, and you are so sweet and kind. I loved you from when first I heard the sound of your voice. And I can cook, if I know where everything is, and I'm clever with a needle, although, you know, we will need a girl to clean—" but then she could not continue because he had kissed her—for both of them, the very first kiss—followed soon by a great number of others.

"Now," she said after some time, and after catching her breath, "we must contrive to slip away, for if my mother suspected she would have me locked up and set the guards on you for a vagrant rogue. There is a small church, a hermitage really, just half a league distant, where we can be married; and once I am your wife she can do nothing."

"But, Nuala, I—I cannot be married in a church," he said, "because, you know, I am a witch's boy. It would not be right." Her face fell, and he asked, "Does this matter to you?"

"Yes," she said, after a moment. "I find that it does. Oh, dear! What to do?" She stood and walked off a distance down paths so familiar that she did not need to feel her way but strode out, and his heart swelled to see the pure grace of her movements. He waited silently, and she came back, standing before him straight as a birch, her eyes dripping tears but smiling. She said, "It is no doubt wrong that I love you, but there it is, I do, and cannot deny what I feel. I want to live with you and share your life, and if it is wrong I will answer it at the gate of heaven after I am dead. In the meanwhile, I will jump over a broom with you or throw a coin backward, or dance in a circle around a fire or what you will, and be damned."

Now a month passed. The diamond being sold, Lump and Nuala lived in an old, tilting house by the docks of the royal city, small but snug. Nuala cooked and sewed, as she had said, but they had no girl to clean, to save money, for Lump was having great difficulty finding work. His only two qualifications—as a mountebank's boy and a magnate—did not signify much to the sort of employers he could approach. Still, as he walked out each day to search, he was cheerful, first because he was in love, and with someone who loved him back, and second because from being an absolutely hideous little boy he had become merely an extremely homely young man. People did not run shrieking from the sight of him. On the other hand, his looks did not help his search for employment. Between two men with strong backs and no skills, the fairer usually will be chosen. Still, he persisted.

One day he was walking by the docks, observing with interest a crane lifting long, thick slabs of white marble from a barge and landing them on straw-lined pallets on the dock. A large red-haired man in a leather apron was inspecting them as they landed, tapping with a small hammer and listening closely to the sound the stone gave back.

Now he turned to a richly dressed, portly man standing nearby, and said, "Master Morion, I do not like the sound of that one. It is flawed, I think."

"Flawed? Nonsense!" said Morion, clearly the stone factor, as the red-haired man was clearly a master mason. "This lot is all from the same cut," continued the stone factor, "and as pure and close-grained a white marble as you will find anywhere."

The redhead scratched his short beard. "You say so, sir, but to my ear the sound is somewhat off. And as it is stone for the dome ribs in the new royal chapel . . ."

"The mason is right, sir," Lump called out. "The stone is flawed, as are two of these others, by an intrusion of mica. They will not bear as they should."

Both men stared at him. Then the stone factor snorted, saying, "Pah! He is a barrow boy. Will you believe him and not me?"

"I am not a barrow boy," said Lump angrily, and picking up an iron crowbar from the ground, he approached the slab. Pointing with the crowbar, he explained, "The flaw runs thus and crossways thus."

"What!" cried the factor. "Get away, you wretched yokel! Do you pretend to see through stone? This is mere prattle!"

"Is it? Watch this, then!" said Lump and, sighting carefully, he brought his iron down on a precise spot on the cut stone. Instantly, the slab cracked and fell into three pieces, and the mica could clearly be seen, glittering in the sun.

"That's enough for me," said the redheaded man. To the fuming stone merchant, he said, "Sir, you may load your rotten stone back on the barge or sink it in the harbor, but none of it will I take. Good day to you, sir. Son, come walk here with me. That was the most remarkable thing I have ever seen. How did you know the stone was flawed?"

"It was obvious to one who has been . . . much about stone," replied Lump.

"Ah! A journeyman mason, are you?"

"Not I, but I would be glad to learn the art. I am at liberty for the moment."

"Remarkable! Well, I am Troon, master mason for the royal chapel construction. What would you say to half journeyman's wages until you can show your mettle? I owe you that much for saving me from that rascal, or worse. I will cozzen the guild, and say you are my cousin, by name . . . ?

"Lump."

"My cousin Lump, and get you on the books. What say you, cousin?"

"Yes," said Lump. "Yes, with all my heart, sir!"

And so Lump began his career as a mason, working on the scaffolding of the great chapel that the king was building in the modern fashion, with forests of figured columns, noble pediments, saints in ecstasy, inlaid floors, and a marvelous dome, said to be the highest yet built. Lump's skill with stone was a wonder to all the workmen and masons. From the first day, he could cut it like clay; and his tools rarely needed sharpening, so clever was he about the grain and the force required. He also had an uncanny sense of what stone would bear, as if he were seeing the material from the inside out. He was able to make several suggestions to the master mason, who took them and was pleased, and thereafter treated Lump as his personal apprentice and introduced him to the art of drawing and using the instruments of the profession and casting elevations.

All morning Lump would work up on the rising stone walls or down in the yard, cutting, until the bells of noon rang out, when he would search the square for the slim figure of his wife, in her blue cloak, a straw basket on her arm, tapping her way with a stick across the cluttered square. Then he would drop his tools and rush to meet her, but always he was anticipated by the nearest laborers, who would surround her and take her basket, and, with many a kind word, guide her tenderly to a sheltered spot and make her comfortable on a tarpaulin or a nest of straw. Her sweetness and gaiety of manner had early won the hearts of the roughest haulers, and she had become the pet of the entire enterprise.

Then she and he would eat the meal she had prepared and talk about the day's doings, and be in love, and afterward she would tap herself away again, Lump following her figure with his eyes until she was lost to view. He was as happy as he ever had imagined being, and thought himself now enfolded in a magic greater that what wizards wield.

Then, one afternoon, on an autumn day with the first hint of chill in the air, Lump was strolling through the city's great market on some errand when he caught sight of a familiar face hurrying by.

"Gretl!" he cried out.

The woman he had called to stopped, glanced at him, her face showing alarm, and hurried past. He pursued her and held her by the sleeve.

"Gretl, wait! Don't you know me? It is Lump, Mrs. Forest's boy."

Gretl looked into the strange face and at last recognized the peculiar yellowish eyes that she had only before seen peering through the slits in a mask. Her face was much worn with care, Lump thought, and she appeared now quite middle-aged.

"Ah, yes," she said in her low voice. "I see it is you. And have you returned? Surely not with your mother?"

"No, I have never seen her since that night when they came to arrest us. But what of you? There is a lodging house and a tailor's where the fencing school used to be. Is Hansl well?"

"No, not well, I fear, but still alive," Gretl answered. "He was taken up the same night and put to the question concerning witchcraft and your mother. It was Mostin, who is now chancellor, that wicked man, who caused the arrest. And he was present during the torment. Of course Hansl knew nothing of where she had gone, but—oh, Lump, they tortured him so cruelly, his poor hands are ruined and he is ever in pain. He cannot fence any longer."

"But how do you live, then? We have little enough— I am a married man now—but if you have need . . ."

"Oh, no, we are well in that regard. We have a small shop on Armorers' Street, where we sell and repair the new sort of pistol. He can still shoot and, you know, 'A fellow must protect his sister . . .' " Here she smiled sadly.

"I will come to see you," said Lump.

"I think not, dear Lump. He is strange now, I fear, and does not like company. Not that he blames you for what happened, but . . ."

"I understand. But give him my kind regards and say that I regret deeply that I did not take up his friendship, nor yours, when it was offered. I was a fool then, and not in my right senses besides. But tell me, my mother said that she would send a message by you, if she lived. . . ."

"Oh, yes, she did!" exclaimed Gretl. "It was, let me see, not three years past this summer. A bird came, a seabird of some sort—large, white, with a black head. It just flew in by the window and walked about on our counter, as if tame. There was a message tied to its leg, saying, 'Tell Lump that we are safe and live by the Minch of Morr.'"

Lump experienced a thrill of relief so deep that his knees trembled. "Oh, thank you for that news, dear Gretl! I had thought she was gone, and so I did not dare to think of her or feel my loss. I must go to her as soon as ever I can. But do you know where is this Minch of Morr?"

"That I do not, nor did Hansl, although we have traveled much. Ask by the docks—perhaps some sailor . . . My dear, I must go now; Hansl is waiting for his dinner. Fare you well." She kissed him on the cheek and vanished into the crowd.

That evening, and for many evenings thereafter, Lump left his house after supper and wandered through the narrow lanes around the docks, stopping in all the sailors' taverns and asking whether any knew of the Minch of Morr. None did, but he persevered.

At last, in one of these smoky places, an elderly

man in a canvas coat looked up from his ale and stared at Lump with his one bright blue eye and said, "The Minch of Morr? Aye, I know it. But there is nought there in trade, and the few that venture so far avoid it as it were their own death."

Lump introduced himself and learned that the man was Captain Woak, master of the brig *Marvelous*.

"Why do they fear it so, captain?" asked Lump, sitting himself opposite the man and signing to the tapster to bring another large flagon.

"Why? Because it is the most infernal spot on the western seas: you have your contrary winds, your plaguey whirlpools; your bloody tide races; and strewn about you have your thrice-cursed rocks sharp as teeth that'll rip the keel out of any ship swimming as easy as kiss my hand. No, nobody goes to the Minch of Morr, not if they can help it."

"But if one wished to go there . . . ?"

"Eh! One would be a devil take 'em fool, then, sir! Ha! But look you here!" The man cleared a place on the table and drew a map in spilled ale. "Here, you see, is the headland of Clinky, pointing nor' nor'west. And here is Clinky Town on the north side, a mean place, too, with barely enough sheep's wool to warrant a ship a year. Now this gut on the south side is the Minch itself, and the headland and all the country roundabout is near as barren as this tabletop, and boggy besides."

"But were I at this Clinky Town, I could walk to the Minch, could I not?"

"Aye, sir, and then you would be nowhere and would have to walk back, with no profit."

"What would it cost to take me and my wife to that place?"

"What? Go to Clinky? Why it would be a voyage all its own, with no freight, long and hard at this time of year." He looked Lump over shrewdly and said, "I could not undertake it for less than one hundred gold magnus, half in advance."

"Why, that is a year's wages!" exclaimed Lump.

"Nevertheless, sir, that is the fare, for it is as near to the world's end as makes no difference. And return," said Captain Woak, and would not be moved.

Lump returned home that evening with a heavy heart and told Nuala all. And she said, "Do not worry, my dear, for I am a thrifty housewife and keep a jar with money against an evil day, which God forbid. I already have twenty-one silver pennies, and this in less than a half year. We will soon have our fare."

"Yes, dear, if soon means a hundred years. Now for the first time I regret the loss of my gift, for in years past I would spend a hundred magnus to feast a dozen men I did not like."

The next day, Lump arrived at the building site to find it full of court functionaries. A crimson carpet was being laid from the road up the steps and into the interior of the unfinished church.

"What is happening, Master Troon?" Lump asked the mason.

"Why, it is the king, my lad. He visits us today, to see our work and goggle at its magnificence. We are all to assemble in rows where yon popinjay waves his little rod. I will make my speech and bow, and then we will all troop through, I and the royal party, and troop out again, and if his grace is pleased, there will be purses handed about and beer and pies for all."

"Is that so? I had heard his grace was tight with coin."

"In former days, yes, but the queen and her brother between them have loosened him a good deal, for they both love show, and, of course, the late wars have brought in much booty. Oh, yes, the gold does flow nowadays, and ain't it jolly for us poor masons!"

"Will the queen come, too?" asked Lump in a nervous voice.

"We'll soon see, laddie. Here is the procession now."

So Lump waited in a long line of journeymen, with the laborers massed behind, while the guards and the outriders and the gilded coach arrived, and the king stepped out onto the carpet. All bowed deep, and when Lump looked up again, there was Aude next to the king, with Mostin, in black with his chancellor's chain, standing a pace or two behind.

He was shocked at her appearance. Ten years had been sufficient to mark her face with her true character; and while she was still beautiful, her face was not pleasant for Lump to look upon. The royal group shifted as Troon pointed out details on the façade. Lump saw that Mostin had next to him a little boy, a lad of ten or so, the babe he had tried to steal. Handsome he was, but the marks of petulance and cruelty were already present on his face. Lump shuddered and had to look away, and he cast his eyes up at the white marble of the façade. The king and his party were right under it now, preparing to enter the building. Lump's eye was caught by a particular ashlar, thirty paces above the ground. He thought, That is wrong—it will have to be relaid, and then it struck him just what he was seeing, and before he knew what he was doing he was running full tilt toward the church entrance.

The king and queen were already under the overhanging pediment. Lump saw the startled faces of the guards, heard their shouts and the rattle of their swords springing free, and then he was slamming into Mostin and the crown prince, driving them under the sheltering porch as half a ton of marble came crashing down, crushing a guardsman to jelly beneath it, at the precise spot where heir and chancellor had been standing.

"They did not recognize you, then?" asked Nuala. Lump was in a tin tub, and she was washing his back, which was covered with bruises made by fragments of the smashed stone.

"I think Mostin might have; he is very clever, but, of course, he could say nothing. It is good that we are leaving, I think. I don't want to have to watch for murderers."

"There was enough in the purse to pay our way?"

"Oh, that and more. The queen was very generous. And, no, my dear, there was not the slightest pang."

"I should hope not," said Nuala. "I have heard that she is not fit to carry my bathwater."

Heart's Desire

They sold up and were gone the next day, to much lamentation at the building site. Troon presented Lump with a set of best steel stone chisels and a certificate naming him a journeyman of the masons, which meant that he could find work anywhere.

As Captain Woak had promised, it was a long and hard journey, although the brig *Marvelous* was well found and dry. Lump was sick much of the time, but Nuala proved a superb sailor. The mariners would lash her to the foremast, where she would laugh and revel in the heaviest seas. Of course, they doted upon her and could not do her enough service, and each evening she would come down damp with spray, her cheeks rosy red, and nurse the groaning Lump with dry bread and thin soup.

After three long weeks of rough sailing they were landed at Clinky Town, which proved, as predicted, a mean place of a few dozen houses. It was agreed that the brig would return for them in the spring.

Lump hired an old cart with a pair of tired bays, all three smelling of fish, and, loading their small baggage, they set out on a sandy track that they were told led eventually to the Minch of Morr. No one ever used it, the people said. There was nothing there, and the country was strange in a way that no one in Clinky cared to specify.

This track, they found, led through an odd, broken country, made of lumpy low treeless hills covered with thin soil; decked with gorse and heather; and cut with shallow, slow-moving streams and ponds. The sky over it was low, and often the clouds reached down to touch the earth with mist. The air was fresh and smelled of salt and mud.

They stopped for the night in the shelter of a stone outcrop. Lump built a little fireplace of rocks and made a fire of turves. Then he took a bucket and went to draw water from a nearby tarn.

He was just dipping his bucket and thinking that, although he had never been in this sort of country before, something about it seemed familiar in a disturbing way, as if he had inhabited it one time in a dream, when he looked up and there was the nixie.

She was crouching on a flat rock, combing her long, pale hair with a fish bone. Her eyes were the color of running water under the moon. She saw him and smiled, showing slightly pointed teeth, and began to hum a tune. Lump felt the familiar warm prickling sensation, the thickening of the air, and saw the little sparkling lights. Before he knew it, he was knee deep in the water, moving toward that long, thin beckoning finger. Then, in one convulsive movement, he upended the full bucket over his head and turned, blind and gasping with the shock of the icy drench, and stumbled out of the tarn. When he looked again, the nixie was gone.

"I slipped and fell in," was all the explanation he gave to Nuala as she rubbed him with warm blankets. It was some time before he could fall asleep, and a little before dawn he woke screaming.

"What is it?" cried Nuala.

"A dream! I felt I was sinking into the earth without being able to stop. Oh, Nuala, it was dreadful!" He tried to sit up and then shouted, "Ah, no! I *have* sunk into the earth! My legs!"

She felt frantically down his legs and discovered that they were buried from nearly the knees down. With a fierce cry she pulled at them, and by dint of much hauling the two together were able to jerk his legs from the earth. Then she began to tremble.

He clasped her in his arms, saying, "Why, what is wrong, my dear? I am safe now, as you see."

"Oh, Lump! All your talk about faeries and enchantments—I only half believed them until now, for I thought that they were fables like the stories we tell to children. But when I felt your legs buried in the ground—I was in terror."

"I am sorry, dear," said Lump. "But why would you tell children things that are not true?"

"I cannot tell you that—my mind is a muddle. Lump, what is happening?"

"Well, I think we are moving through a land where the old magic is still strong, and some earth magic must still cling to my body, from my past enchantment. I have felt it ever since midday. And look! This high stone we are under is not a natural solitary, but a carved image, very ancient and much worn."

It was so. The first glow of false dawn revealed the figure of a woman, great of hip and belly, with a belt of round beads and a blank knob for a head. Lump rose and inspected its base. "And here are the remains of flowers, larkspur and red valerian, which do not grow on these moors. This is a shrine, what you would call a witch's shrine. I think this is proof my mother is close by."

"Did she leave the flowers, do you think?"

"She did, or the fay. This country must be thick with them, and I imagine many of these little hills are their forts. And . . . I saw a nixie by the tarn. I didn't tell you, for I thought you would be frightened."

"You were correct," she said. "Come, hold me again! That is better. Are we in any danger, do you think?"

"A little," he answered. "We might encounter a troll."

"A troll! Merciful heaven! What would you do if we did?"

"Do? Why, I would run like a deer, of course, leaving you to be gobbled up. In any case, trolls shun the day, the night is almost over, and I expect we will be at the Minch and my mother's place this very day."

"Good. I am a-jangle about meeting your mother, which is common enough among us brides, but I should think truly excusable in those who have married a witch's boy. Will she like me, do you think? I wish her to."

"What a question! The whole world loves you, and besides my mother loves all—polecats, beetles, and deadly nightshade together. It is hard to avoid her love, in fact, though I own I tried hard enough. I thought she could not really love me, since she so loved everything else. But I will make it good, if I can."

The next morning they crested the last of the little rises, and there stretched before them was the gray sea and the crashing, roaring surf. They rode rattling down a cobble beach until they saw a line of smoke and a small round boat tied high up the beach. There was a cut in the dunes, and at the head of it, they found a group of buildings fashioned of oblong beach stones with turf roofs: one large cottage, one smaller, and a barn. They saw also a little meadow behind these on which sheep grazed; a pond with ducks and geese of many types; a garden plot; and several plowed fields, wet and bare now with oncoming winter. Lump brought the cart clattering up to the front of the larger house, helped Nuala down, and knocked on the door.

There was more gray in her hair, and she seemed smaller than he remembered, but otherwise she was unchanged, standing there in the doorway in her plain brown dress, with a blue pottery bowl of risen dough in her arms. Her face was calm and her carriage was straight as ever. She did not seem surprised to see them.

"So. You have come at last," she said. Her stone-colored eyes took him in, and took Nuala in, and then she moved away from the doorway and bid them enter. But Lump swept her up in his arms and held her close, burying his face in her hair.

"I am sorry," he cried, "more sorry than I can ever tell. I lost my Name, and your gift that you paid so dearly for, and I was trapped in the earth, but a bear came, and I was freed, and now I am married and have a trade." He stepped away. "This is Nuala."

The woman embraced Nuala and kissed her, saying, "You are most welcome, my dear. Come enter, and I will make tea. The wind grows cold."

So they sat by the warm peat fire and drank, the bread baking all the while, and Lump told everything that had happened to him since they had parted. And then he asked, "But what of you, Mother? What happened after you fled?"

"This is soon told," said the woman. "We escaped, needless to say, and fled north, and then Falance went for a soldier, and we joined the war."

"The war! You?"

"Well, I was what they call a camp follower. I helped with the wounded and robbed corpses. You know, I have always admired the ravens, and it is much the same sort of life. Also battle is exciting, though stupid, like a stampede of elk. As for Falance, you know he loves to kill—it is his nature—and I did not want to deny him. He made a fine-looking soldier, too, with a plume, dangling cartridges, and boots to the hip, his mustache waxed to points and his hair in tight braids. We were of the White Dragoons. Seven years we followed the drum, and then some doctors noticed that their patients died while mine lived and kept their limbs, and an accusation was lodged against me, as happened before, and we had to desert. Falance was obliged to do extraordinary slaughter to get us away, and when we were safe I said to him, 'My dear, this has been instructive, to be sure, but it is clear that we cannot live among ordinary folk ever again. We must go where none dwell,' and I had, of course, known of this place—"

"Why had you?" Lump asked. "Scarcely anyone else has."

"That is its virtue. But it is famous among witches, a holy place. There have been sisters in this house time out of mind, and the place is dense with magic. When the world was young, the causeway to Lyonesse started here. Then all the ground roundabout was thick with faery forts, and at night the glow of their lamps obscured the moon, while on the seaward horizon the spires of Lyonesse shone blue and green. Now most of the forts are empty, and Lyonesse is long sunk beneath the waves, but there is weird enough to keep away the curious, as I daresay you noticed."

"Yes, we did, and we saw the stone mother."

"There is that, too. It was old, old when Lyonesse was first made. It is comforting to think that Her spirit is strong at that place, although, you know, She is still silent with me."

"That is unjust," Lump said.

She smiled and patted his hand. "Lump, you know well, we do not look to Her for justice. That is the business of another sort of being. In any case, here we are and here we will stay. We live simply and keep the seasons, solstice, then Beltane, then solstice, then Samhain, then solstice again. I have a little boat."

"We saw it."

"Yes. Falance made it for me. It is not a very good boat, I fear, a boat made by a *cat* after all, but it serves. I row out through the surf and I fish, and think of dead Lyonesse and of Her. On the sea She is very close, you know."

She turned to Nuala and asked, "Child, how long have you been blind, and how did it come about?"

Lump listened as his mother and Nuala spoke about this and other things, easily and without restraint, as if they had been friends for many years. He was so happy that he could hardly keep his chair.

Then the door burst open with a bang and there stood Falance, his green eyes and his hair wild, breathing smoke in the cold air that blew around him and holding in his hand a long, gleaming saber.

"Falance, what is this?" cried the woman.

"I thought . . . ," gasped the cat. "I heard horses from beyond the hill. I was chasing sheep, and I thought, you know . . . dragoons."

"In a *cart*, Falance?"

"I beg pardon, my lady," he said, putting by the blade, and then his eyes widened and he exclaimed, "By my tail! It is Lump! Lump has come back!"

At this Nuala's face blossomed in a smile, and she rose and tapped her way up to Falance, and curtseyed, saying, "You are the cat. I am Nuala, and I am delighted to meet you. You are a wonder to me, sir."

"And to myself, often, my lady," Falance responded, making his bow.

"Do you keep sheep, now, Falance?" asked Lump, grasping him by the hand.

"Of course I keep sheep. I would be ashamed for the cats could I not do what any *dog* can do. Well, well, I expect all the stories are told already; you will have to tell them all over again, for me. Madam, by your leave, we must have a feast tonight."

"I will get a goose," said the woman, and went out of the house.

"Falance," said Lump, "I wish to beg your pardon for the ills I did you when I was a boy. I was confused and did not know how to be a friend."

"Pah! That is forgotten entirely, for who cares where a kitten messes? Lick it up and forget it is our way." He clapped Lump on the back. "And truly, I am glad to see you grown a man and with a pretty mate, too. I despaired of you, I confess. But she? Never!"

The woman returned, carrying a large gray goose in her arms. She took it into a quiet corner and spoke to it, and listened while the goose spoke to her, and then she killed it, swiftly and gently.

In the evening the four of them sat down to a laden table, the goose brown and steaming, stuffed with oysters, and on the side potatoes, cabbage dressed with poppy seed, and pickles and the new bread. The woman took a pinch of earth from a little pot and said the Witchs' Grace: "Oh, Mother, we thank thee for this meal, Your body, and this drink, from the River of Life. Oh, generous, giving all, asking from us only death and changing form. Food we eat. Food we are. In the Pattern of Thy carefulness, until the Last Day."

Then she put the pinch into her mouth and swallowed it, and they feasted; and after the plates were cleared away, Falance brought out a stone bottle of barley wine he had made, and they drank, and each told stories and jokes and fables, although many of these last were strange to Nuala's ears.

"That is not how the story goes, my dear," she said to Lump, after one of these. "Goldilocks is a little girl and the three bears are fierce and she runs away in the end."

"Nay, Goldilocks is a great ogre with one eye, and the little bears invade his house looking for porridge with honey on it, and the *bears* must run away in the end. I know it is so because I had it from the bears; and who should know, if not they?"

The little house rang with laughter late into the night, until at last Nuala's head slumped forward on the table, for the wine was very strong and she was not used to it. Then Lump bundled her into a blanket and laid her in the bed in the loft of the witch's house, and built up the fire, and went back to talk more to his mother. She was alone.

"Falance has gone to his cottage," she said. "He learned to drink in the army, but still has no head for it, for which we may be grateful.

"You have come to ask me about Nuala."

"Yes. Can anything be done?"

"Not by herb or ointment, I fear. The injury is beyond the reach of that art. But there is one thing else." She went to a cabinet and drew out a small bundle wrapped in many layers of colored yarn.

"This is my last spell. It is called the Smoke of Heart's Desire. It is burned, with certain words said, and who sniffs the first smoke of it falls into a trance, and when he wakes, he has his heart's true desire. I offered it in pawn but found no takers."

"What! But surely it must be of all things the most valuable."

"Not so," said the woman. "For, understand, it gives us not what we *say* we want, or *imagine* that we want, but only the deepest desire of the heart, which is hardly ever the same thing, and also it takes a wise person to know what it truly is. It is therefore of very uncertain effect. I knew once of a duke who used it, as he thought, to obtain a greater realm, but when he awoke he was a hound chained in a kennel."

"I don't understand. Why ever would any man, not to say a duke, wish to be a dog?"

"I don't understand either, but it must be so, else so many men would not act like dogs, or worse."

"But surely Nuala has no greater desire than to see."

"That may be, but I do not know her well enough to say. It may be she wishes in her deepest heart to dwell in her heaven or to have you become a handsome prince. And you, Lump, do you still wish to be a handsome prince, as you once did?"

"To be handsome I would not mind, although, you know, since I have . . . come back, I find it is not as bad as I thought, to go unmasked." He rose and paced for a while, thinking. Then he sat again and sighed and said, "But, if you will, I would like to try, for if I do not, I will rue it forever and forever doubt my own heart. And I would rather die than that."

She nodded and patted his cheek. Then she assembled her materials—a brass censer with tripod legs, some colored chalks, her skin-bound book, and a candle. She placed the Smoke of Heart's Desire in the censer, made her marks, and began the enchantment. To Lump, the smoke smelled of vinegar and hops and something that was neither, but sweet and pleasant.

Waking, he found himself on the stone flags before the still-warm hearth, with sheepskins piled on him. He rose, groaning, and blinked in the thin sunlight that filtered through the fish-skin windowpanes. Suddenly, the memories of the previous night came rushing back, and he raced out the door to the duck pond, his heart in his mouth. Kneeling, he stared at his reflection in the water.

"Oh, ugly face, I bless the sight of you," he said aloud and then raced back to the small room where Nuala lay. She slept still and he sat down at her side, watching.

Soon she murmured and yawned and opened her eyes. "Oh, Lump, I had the strangest dream. I dreamed I could see again, and—" She stopped and laughed. "But I am still dreaming. It is a dream within a dream, for I can see your face. How beautiful you are, my dear; so often my hands have walked the lanes of your face, but I could not see your eyes, which are like gold. Are they gold in truth? This is such a bright and vivid dream; I will try to remember it and tell you about it when I awake. Oh, but you are crying! Why do you weep, Lump?"

"I weep from happiness, my girl, because it is not a dream, or no more of a dream than is this our life. You *can* see, through magic. My mother made her last enchantment, and it was to give me my heart's desire, and this is what my heart truly desired, it seems."

Then they both wept and embraced, and then Nuala leaped up and thrust her head out each window in turn feasting her long-thirsty eyes, crying, "The sky! Ducks! Birds! Sheep! My face, oh, I am awful to look at, my hair is undressed! Is that the sea? It is so large! Fields! Oh, the colors! A meadow! Lump, I must run through the meadow. I have not run through a meadow in twenty years."

With that, she dashed out of the house and away, springing and leaping, as lithe and sprightly as a deer, and watching her Lump thought he would faint from the pure joy of it.

"Mind the sheep turds!" shouted Falance, who had emerged from the barn with the woman, and they all three watched Nuala run.

"It is like the fay dancing," said Lump, "but not

like. It gives, yet takes nothing away."

"Yes, for your heart is mended now," said the woman.

He turned to face her and pressed her hand between his own. "There are no words to thank you, Mother," he said, "for this and the other gifts you have given me. But, I wonder, did you never think to use the smoke to get your own heart's desire?"

"Ah, but I have it already," she said.

"You do? What is it?"

"It is you, of course, ninny. Now, get that mad girl out of the meadow before she chills herself. It will not do her baby any good should she fall sick."

"What baby? You mean she is with child . . . but she has told me nothing!"

"She doesn't know yet," said the woman. "Hm. I am still something of a witch, I find. Falance! Finish milking the goat, and I will make us all hot porridge."

They stayed the winter, and left in the spring, as planned. In the brig *Marvelous*, they sailed back to the crowded lands, but not to the same kingdom, and there Lump took up again the tools of his trade. With Nuala he had three children, two girls and a boy, and fortunately they took after their mother as far as looks, although the boy had yellow eyes. Every year they journeyed back to the Minch of Morr to show the woman her grandchildren. She did tricks of all sorts to amuse them, but never again true magic.

A year after their youngest was born, King Magnus II died, of a flux most said, of poison, said others, and Magnus III, whom Lump had sought for his own, took the throne. Within an hour of his accession, the chancellor Mostin's head stood staring and bloody on the castle battlements and the Queen Aude had been shut up in a tiny tower room, walled and floored and ceilinged with mirrors, which no one ever visited and from which she never again emerged. The new king, who became known to history as Magnus the Cruel, provoked a rebellion by his exactions and profligacy, and died an exile, still young, and that kingdom passed into other and kinder hands.

Lump and his family returned to the royal city then, and stayed there all their lives. Although they did not live happily ever after, for they often quarreled about religion and who loved whom the best, they were happier than most families. He gained wide fame as a builder of fortresses and palaces, bridges and monuments, and one cathedral, to please his wife, as he told it. It was said that he could make stone flow like water; and to this day you can see his work still standing, although it has been a long time, and magic is now quite gone from the world. Connoisseurs can tell his buildings by the little colophon he placed in a hidden spot on each one, which says LUMP MADE ME, although he soon stopped calling himself by that name outside his family. But others remark that they can always tell his structures because they seem to grow like mountains from the very earth, the same earth that was his playground when he was the witch's boy.